BLACK SHADOW
DETECTIVE AGENCY

INFERNAL ANGELS

COUNT S. A. OLSON

Copyright © 2024 Count S. A. Olson.

All rights reserved. No part of this book may be reproduced, stored, or transmitted by any means—whether auditory, graphic, mechanical, or electronic—without written permission of both publisher and author, except in the case of brief excerpts used in critical articles and reviews. Unauthorized reproduction of any part of this work is illegal and is punishable by law.

ISBN: 979-8-89419-506-3 (sc)
ISBN: 979-8-89419-507-0 (hc)
ISBN: 979-8-89419-508-7 (e)

Because of the dynamic nature of the Internet, any web addresses or links contained in this book may have changed since publication and may no longer be valid. The views expressed in this work are solely those of the author and do not necessarily reflect the views of the publisher, and the publisher hereby disclaims any responsibility for them.

One Galleria Blvd., Suite 1900, Metairie, LA 70001
(504) 702-6708

THE ANGEL AND THE DEMON CAPER

CHAPTER

"Looking deeper into the week it looks we're going to see some snow making its way into the Twin Cities come Halloween. However it doesn't look like there will be enough to make it hard for those little ghosts and goblins to make their way to your door. So be sure to stock up on enough treats for the kiddies."

I clicked off the radio, the weather report was all I had really needed. I really didn't care about the trick 'r treaters since I wasn't going to be home. There was going to be a massive party at the Mystic Wolf on Samhain, known to most as Halloween. Not everyone was going to be there since it wasn't a major holiday for several pantheons, but the party was still going to be huge.

It was going to be Jamie's first Samhain party and I knew it was going to be the wildest party she had ever been to by far. She kept thinking that it would be like a normal Halloween party. It seemed that no matter how many times I tried to explain it to her that I couldn't get her to understand that this was going to be like a New Year's Eve party on steroids. For many pantheons October 31 is their New Year's Eve; add in the fact that the vast majority of the people who were going to be at the Mystic that night were from varying magickal, divine, and infernal realms (I doubted that anyone from an elemental realm would be there), or were pagans from this side of reality, things were going to get wild. Plus Brisbane had given me a heads up on a new liquid memory drink he had come up for that night, the 'Sugar Buzz', which was based on his earliest memory of getting hyped up on candy he had collected trick or treating.

Well at least she was taking the whole costume thing seriously. When I had gotten in after hitting the nearby Thai place for take-out I had seen her browsing a website full of costumes. I was also happy to notice that most of the costumes showed a fair amount of cleavage and or leg which meant they would look great on her. Of course there was no chance of her competing with Aphrodite or Freya in the looks department. The two of them usually came in outfits that could easily spark a riot at some parties. Still I was looking forward to seeing her in whatever costume she chose. I may be a half-Daemon but even I'm affected by a good looking woman.

I heard a knock on the outer office door which was answered by Jamie asking whoever it was to come inside. I wasn't too worried about what was being said, Jamie was good at her job so there was nothing to concern myself with until she called me on the intercom.

The intercom buzzed. "Boss?" she said across the line.

"Yes?"

"I have a Sasha Sumer out here, she said she needs to talk to you." That sort of surprised me because I thought I knew who she might be talking about, and if it was who I thought it was, something was seriously wrong.

"Is she about five seven, Arab looking, and insanely beautiful?" I asked.

"Uh, yes."

"Then send her in right now, it's almost definitely important."

Are you thinking she's one of the waitresses from the Mystic Wolf? Shadow, my crow familiar, asked me, his voice in my head only.

"Who else," I replied to my familiar as the door opened.

"Mr. Black? I need your help," she said as she entered my office. As she stepped inside her human facade was replaced by her natural, daemonic form, that of a lovely succubus. Sasha wasn't her real name, it was just the one she had currently adopted to fit in. Only one human knew her true name and that was Brisbane. To know a Daemon's true name was to have power over them, so they didn't give it out very often.

"Well, have a seat and we'll discuss your problem," I said motioning her to the chair across from me. She tucked her wings in and sat down with some hesitation, obviously both nervous and upset.

"Well first let me thank you for seeing me, I..." I cut her off.

"Don't thank me," I said. "You've come to me as a client so you can thank me after this is all settled. Now what is the problem?"

"Well a friend of mine has disappeared, and I'm terribly worried about her. I want you to find her for me." I was immediately surprised by this. For one thing I knew that it was rare for daemons from the infernal realms to really form attachments to others, my dad being an exception, but this was something different. I had never seen a daemon this upset about missing a friend before; even my dad hadn't been this upset when my mother had been killed over three centuries ago.

I nodded to show that I was going to take this seriously, I may find this situation unusual, but that didn't matter. Sasha was just another client right now which meant I would treat her with the same respect I do all my clients. I took a notepad out of a desk drawer and got ready to start the initial questioning that would help me find a place to start. "So what is your friend's name?" I asked her.

"Kara Odinsdottir," she said quietly. My first response was to drop the pen I was about to use to take notes with. If she had just said what I thought she had, those two words had just turned this into the most outlandish case I had ever started.

The hell!? I heard Shadow exclaim in my head. *It can't be.*

"Let me make sure I have this right. Am I correct in thinking that Kara's last name, Odinsdottir, is Icelandic in origin?"

Sasha nodded quietly. "Yes," she said in barely more than a whisper. She seemed almost ashamed of the answer.

"Am I also correct when I translate it as 'Odin's Daughter'?" I asked. Again she gave me another barely audible 'yes'.

I leaned across my desk to get a better look at her, if she was lying to me I would know. "So what you mean is that this friend of yours that you want me to track down for you is a Valkyrie, correct?"

This time when she said, 'yes', I could see tears welling up at the corner of her eyes. I dropped back down into my chair. Never in all my years would I have thought I would ever see a Daemon from one of the infernal planes brought to tears, but the reason for those tears was completely unreal. My client, a Daemon who's nature caused her to fit neatly into what most people thought of as a classic 'Demon', was asking me to find a Daemon from a divine plane, or what many people would call an 'angel'. This was so utterly beyond belief that it couldn't have been made up. Had anyone else told me about this case I would have called them liar, but this was no lie. I would never have expected that a succubus could even cry, not even fake tears, but these tears were not fake, they were genuine. She wasn't just upset, she was scared.

I reached into my desk and pulled out a couple lowball glasses and pulled out a bottle of what I sometimes referred to as nerve medicine, more commonly known as cheap bourbon. I poured a couple fingers of the liquor into each glass and pushed one over to her. "Here, this might help calm you down?"

She took the glass and took a quick sip. "Thanks," she mumbled.

I picked up my pen and got ready to write again. "Okay how about we start with the relationship between you. What do the two of you mean to each other?"

Instead of saying anything the succubus reached into her jacket pocket and took out a picture. I looked at it, then looked at my client, then back again at the picture. I was having a hard time believing the picture, but if it was genuine it explained a lot, and from the way Sasha was acting I knew it was genuine. The picture showed Sasha and the Valkyrie hanging on to each other in what could only be described as a loving manner, and both obviously smashed beyond belief, in the Mystic Wolf during some party. "Which party was this?" I asked her.

"Last Spring Equinox," she said taking the picture back.

"What happened between the two of you?"

"Well I was off duty and the two of us got to talking, and drinking, more talking, more drinking and, well, you saw the picture. I remember getting in her car and going to her place. When we got there we did a lot more drinking. The next thing I remember is waking up next to her in her bed. I was so drunk that I don't remember what happened, and she says she doesn't remember either, but whatever did happen I don't regret it," the Succubus reached out her hand and I gave her back the photo. "Since then we've been, well, close."

No, no, no! Shadow yelled in my head. *Valkyries don't get involved with Succubi! It's... It's...*

I raised a hand to shush him. "How close?" This was going to be an interesting conversation. I wanted to know what kind of relationship could form between two Daemons from such different realms.

"Well when I'm not at school in this realm I'll usually try to spend at least some time with her." I remembered her saying something about going to college when I had met up with Detective Wallace from the St. Paul PD a few months ago. "She is also a regular customer and she hasn't been around for a couple of days which is what got me worried in the first place. She's normally in at least once a day." I cut her off a bit too soon.

"Is it possible that she just left for somewhere and didn't tell you about it?" I asked. I didn't want to waste my time and her money searching for a Valkyrie who had simply returned to Asgard.

"Not a chance. You see I have a key to her house and well someone ransacked the place." I simply stopped writing and looked at her again.

"Why do you have a key?" Right now that seemed important because it was possible that someone had taken serious displeasure at the idea of two Daemons from different realms fraternizing.

"As you may remember I'm going to school for elementary education." I nodded. "Well I'm planning to start my student teaching in January. Since Brisbane has been giving me more freedom to leave the Mystic Wolf and spend time in this realm I've been looking for an apartment..."

"And she's been letting you stay with her while you search." I said.

"Yes... She's been great about letting me crash in the guest room." The hesitation was obvious.

Talk about a lie! Shadow screamed.

I turned to look at the bird. "Shadow. Stuff it," I snarled.

I then turn my attention back to my client. "You haven't been sleeping in the guest room have you?" I was fairly sure I knew the answer already. I didn't like it when clients lied to me, but in this case it was understandable to some extent.

"What? Yes I've been using the guest room." Her voice was clear, either she was a good liar or she was telling me the truth. However seeing as she was a succubus I wasn't inclined to believe her.

Liar! She's lying!

"Shadow! I said stuff it!" Shadow can often be helpful but there were times I wish he wouldn't talk. This was one such time.

I then looked at Sasha again. "Sorry about that. Now back to you. Look I personally don't give a damn if you have been using the guest room or not. However someone else might." I didn't want this to be a case of Odin being an ass and getting pissed with one of his servants spending what could be called 'quality time' with a daemon from another realm. However old one-eye had some interesting ideas of what was acceptable behavior when dealing with the relationships of others. The guy had once been a jerk to his own son, Thor, and told the guy that his wife, Sif, was sleeping around. Thankfully Thor trusted his wife, and rightfully so, considering that I've seen her chew him out for forgetting their anniversary on a couple of occasions. However Odin can be an ass at times, especially if he felt a Valkyrie wasn't doing what he wanted them to. Hell he had put Brynhildr into an enchanted sleep for basically mouthing off. Well more than that really, but that's the way she tells it.

"Look I don't care if you believe me or not, but I'm telling you the truth that I've been using the guest room." She sounded pissed that I had accused her of lying to me. "Look I know what I told you about sleeping with her would make it sound like that it's repeated but it hasn't." She then quietly added. "Not that I wouldn't mind it."

"Okay I'll believe you." It wasn't my business what my client's relationship with the Valkyrie was. She was going to be paying me to find her friend and the money was what really mattered. "Now let's get back to what you found at the house."

"Well as I said the place had been ransacked. Everything had been thrown around, and a lot of it was broken, there were also holes in the walls and a lot of nasty burn marks. Truthfully I doubt you could have made much more of a mess out of the place if you had set off a bomb in it." That was a bad sign. If someone had made a direct attack on a Valkyrie, who were skilled warriors, and won it meant that they were dangerous. "I looked around a little but I knew right away that I should call you so I didn't touch anything. I didn't want to disturb anything for you."

"Thank you." I was glad she hadn't called the cops. Those idiots would have really mucked the place up and it would have been much harder to find anything useful.

"Now before we go any further I need to bring up the matter of payment, and I'll need you to sign the contract," I said.

"Okay," Sasha started with a swallow. "How much is this going to cost me?"

"Seven hundred a day plus expenses, and I'll need a five day retainer up front," I told her as I pulled open a desk drawer and reached for my standard, middle of the road contract. I charged by what I think people can afford; some people can afford to pay me a lot, others not so much. Sasha was a waitress at the Mystic Wolf which, considering how much Brisbane told me their tips averaged out to, meant she had fairly deep pockets.

"Okay, that won't be a problem," she said as she cut me a check. "Can you just hold it for a day so that I can make sure that there is enough money in the account for the check not to bounce?"

"I have no problem doing that," I said. "Just date the check for tomorrow and it won't be a problem."

"Thank you." She handed me the check.

I put the contract in front of her. "Now please read this carefully and sign it. I don't need your true name, your human one is fine since it is on all your legal records." She read through it carefully, and signed on the line I indicated. I wasn't sure if she would understand all the legalese the contract was written in until I realized that since she was in college it was a good chance that she would have figured out a fair amount going through loan applications.

"Here you go," she said pushing the contract back to me, and held her hand out for me to shake.

"Okay you've just hired yourself a private eye," I said shaking her hand. "Now let's go a little deeper into what has been happening between you."

"What do you need to know?" she asked.

"How about we start with the basics of where she lives and what she does for a living." First rule of being a detective is always start with as much information as you can. "I know she works for Odin but I'm fairly sure that he doesn't pay well enough for her to not need another job if she's living on this plane."

Sasha gave a trace smile. "She always complains about Odin not paying enough, so you're right about her needing another job. She's a anesthesiologist for United Hospital, and she loves her job."

Well that gave me one place to start with, I could track down her coworkers and see what they knew. "And where does she live?"

"She has a house in the Como neighborhood of St. Paul." Fairly nice part of the city, not the best part of the city, but nice enough without being too expensive. She then gave me an exact address which wasn't too far from the Como Zoo.

"Did the two of you ever go to the zoo?" I asked her, more out of curiosity than anything else.

"Every once in a while," she said. "For the most part Brisbane limits my time on this plane to going to school, along with the normal days he gives all of us Succubi who work there. However I got him to give a few more days so I can have a chance to start looking for an apartment as well as get used to regular life out here. Kara even taught me how to drive a car, and Brisbane had someone create a legal driver's license for me."

"How about enemies?" I asked. "Do you know if Kara had any enemies? Well other than the typical ones of, and in, the Norse Pantheon."

"Well as far as I know there are only the general ones," she said. "I mean she's probably gotten people pissed off at her, she can be a little... err... abrasive, at times. But I can't imagine that she'd get anyone powerful enough to take her out pissed off enough to do this."

I nodded in thought. Taking on a Valkyrie was nothing to be taken lightly, it meant pissing off a major God. However it didn't make sense for a Valkyrie to disappear like this since Odin would be quick to get involved. If Odin had done this to punish his child for taking up a relation with Sasha he'd have gone after my client as well, or at least I thought he would. Plus he would have simply ordered Kara to cut contact, a smash and grab wasn't his style. Even Brynhildr hadn't been taken like that when she had openly disobeyed him. No, someone was either making a move specifically against Kara or they might be planning to go after other members of the pantheon soon.

"Anything different in the way she's been acting over the last few days?" I asked. It's possible that something had happened that she simply hadn't wanted to tell my client about.

"Not that I noticed," Sasha said. "However she's always been a bit hard to read. That's why she often times rubs people the wrong way. It can be hard for people to tell whether or not she's joking or whether she's just being a bit bitchy and or sarcastic. Hell even I have a hard time catching whether or not she's being serious or not and we're close."

This was getting me nowhere. Sasha was doing her best to be helpful so that wasn't the problem. The problem though was that none of this added up. This had been a smash and grab, so whoever had done this was no one to be trifled with. It wasn't Odin's style, at least I didn't think it was. Still it was possible that someone else in the pantheon had taken it upon themselves to punish Kara for her relationship with Sasha. I mean it's not like minor members of differing pantheons to have much to do with each other unless it is directly happening at the Mystic Wolf, and even then things tended to be a bit tense, especially among the European pantheons. However that still didn't explain the fact that no one had gone after Sasha, but...

I was hit with a sudden revelation. The reason that whoever had gone after Kara had left Sasha alone could easily do with the fact that Brisbane would have immediately gotten involved. Going after one of his employees would have gotten a lot of people involved. Not only had Brisbane in a sense formed his own pantheon within the bar, but an attack on the bar, directly or not, would get just about every pantheon out there involved. If Sasha had been attacked and Brisbane able to point out the culprit whoever had done it would have to deal with a lot of angry gods and all sorts of others. No Sasha was probably safe from whoever had attacked the Valkyrie.

"Okay all I need from you then is the key and I can get started," I said.

Sasha quickly jotted down the number at the hospital where I could reach Kara's supervisor and gave me the key. She then looked at her watch and I saw a look of mild panic cross her face. "Shit! I'm going to be late for class, and I didn't drive."

"Don't worry I'll give you a ride to school," I said.

"Thanks," she said. "I've got class in thirty minutes and we have a test today that I've spent the last three days studying for."

"Well come on then let's go," I said. As I stood up I reached into my gun safe and grabbed out my shoulder holster and slid my Colt 1911, 'Ace of Spades' into it, along with a couple magazines of specialty bullets. In this case I didn't know what I might be up against. I threw my suit coat on over the holster and then a trench coat over that. Lastly I grabbed my old fedora off the coat stand and motioned Sasha out the office door ahead of me.

Not without me you don't, Shadow said and hopped on to my shoulder.

As we left my office Sasha resumed her human facade. I told Jamie that I had taken the case and then giving her the check told her to take it to the bank tomorrow. As Sasha followed me to my '41 Buick Special,

I asked her a few more questions regarding her relationship with the Valkyrie. I didn't expect to learn anything useful for the case, I was just being nosey.

Once we got to the car Shadow hopped off my shoulder and took his normal spot on his perch in the back seat of the car. Sasha slid into the passenger seat and we left the parking garage. In the light traffic we reached the college and I dropped my client off as close to the building her class was in as I could, then headed off to work on her case.

CHAPTER 2

After I dropped Sasha off at her college I made my way over to the Como neighborhood. Como is made up of mostly relatively newer houses of the small variety, but when you get close to Como Lake there are some older and much larger houses. The area's clean with little crime, a nice place to live. There is the hundred plus year old city zoo, which is connected to a small amusement park. Across from the street is a miniature golf course and a new water park. All in all it's pretty much the ideal place to raise a family. I could picture Sasha wanting to spend time here, maybe even living here, since she seemed to like kids, well at least enough to want to teach elementary school. It was still something that I was having a hard time wrapping my head around. She was a Succubus, her very nature said that she was supposed to seduce men and use their lust to destroy them. Yet she seemed to have broken from her nature so strongly. Who knows maybe she was tired of pointless sex and wanted something more? Maybe she even wanted to be a mother.

That last thought caused me to wonder what kind of mother a daemon like her would be like. Daemons can't have children naturally so she would have to adopt. If she settled down with Kara, which I had no doubt she wanted to do, that could make things difficult because of the stupidity surrounding people's ridiculous prejudiced views of gay couples. A child raised by a pair of daemons, one from a divine realm and the other from an infernal realm, that would be confusing for the kid. As far as I knew Succubi have little, if any, contact with whichever elder daemon spawned them. However Valkyries always maintain contact with Odin, meaning that any kid they adopted would be the adopted grandson or granddaughter of the All Father. Wouldn't that make for an interesting family reunion. They'd have to keep a lot of stuff secret from the child until he or she got older otherwise people would think that the child was nuts. I could almost imagine the parent teacher conference.

'Your child has been telling ridiculous stories in school. They've been saying that their grandparents are Gods. Now I know every child thinks their grandparents are great, but you shouldn't encouraged them to have such ridiculous notions about them.' I mean, what would the response be like?

'Well you see his/her grandparents are Odin and Frigga.' Someone would try to lock up Kara and Sasha for being nuts.

Oh well I'll let those two figure something out on their own, if something like that was to happen. Until now I've only known Sasha as a waitress and while I've probably seen Kara at some point at the Mystic Wolf I've never been introduced to her.

I've met most of the Norse Pantheon over the years, or at least the Aesir and Vanir proper and even a couple of the Jotunns. However I've never actually met any of the others, even though I've seen some of the dwarves with Freya trying to buy her favor with jewelry, and Valkyries near Odin. When that's going on though I always leave them alone. Pantheon business is best left to members of that pantheon. That being said I was going to have to talk to Odin today regarding Kara no matter who he was talking to. If he could give me the information, I'd refund Sasha most of the check. However right now I would at least earn some of that check and look around the house to see if I could find something that would lead me in the right direction so as not to bother Odin.

Can I talk now? Shadow asked.

"Yes. It's just rather irritating when you start yelling like that when I'm talking to a client." There were times when Shadow's input could be useful but that had not been one of them.

Sorry about that. Shadow sounded mollified. At least he wasn't going to hold a grudge which was good. Especially for my much beloved fedora. *'Do you believe Sasha when she denied that she is still sleeping with Kara?'*

"She has no reason to lie about it, especially since she flat out admitted to the fact that she would like to be," I said. "No, I'm fairly sure she was telling the truth."

Do you think that, that may be the cause of this? Shadow asked.

Now I was fairly sure that Shadow wasn't homophobic, but he had watched a lot of political TV coverage during last year's presidential campaign. "Are you saying that you don't approve?" I asked.

I don't give a damn either way, however someone else may have. Shadow had a point. *It's possible that a God or Goddess, or even other Valkyries may not have approved of their relationship, or at least perceived relationship, and had taken it upon themselves to do something about it.*

"I had thought about it," I said. "However anything that was done in pantheon would have had to have been done with the approval of Odin. Unless something turns up that indicates otherwise I'm going to rule out the residents of Asgard. The only other possibility that would make sense for in pantheon, really, would be other Valkyries. As you said, they may not approve of one of their own mixing with a Sumerian daemon."

I guess you do have a point. Shadow conceded. *But if it wasn't an in pantheon job who else would be nuts enough to pull a stunt like this? I mean Valkyries are tough pieces of work, she wouldn't have gone down without one hell of a fight.*

"I'm going to leave any further speculation until I take a look at Kara's house," I said. "However if what Sasha said about the state of the house was true then you're right about the fight. I know I wouldn't want to take on a Valkyrie in a fight even if I knew for a fact that I'd win."

Do you think you could beat a Valkyrie in a fair fight? Shadow asked sounding genuinely curious about my answer.

"In a fair fight? Probably not." I admitted. "Of course since when have I ever fought fairly?"

Probably never, Shadow said. *You're very much like your father in that respect. I doubt any Daemon from one of the infernal realms would ever fight fairly.*

I gave a sharp bark of laughter. "I know I sure as hell wouldn't. I always try to stack the deck as far into my favor as possible."

Probably saved your neck more than a few times.

I pulled up in front of Kara's house and was struck immediately by how normal it was. It was a fairly small-- one and a half story-- white house that looked like many of the houses in the neighborhood. However it looked a bit older, it had probably been built somewhere in the late twenties, early thirties. It had a white picket fence; under the front windows were bushes of some sort. From the way the yard looked on either side of the sidewalk leading to the door I guessed that flowers had been put to bed for the winter. Sort of mind boggling in a way to think that a shield maiden, a warrior like a Valkyrie, would be so domestic as to plant tulips in the spring.

Not what you expected is it, Shadow said.

"Truthfully I didn't know what to expect," I said. "But this is about as different from Asgard as a Valkyrie could probably get."

I guess she just wanted a change of pace.

"You know, if it wasn't for knowing that Sasha was in school for elementary education, I would have sworn up and down that a Daemon couldn't go against their nature this far." From picking out the fallen warriors to bring to Valhalla to living in a part of St. Paul that was so far from the heart of it that it could almost be considered a suburb. "This is just plain surreal."

Could be worse. Shadow said cryptically.

"How so?"

Shadow did as close to a smile as is possible with a beak. 'She could have plastic flamingos in the front yard.'

"That would be just plain disturbing."

Well how about I take off and see what I can see. Shadow suggested.

"Okay. However I doubt that you'll find much."

I'll give the area a couple of passes, he said. *If I don't find anything by the end of the third pass I'll get my feathers back here.*

"Sounds good."

I got hit with a blast of feather tossed air as he leapt off my shoulder and pumped his wings for a hard take off. He knew his job well enough that no further orders were needed. I seriously doubted anyone powerful enough to take on a Valkyrie would be dumb enough to leave a trace of their passing. However my familiar might very well get lucky.

With Shadow taking a look around the area I got down to doing my own work. I walked around to the backyard and saw that Kara had put in a nice brick patio which was partially shaded by a red oak. The furniture was covered up with tarps in preparation for the oncoming winter and judging by the bulky shape that one of the tarps had taken I was willing to bet that it hid a large, and probably expensive, grill. The whole thing was almost too stereotypically normal. If I found a 'Kiss the Cook' apron, or something like it, in the house I just might scream. The scary part was that if invited to such a party I wouldn't be shocked to see a group of armor clad, black winged beauties tossing back bottles of beer and talking about the butt kicking the Saint Paul Saints had just handed the Toledo Mud Hens. Don't ask me why, but the magickal community in the Twin Cities has an almost irrational fixation on the local, AAA baseball team.

What was more interesting about the patio than my idle speculation on what a cook out party of Valkyries would look like was the fact that the masonry was covered in broken glass. A couple of windows at the rear of the house had been blasted out, and the fragmented glass was stained grey. It would be a pain to clean it all up, she would probably have to call in a service to figure out a way to get it off the grass. Might be simpler to dig up the whole thing and put in new sod. I wonder if her home owners insurance would cover that.

I was about to head into the house when I noticed that the garage door was hanging from a single hinge. On closer examination I could easily tell that the door had been wrenched open with tremendous force by the fact that the wood of the frame was splintered. There had been no subtlety in the way it had been opened. It had been a sheer matter of raw, dumb strength inflicted upon the door.

I entered the garage and was hit by the usual scent of grease and oil that comes from power tools. The gas powered garden tools had been thrown about, probably more in frustration than anything else. Whomever had been here had also done a real number on a beautiful, classic, blue Mustang. The poor thing had been thoroughly trashed; Kara was going to be seriously pissed about this when I found her. Of course I needed to find her and bring her back home safely before she would get a chance to be pissed about her car.

There wasn't anything else of interest in the garage so I decided to go into the house and take a look around. I figured that there was probably no one in the house so I didn't bother to reach for 'Ace of Spades' and left her tucked away in her holster. I found myself walking into the kitchen.

The place had been demolished. The granite counter top was broken in several places and had crashed to the floor at points. Cabinet doors were either hanging awkwardly from broken hinges or ripped off entirely. Knives from the empty butcher block were scattered, many imbedded in the wall. Broken dish ware and glasses littered the floor. Someone had slammed what appeared to have been some sort of broad sword through the refrigerator door. Judging by the amount of the blood that had been liberally used to paint the floor and walls there had been one hell of a fight here.

From this point I made my way into the dining room. If the kitchen had been destroyed the dining room had been bombed. The dining room table had been turned into only so much kindling and judging by the wreckage someone or something had been smashed through the top of it. The chairs had either been hacked on or seemed to have been used as improvised clubs, and usually both. There was a cabinet that had contained knick-knacks and probably what would be considered the fine china, knocked over. There were fragments of ceramics and fragile glass trapped, mostly under it, but some had spread out over the rest of the floor. There were holes in the walls and judging by the size and depth I was willing to guess that they had been made by someone's head or fist smashing into the drywall. Again, just like in the kitchen, there was blood everywhere.

From the dining room I entered the living room. I felt sorry for the insurance adjuster who was going to have to figure out how much they owed Kara. There was a massive, top of the line, flat screen with a huge hole in it, and the home theater set up was mangled beyond belief. Some sort of fireball had hit the couch which left a massive scorch mark almost dead center and the wall had taken part of it. When an insurance investigator saw it they'd probably attribute it to someone letting off fireworks inside the house. An easy chair had been smashed to pieces with springs and metal showing at the most awkward angles possible for furniture.

At some point something had hit the ceiling during the fight and broken the ceiling fan. Judging by the possible angle of a throw like that they had been thrown into it after someone had used them to massacre a defenseless bookshelf. The blood had soaked into the carpet making me guess that someone, or someones, had bought the farm during this part of the fight. I wondered what the bedrooms looked like and made that the next stop.

The first bedroom I looked in had been spared for the most part, at least compared to the rest of the house. The bed had been flipped, and the closet doors had been ripped off their tracks but all in all it wasn't too bad. There was some blood on the floor, but not enough to cause me to believe that there had been much fighting here. My guess was that this was the guest bedroom. But that confused the motive. With so little blood that probably meant that this room had been tossed after the fight. So why did someone want to search after the fight? The only reason would be that the Kara wasn't the target. So if it wasn't Kara then either they were after something she possessed or someone else. And the only other person who would normally be there was Sasha. Had my client been the target of this smash and grab, with Kara just having been in the wrong place at the wrong time? Maybe the answer would be in the next bedroom.

The next bedroom had been destroyed. From the looks of things this is where the fight had started. There were holes in the walls that were rimmed with blood. The dressers had been demolished and it was only the clothes that kept them from collapsing completely. The bed was a shambles; the mattress had deep burn marks and was slashed up. The windows had been demolished and were surrounded with black burn marks, which explained the smoky grey staining of the glass fragments that littered the patio. I wondered if it had been the concussive blast of a fireball that had broken the windows or if somebody had been thrown out of them.

Sensing something magickal from the demolished closet, I took a closer look. The clothing racks had been yanked off and the clothes strewn about the floor. However I wasn't interested in the expensive shoes and little black dress. I was interested in a spatial fold that was in the back of the closet. With a little effort I reached into it and found a golden chainmail shirt with a matching shield bearing the symbol of Odin's raven banner and a golden spear that had probably been made by dwarves. However, her sword was missing. Considering that I hadn't seen the sword anywhere in the house it was a damn good bet that it had been taken as well. Had the attackers been after the sword? Unlikely. There are easier way to get a powerful, magick sword that don't involve kidnapping.

I could understand why the spear was still there. If Kara had been surprised and had needed to grab a weapon quickly the sword was the obvious choice. The spear was far too big to be used effectively in the small house. Likewise the chainmail would have taken too long to throw on even if it was just a shirt. Putting on a shirt would have left her vulnerable temporarily and considering that it was possible that the fight had started in the bedroom she would have needed to press any momentary advantage she could have gotten. The same was true for the shield, she simply wouldn't have had a chance to properly set the shield and it would have been clumsy inside the house. The logical step would have been to go immediately for the sword. From the look of things she had pressed the battle out of the bedroom and into the living room and caused massive damage along the way. So the question was why had her attackers even come here.

I decided to take a further look around. My next stop was to the bathroom. There was blood on the floor, but like the first bedroom not enough to suggest that there had been any real fighting in here. The door to the shower tub combo had been ripped from the frame and shattered but that was about it. It was looking more and more like Kara really hadn't been the intended target of the smash and grab.

I took a cursory look through the basement and attic and found the blood trails like I had seen in the guestroom and bathroom. Both had been demolished looking more like it had been done out of frustration than anything else. Whoever or whatever had been the target of the smash and grab hadn't been here and the attackers had been pissed. It was probably the same reason that Kara's classic had been destroyed in the garage.

The only possible target of a smash and grab would have been my client. It was possible that she was supposed to be here and that Kara wasn't. It was possible that whoever had grabbed Kara had made a tremendous fuck up and gotten the timing wrong. Or the time table had been altered by a mere chance of luck. Whatever the reason the whole thing had gone south in a hurry. That didn't get me any closer to an answer about who had done it. Shadow suddenly broken my train of thought.

Master? my familiar asked from a long way off.

"Yes?"

I found something that may be of interest.

"Do tell," I replied heading back to the living room which showed the greatest amount of damage.

I think I found the remnants of a fairy circle, Shadow replied. That was worrying.

"What do you mean you think?" I asked him.

I can't tell for certain, the area has been hit by the weather a little but I can make out a trace scent of burned mushrooms. That was a distinct sign of fey activity. Fey circles are avenues from which they enter the human world. They are always ringed either with mushrooms, or if they are in a long standing mound ringed by stones. If a ring of mushrooms had been burned it meant that a group of fey had been here and didn't want anyone following them back through. The only fey that use circles of mushrooms are those from the British Isles, often known as Arcadian fey. If it had been Arcadian fey there was a very good chance that I'd find some more evidence if I took a closer look at the furniture.

"Okay head back here, I need to check something out." I commanded.

Arcadian fey are allergic to all things iron, including steel so if it had been fey there would be trace of bronze on the metal pieces of furniture left by their bronze weapons. As long as I wasn't mistaken a Valkyrie's blade would have gone straight through the metal without any scratches. However I seriously doubted a Fey's bronze blade would have been so lucky. Since I was already in the living room I bent down to examine the furniture. Indeed there were markings on screws, springs and pieces of framing that appeared to have been made by bronze weapons. However I was confused, there seemed to also be a trace amount of steel. I was still fairly certain that Kara's blade wouldn't leave those traces. For that matter I was fairly certain that her blade wasn't even made of steel but instead a type of Dwarven gold. Had the Fey been helped by a human?

That was confusing to say the least since Fey usually want nothing to do with humans. There are exceptions to the rule of course. There are of course changelings, human babies that are stolen by fey and replaced with one of their own. Changelings develop Fey like abilities but are immune to the effects of iron. The other exception would be that the human had been ensnared by a Fey queen, maybe even king, and had been taken to Arcadia to live out their lives until whomever had taken them got bored with them. The most well-known case of that happening was, of course, Rip Van Winkle. Like changelings they develop Fey like powers the longer they live in Arcadia. Either way one was rare nowadays but time travels in odd cycles in Arcadia so who knows when that had happened. The human could have been taken centuries ago and only aged a couple of years. Or they could have been gone only a few days and grown older by years.

I'm here, Shadow called out.

I let him in through the front door. "What do you think?" I asked.

How many people died in here? Shadow asked looking around.

"Probably a lot." It was the most accurate estimate I could give. "So a fairy circle?"

That's what it looked like, Shadow said with a dip of his beak. *Do you want me to show it to you?*

"Not really. If they blasted it after they left I won't be able to run a trail on it and figure out where they had gone," I said. "Which of course leaves me the problem of tracking down which court it was."

As I said I'm not even sure it was a true Fey circle... Shadow started before I cut him off.

"I checked the cut marks. For the most part they were made by bronze weapons."

That means Arcadian Fey alright. Shadow looked around than looked back at me. *What do you mean most of the cuts were bronze? Not all of them?*

"Some were steel, and I'm fairly sure they weren't left by Kara's sword."

So the Fey were working with a human? Shadow sounded confused with idea and had every right to be.

"That's about the size of it."

So what is your guess? Was Kara kidnapped or was she killed outright?

"If she had been killed I would have found out about it by now," I said. "Odin would be on the war path right now and everyone would have heard about it."

So what did happen, and why?

"I have a feeling that Kara wasn't the target. The place had been searched after the fight." The evidence spoke to only one conclusion. "I think that the true target was Sasha."

So what's the plan?

"I have to call the cops, they're going to want to see what happened here even though there isn't any point to it. However someone else might call the cops ahead of me and I'll have to confess to knowing that something happened." The problem was that there was a member of the occult community in missing persons in the Saint Paul PD, and he was a friend of mine. "That of course means I'm going to have to give Wallace the run around for a while."

What else?

"My next call will be to the Countess. I'll probably need an army to help me right now. First things first." I pulled out my phone and called Sasha.

"Hello?" the daemon asked when she picked up the phone.

"Sasha, it's Black. I want you to go to the Mystic Wolf as soon as you can. Stay in Brisbane's office until you hear from me." The Mystic Wolf was one of the safest places in any reality. People don't cause trouble there, including Gods, and there Sasha was an Arch-Angel herself.

"What's going on?"

"Trust me it's better if you don't know right now." I didn't want to cause her to panic, at least not too much.

"Okay I'll go there after class."

"No, go there now!" I said sharply.

"You're scaring me, Black."

"Good."

"Okay I'm going. When are you going to meet with me again?" Sasha was starting to sound scared, which is exactly the way I wanted it.

"I'll send Jamie to pick you up." Nobody messed with Jamie. It was well known that she worked for me, and she was protected by my well-deserved, and very nasty reputation. "Now I've got all sorts of other calls to make." I hung up on her.

Who's next on the list? Shadow asked and I ignored him and simply dialed.

"Hello Yvette?"

CHAPTER

I arrived at the Mystic wolf at four-thirty with about four hours before I met my friends at my office. I was surprised by how the bar's resident head God, the owner and head bartender, Brisbane, had formed the bar that night. As opposed to its many normal incarnations, tonight it had been given the form of an old and massive hunting lodge. The wood floor had a weather beaten look to it with the boards being slightly uneven, and quite wide. The furniture was the rough cut trunk style with the legs of the tables and chairs still having stumps of the branches on them. The tops of the tables had to be at least four to six inches thick and I couldn't help but think how painful if a patron got rowdy enough for Brisbane to use the offender to break one of them, which was often a punishment for being too rowdy. From the ceiling hung chandeliers made of antlers and along the walls were numerous hunting trophies.

The Succubi waitresses, as usual, were dressed in sexually provocative outfits. Their shorts were cut so high up they barely counted as Daisy Dukes, and their black and red checkered, flannel shirts, with the bar logo embroidered on them were tied under their breasts showing a fair amount of midriff. They had their typical mini-aprons tied just above their hips for their check pads, and order sheets. I had wondered how long their union steward had argued with Brisbane on the style of the night's uniform. I'm sure if it was up to the waitresses the only thing they'd be wearing were the aprons, and only that for carrying things. However Brisbane, with the help of a good fashion designer who also had a degree in psychology focusing on sexual therapy, had finally gotten them to realize that certain clothing could be sexier than full out nudity. She had helped the Succubi's union steward, who then went to the rest of the daemons, understand that only hinting at the treasure that lay beneath the clothing would drive people up the wall with lust. It was the focus group of soon to be patrons that had cinched the deal. Unfortunately every one of incarnations of the bar came with arguments about that theme's uniform style.

I was about to stop one of the waitresses and ask her if Odin was in tonight when I heard Shadow whistle next to my ear. "What is it feather brain?" I asked him.

It's her, he said in what I could only describe as a smitten tone of mind.

"It's who, Shadow?"

Her. The most beauteous bird ever. That's who, he replied.

"The phoenix?"

No, not her. Shadow sniffed dismissively. *Phoenix looks like a trollop. She has no class, all glitz and glam that one. No, I'm talking real beauty. The kind that goes down deep.*

"I give. Who the hell are you talking about?" I asked.

Muninn, that's who. The most beautiful bird to grace the skies. The dumb crow sounded absolutely besotted.

"Oh good, Odin is here then. Where is this bird you've got a crush on?"

Over there, he said pointing with his port wing. *And please don't tell her that I've got a crush on her.*

"Sure, just don't make it obvious," I said as I made way over to the All Father. Muninn wasn't the only raven with Odin, his other raven, Muninn's mate, Huginn, was with him as well. How Shadow could tell the difference between the two ravens was beyond me, however, he could.

Odin was sitting with his back to me as I approached him. At first I was surprised when he didn't turn to look at me, until I remembered where we were. The Mystic Wolf is not really on Midgard, it's its own realm, and therefore Odin wasn't all seeing here. Nearby I saw a group of dwarves waiting patiently to talk to him, and soon I saw that he was already talking to one that I assumed to be the spokesmen. Well too bad he was going to have to wait.

As I came around behind the Dwarf I grabbed him by the shoulder and spun him around to look at me. "You have three seconds to scram before you find out what your fingers taste like," I snarled.

The Dwarf looked back at Odin who merely shrugged as a sign that the Dwarf was on his own. The Dwarf turned back to look at me and saw that my eyes had started to glow as a sign of my half daemonic nature. Probably armed with the knowledge of my well-earned reputation for extreme viciousness he got up and left.

Odin looked at me calmly as I sat down like nothing had happened. Odin's two wolves, Freki and Geri, were laying at the All Father's feet and growled slightly as I took the seat but Odin waved them off. "So what has you in such a professionally unpleasant mood?" the God asked.

"Kara," I said simply.

"What about that particular daughter of mine deserves this kind of mood." I then saw the God's facial expression change. "Before you answer let me guess. This is in regards to the relationship between her and that Succubus."

"Something like that." My guess was that Odin must not have been sitting on his throne, Hlidskjalf, when Kara had been taken. It was also possible that he had been too busy to use it to look throughout the realms of Yggdrasil since the disappearance either. It was a fair bet that since he hadn't already contacted me himself he didn't know.

"Well before you ask let me explain a few things. Had this sort of relationship formed between two of my servants I wouldn't care in the least. That being said I'm not about to act against the two of them. Kara is old enough to make her own decisions about these sorts of things. If she wishes to take a Sumerian Succubus for a lover that is her concern," Odin said.

I waited for a second waiting for Odin to take a drink of his mead. "So you have nothing to do with her disappearance then?" I asked, and was greeted with the sight of the God spitting out a mouthful of the honey wine.

"She's what?!" the God bellowed.

"Disappeared." There was no real need to elaborate.

"What happened?" Odin didn't seem so much as worried as he did pissed.

"It looks like a typical smash and grab," I said. "And I can tell you that she put up one hell of a fight. There was blood everywhere and I'm guessing at least one person is probably dead. However judging by your reaction Kara isn't one of them."

"If she was and I didn't know who killed her you'd know by now as I would have hired you to find out." I knew Odin was angry and he had every right to be of course. "I want you to find out who did this and let me know so I can perform a Blood Eagle! No one attacks one of my Valkyries and lives!"

"I already knew you'd say that." I didn't have to be a God to know that would be this God's reaction.

"Do you have any idea of who could have taken her?" Odin asked. His voice betrayed his anger that someone had dared to attack one of his daughters. Whoever had done this was a dead man, or woman for that matter, and it would be a painful death. I had seen a Blood Eagle performed once and it made even me, a man who has no trouble with drawing blood during torture, squirm. The offender is laid out and tied down, then the executioner takes an axe and lays open the victim's back right below the shoulder blade. I know from seeing it that it isn't always fatal, but the next part will kill just about anything. Once the victim's back has been opened the executioner reaches into the broken ribs and pulls out the lungs and displays them as if they are wings, hence the name. When I fought in the Knight's War back in the forties, and

World War II raged on, I saw it done to a Nazi. It's a messy death, but it looked as if I'd see it performed one more time.

"I have a solid theory as to who took her..." I started before Odin cut me off.

"Who?" The tone was ominous.

"The furniture showed signs of being cut by bronze weapons, and the only ones who fight with bronze weapons are the Fey of the British Isles." It is common knowledge that those Fey are highly sensitive to all things made from iron.

"So it was the Fey," the God growled.

"Not quite so fast." Odin needed to know the rest. "There is something more..."

"And what is that?" Odin asked me before I could finish my thought.

"Am I right in thinking that a Valkyrie's blade would have cut straight through the furniture without being scratched by the metal in it?" This was important. If I was right it meant dangerous things, not just for Kara, but for any Fey court not aligned with the court that had attacked.

"You are correct," Odin said confirming my knowledge. "Why?"

"There were signs of steel weapons having been used." I knew that would confuse the All Father.

"I thought the Fey of the Isles were allergic to all things iron." Odin's statement was really a question so I answered it.

"They are, however my guess is that they have at least one Human working with, or rather for, them," I said.

"I thought that the Fey had nothing to do with Humans." Another statement that was really a question.

"For the most part they don't but there are exceptions to all rules," I said. "There are two possibilities. One is that the human was taken as a child and replaced by a changeling, then was raised by the court. Changelings are rare these days, but that doesn't mean that you don't still find old ones. Just like everywhere else time travels at a variable rate in Arcadia."

"And the second possibility?" Odin growled.

"The Human may be a great warrior that a queen, or possibly king, of a court may have taken a shine to and entranced." Either possibility was worrying.

"The warrior must be a truly great one if he defeated my Valkyrie," Odin said. My guess was that he didn't know what happened to Humans who spend too much time in Arcadia.

"You have to keep in mind that the longer a Human is in Arcadia the more they change. They start to gain the magickal powers of a faerie but without their weakness to iron. Any such Human is dangerous, and they are also dangerous to other courts." This thought made me wonder who had taken Kara and why. It could be possible that the taking of a Valkyrie was a show of force to other courts. I quickly dropped that idea, it was a stupid play to get a Valkyrie involved, that entailed getting all of the Aesir involved. No, Kara had been a problem and whoever had been involved panicked and grabbed her when they couldn't find Sasha.

"So you are looking at possibly meeting one of these Humans?" Odin asked.

"Unfortunately yes, plus a possible army of other Fey. However we can worry about that in a second," I said. "I need help from you in the here and now."

"And that would be?" Odin probably knew what I was about to ask for, he just wanted me to ask for the sake of his ego.

"I need your help finding Kara in the first place."

"You do of course know that I can't simply look for her, don't you?" Odin asked. "I am not all seeing, despite what my followers think. Since Arcadia is not part of Midgard, and therefore not connected to the World Ash, Yggdrasil, I cannot peer into its depths."

"I assumed as much." I had been fairly certain that that was the case. "But is there anything you can do for me?"

"There are two things I can do to help you." The God slapped his hands together and when he opened them there lay a gold ring in his right hand. On the outer side of the ring was etched the symbol of the Raven Banner, which is often, and apparently rightly, connected to the Valkyries. On the inner side was Kara's name written in the oldest of all the Futharks, the written language of the Norse Gods. "When this ring comes close to Kara it will start to vibrate. The closer you are to her the more it will vibrate."

"And one ring to rule them all," I muttered beneath my breath, but apparently not quietly enough.

"Please, no Tolkien," Odin sighed. "Do you want the ring or not?"

"Trust me when I say that it will make this far easier," I said taking the ring from the God's hand. "Now you said you could do two things for me?"

"I did, didn't I?" The All Father seemed to muse on this question. It is one of the most infuriating things that Gods do. It often seems that the more you need the help of one the slower they are to act. It's good for their ego, but it does tend to get a lot of people killed. "Considering that this group was able to capture one of my daughters, even if they did suffer casualties, I'm sure they will be more than you can handle by yourself."

"That is true enough," I said. To say that I wouldn't be able to handle that many Fey by myself was an understatement. Even armed to the teeth they would overwhelm me within minutes, especially since they had at least one human who was probably very dangerous. I could always count on the support of Countess Bloodwolf who would go insane if I attacked a Fey court without her for back up. Not only would I have the Countess but I would probably have a small army of her toughest enforcers. However I wasn't sure if they would be enough.

"So here is what I'm going to do. As soon as you find Kara I want you to contact me and I will send the rest of my Valkyries to aid you in the battle." All that I could think of was the fact that, that was going to be some serious cavalry.

"Once I determine where in Arcadia Kara is being held, how am I going to be able to contact you?" Trans-dimensional phones are hard to come by and incredibly expensive when you can find them. I was also fairly certain that a God like Odin wouldn't bother with something like that. Too new-fangled.

Odin looked at Huginn. "Feather please," he said holding out his hand. The raven preened himself and picked out a loose flight feather, and placed it in his masters' palm. Odin handed me the feather. "Once you've found my daughter write her location on a piece of parchment with this feather and then burn both. I'll receive the message and send the rest of my daughters to aid you in your fight."

Gods never do anything in such a way as to make things easy for the mortals serving them. It's for similar reasons that oracles and prophecies are so irritatingly hard to figure out. "Thank you for your help. I'll find her as quickly as possible," I said as I took the feather and put it in the interior pocket of my suit coat.

"There really isn't much else I can do for you, so I'll simply say find her as quickly as possible. If at all possible capture the fey who is responsible for Kara's abduction and bring them to me. I will make a show as to what it means to cross me." Odin's voice had become level in a way that screamed that people would suffer at his hands before he sent them down to Loki's daughter, Hel.

"I'll do my best, but I can't promise about being able to make a capture." I would at least try, I owed the God at least that much for his help.

"Now if you'll excuse me I have business to attend to that you interrupted." I had turned to leave when Odin suddenly said something to me. "Oh and so you know, Muninn is now fully aware of Shadow's interest in her."

I was about to ask Odin what he meant until I heard Shadow speak to me. *Sorry I couldn't keep my mind off her. She must have picked up on it.*

I laughed. "He knows now All Father." I then turned to my familiar. "She is, in a sense, a minor deity in her own right. I'm not surprised that she figured it out."

There was a brief pause where I expected Shadow to defend himself, but when he didn't say anything I looked up to see that he was once again staring at Muninn. The raven winked which confused me until Shadow spoke to me. 'If everything is settled by then I'll need to take a night off in two weeks from Friday,' he said.

"Why?"

I've got a date. I was certain that if he could have, that crow would have been grinning like an idiot.

"If that's the case she has absolutely horrid taste in men," I said as I headed for the bar proper.

What's that crack supposed to mean?

I didn't bother to answer. I would let the idiot stew for a bit.

As I approached the bar I saw Brisbane washing a glass. The bartender was an imposing figure. He stood as tall as Thor and was built like a pro-wrestler. His shoulder length white hair was pulled back into a ponytail and his piercing blue eyes could make anyone feel nervous of starting trouble. Yet despite that intimidating appearance his almost constant smile softened everything and showed his truly friendly nature. However piss him off at your own peril, because if you caused trouble a table would be broken when he hit with you.

Even other Gods didn't cause trouble when in his realm. Here he was in charge. Here he was the head God, with the other bartenders as minor deities, and Succubi waitress his servants. The staff of the Mystic Wolf were their own pantheon, and the bar was both realm and temple. The only difference between the pantheon of the Mystic Wolf and other pantheons was that as long as you made the correct offering you got what you asked for, just make sure to tip the waitress.

When I got to the bar Brisbane was serving a Dragon a Strawberry Volcano. The illusion had yet to erupt so it wasn't quite ready to drink. I flagged the bartender turned God and he made his way over. "Hey Black. What's your poison today?"

"Information, but make me a Midnight Bath just to make it look normal." I didn't want anyone getting suspicious.

"Not a problem." Brisbane turned around and grabbed the ingredients to that particular memory and mixed up a night of skinny dipping in a small pond.

When he turned back 'round and placed the drink in front of me. "So what do you need to know?"

I pushed him the picture of Kara that I had picked up at the condo. "You know this woman?"

Brisbane nodded. "Of course, that's Kara, one of Odin's kids. Sasha tries to hide it but she's got it bad for her. Who'd have thought, right?" Brisbane said as I took a pull on my drink. The feeling of the rebellious water on naked skin hit me as I was encompassed by another person's memory, brought to me courtesy of the drink.

"Yeah she showed me a picture and it definitely caught me by surprise." It wasn't surprising that Brisbane had the same reaction that I had.

"So what can I do to help?" One of the Succubi, Cassandra, walked up and gave the God a new order to start on. He turned his attention back to me once the Daemon was out of sight. "Mind if we talk while I mix drinks?"

"You're the God," I replied. Brisbane had a business to run and I knew from experience he could both talk and mix at the same time. While I waited for him to start talking again I took another pull at my drink.

"So what do you need to know?" he asked as he started pulling bottles of the back shelf. "I don't know too much about her. Well other than what Sasha's told me about her."

"Well she's disappeared. Rather violently at that," I said. "Actually I'm not so much interested in her right now, as I am in Sasha."

Brisbane turned back round holding several bottles in each of his large hands. "A Valkyrie disappears and you're more interested in her friends than you are in her? What sort of angle are you playing?" he asked as he started pouring four completely different drinks at the same time.

"I think that the attack was meant as a way to grab Sasha, but she wasn't where they thought she'd be, met up with a pissed off Kara, and defeated her in a rather bloody battle. Then panicking they took Kara, possibly to use as leverage to get at Sasha later." The theory stood up to everything I could throw at it as the only plausible motive. Everything else screamed even more stupid and insane. I finished the drink as I waited for Brisbane to bring his attention back to me.

"So what you want from me is a list of anyone that maybe showing special attention to Sasha?" Brisbane had always been a quick study.

"Exactly."

Brisbane sighed and ran a hand through his hair. "How do you want the list? Alphabetically might be your best bet. Or do you want it in order of someone stupid enough and with the power needed to make a play like that?"

"You're serious?" I hadn't counted on there being that many possible suspects.

"Extremely." Brisbane's voice was deadpan in the delivery. "You see all of the girls have, in a sense, their own followers. It's sort of like priests focusing their worship on one God of a particular pantheon. Even though they worship all the Gods in that pantheon, they focus on one God or Goddess in particular. It's the same way with the waitresses. Their followers know when their shifts are, what section of the bar they serve, they leave them larger tips than they do for any of the other waitresses that may serve them on a night. Hell the girls just started selling their own novelty, holy symbols."

"Now I know you're kidding." I was hoping he was kidding, but I had the distinct feeling that he wasn't.

"Hold that thought." Brisbane loudly whistled a quick series of notes, which was the call for Cassandra. When she arrived he gave her a tray with the drinks he had just poured. He then turned his attention back to me. "Here, I'll show you."

The bartender motioned me to follow him. He led to the end of the bar to where a glass case held all sorts of bar themed merchandise. The case had quadrupled in size since I had last seen it. The new three-quarters were loaded with samples of merchandise I had never seen before. There was a set of thirty pairs of necklaces, one silver the other bronze, each with a different symbol on them. The rest of the merchandize included glasses, several styles of shirts, jackets, and assorted items with the different symbols. It was almost like looking at sports merchandise for different teams, but from what Brisbane had just told me... "Each one of these is for a different waitress?"

"They hired a graphic artist to come into the bar and work out the different symbols. Took forever. The artist would do an interview for an hour with each girl, and then she disappeared for two weeks and came back with the designs. After another month of retouches everything was ready for them to finance a first run of everything." Brisbane sounded as if he had regretted letting it get this far.

"Why haven't I heard about this before?" I asked.

Brisbane shrugged. "The waitresses realize that some of the people don't care, you and Countess Bloodwolf being two of them. So they've never tried to stake a claim on you. However you guys are in a minority. Even some of the Gods have picked out one waitress as their favorite, so sometimes you'll catch them wearing one of the necklaces." I gave Brisbane a hard look trying to see if he was joking, and quickly realized that he wasn't.

"Considering how many troubles have gotten started over the years because a God couldn't keep it in his pants I guess that it shouldn't be that much of a surprise," I commented. "So do you have a list of who purchased any of the stuff related to Sasha?"

"Of course, it helps to know who likes which waitress. Just give me a couple of minutes." He looked down the bar and called out to another drink slinger, his adopted daughter, Sam, to keep an eye on the bar for a little while so he could run back to the office.

A few minutes after he disappeared into the office he came back with a printed copy of the people who had purchased merchandise with the image of Sasha's 'holy symbol'. "Here you go," he said handing me the list.

The list took up several pages and the type set wasn't large. After each name was a list of what sort of merchandise they had purchased which could be helpful. Then I noticed that many of the names had more than one of the same items purchased. "Let me guess. A lot of these were purchased as gifts?" I asked.

"Unfortunately for you, yes," Brisbane said. "I wish I could be more helpful, but that's the best I can do."

"Well it's a start," I said. I looked at my watch and saw that I still had about three hours before I was supposed to meet everyone at the office. "Do you mind if I take this with me?"

"Sure I've got the file on my computer and it's not like anything on there is private information considering that these guys proudly wear their symbols," Brisbane said. "Is there anything else I can help you with?"

"This should do it. I'm just going to sit down in a booth and try to eliminate some of these suspects," I said.

"I'll send a Succubus your way then." I gave Brisbane a quick wave and looked for the nearest empty booth.

It took me a while to spot one, not aided by the fact that I had never seen the bar look like this before so I didn't know what the seating arrangement was like. A few minutes after sat down, Lori, a blond bombshell of a waitress, brought me a menu. "Can I get you something to drink, sweetie?" she asked, her voice sounding like set of small crystal bells.

"Whatever's on tap," I said to get a rise out of her, since there are more than forty beers on tap.

"Black, you know that doesn't really narrow down the choices," she said, the bells gone. "Now what do you want?"

"You pick beautiful." As soon as she turned around she purposefully gave me a quick, light lash of the tail across my arm, leaving me with a distinct and suppressed urge to goose her. Succubi are hot as sin, and flaunt it, but there are rules that they have to follow. They love pushing the rules as far as they can safely get away with, but they're careful not to break them. They wouldn't dare. They like working in the Mystic Wolf too much to risk it.

I laid out the papers and took out a pen to start checking off my list of possible suspects. My guess was that I might be able to spot a good suspect based on a few traits. The first trait would be by their name on the scene. I was fairly sure there would be a ton of names on this last that wouldn't have near enough power to try something like this even though they were Fey. The next thing to look for was the person's connection to which court. My guess was that I was looking for a court whose ruler was single, or where the rulers were on the outs with each other. I start checking off names of Humans who wouldn't have the power to try a stunt like this since I was looking for Fey, until I was hit with a sudden realization. It was just possible that a Human had been able to strike a deal with the Fey. That reopened the floodgates of possibilities of the people who could have pulled this off. It also opened up a whole new possibility of why this had happened, and I just had to hope that I had the right reason.

I was about to start the process of elimination again when Lori brought me my beer. She looked at the papers and gave me a questioning glance. "What are you sniffing around Sasha's regulars for?"

"I'm working an angle on a case, and I want this to be discreet," I said casually. A thought then struck me and my voice took on a menacing note to match my darkly glowing eyes. "So a word to the wise kid. You tip off anyone on the list to what I'm doing and I'll make sure Brisbane banishes you. Do we understand each other?"

"Whoa, whoa, whoa." Lori held her hands up as if to ward me off. "They're not my regulars. I have no interest in them."

"Good girl."

I watched her nervously walk off. She, like all the other waitresses, knew how deeply I was connected to their boss. If I threatened to have someone banished they knew that it wasn't an idle threat. I had helped Brisbane gather the right sort of people to get the Mystic Wolf off the ground. If I asked him to banish a waitress there was a pretty damn good chance that he'd do it.

I worked until seven and felt I had made some progress when I left for my office.

CHAPTER

When I got to the office I saw Jamie doing a bit of tidying up. "Hey boss. How's the case going?" Her tone was cheerful; she had an almost irritatingly cheerful personality. Considering how she had been thrust into the dark undercurrent of society that I travel in she seemed to love it. She had come to me originally as a client who was going to be murdered as a message to someone who had welched on a debt owed to a shylock who dealt in magick. Now she was my happy, and sometimes over worked, secretary.

Shadow flew off my shoulder and straight into my office where he turned the antique radio on with a quick twist of his head. A second later it was on an oldies rock station and his head was bobbing to the smooth tunes of CCR. *I've got a date!* he said loudly in my head. He'd been saying it every once in a while since he had his little talk with Huginn at the bar.

"It looks like it's going to end up getting messy," I told her, ignoring Shadow.

"Oh? Your usual death and mayhem?" She wasn't even shocked by the idea of me killing people. It was part of my trade; in this world you didn't solve a case and hand it over to the cops. In this part of society you made sure that justice was served with a message that would stick.

"Looks like that. Odin is pissed off. There's an army after my client," I said as I headed into my inner office and opened my desk drawer looking for my bourbon. I found the bottle three-quarters empty. "And I'm almost out of bourbon," I finished.

"I'll pick some up on my way home," Jamie said.

"Actually could you pick up Sasha from the Mystic Wolf and bring her here for me?"

"Sure, that shouldn't be a problem," Jamie said. "So I'm going to guess that she could be in some danger?"

"You could say that," I replied. Jamie didn't scare easily anymore. "So take this." I reached into my gun safe and pulled out 'Lady Bell' a monster of a .357 and tossed it to her.

"Am I really going to need this little lady?" she asked almost casually.

"Couldn't hurt."

"Okay then I'll be back in a little while." She waved over her shoulder as she left the office.

I headed back to my office and went back to studying the list of names Brisbane had given me. I was still hoping that someone would stick out at me like the proverbial sore thumb, but I had no such luck. This was probably going to end up a slog.

By the time my first ally arrived I had just finished a revised list of possible suspects. It was vague at best as much of it was purely guess work. The list I had been given had contained, literally, hundreds of names. I had narrowed it down to just shy of thirty. I had some pictures of a few of them. Never hurts to have juicy pictures of the major players for this specific reason. A few of them I didn't have pictures of because their nature made it hard to get a good picture. The printer was spitting out the last of the print outs I had made of suspects and pictures when my first friend arrived. It was Sarah, a former cop I had brought on to the scene.

Sarah 'Scar Face' was fairly new of the scene, less than two years. Her claim to fame was that I had rescued her from a serial killer that she had encountered during a traffic stop. Her nickname came from the thready scar that ran from above her right eye and down her face to her cheek which had cut deeply into the eye itself. I hadn't been able to save her eye and had instead replaced it with a magickal eye that allowed her to see into the hidden world that she now operates in. The problem was that she has yet to make her bones on the scene and has developed a bit of a Chihuahua complex. She doesn't seem to understand how much of a small fry she is and that I won't always be around to keep her safe. Currently no one has tried to take a swing at her out of fear of my retaliation but it won't last. I'm fairly certain that it will only be a matter of time before I'll be reading the eulogy at her funeral.

My other concern with Sarah is that she has developed an unhealthy romantic interest in me. I try to discourage it as much as possible which isn't easy. I try to help her as much as possible as I feel some responsibility for her. I do this not out of a romantic interest in her but more as if she was my kid sister.

Sarah and I had been making pleasant chit chat for a while with 'Scar Face' scratching Shadow's head when the woman Sarah viewed as her rival for my affection walked in. Yvette, more commonly known on the scene as Countess Bloodwolf, is a dangerous person in the extreme, and she despised Sarah. As far as the Countess was concerned 'Scar Face' was a day old kitten in a world of tigers, and she feared that it was going to get me hurt.

The Countess and I went back decades, all the way back to 1943 when I, along with an ally platoon, raided a Nazi experiment facility. They had been trying to cross Lycanthropy with Vampirism to create a super soldier. Yvette was the sole survivor of the experiments and, at the age of seventeen, had become one of the nastiest Nazi killers that the Allies had. That all happened during the Knights' War, the occult part of World War II. When she had moved to the US after the war there was an almost uncontrollable, underground war raging between various factions and clans of displaced werewolves and vampires. Most of them had come from Eastern Europe and had divided not only along species lines, but also by regional distinctions. Yvette decided that that just wouldn't do and decided to organize the mass of them. Over the span of three decades the two of us culled the ranks of trouble makers so that she could unite them as the Court of Night. She ruled the court with an iron fist, or more appropriately a silver one. Now she rented members of the court for use as enforcers for all sorts of unsavory characters.

Many people considered her as one of the bad guys however she was a business woman with an army at her disposal. All the people in the know realize that I am just about the only person who can keep her from becoming the shadow master of not just the Twin Cities, but in fact the whole country. She has her agents all over the place and if she wanted to she could probably flip a switch and become the true master of the US. Not a single person on the scene dared to cross her that wasn't a God, and I think she even makes some Gods nervous. However the two of us owe each other so many favors that we had stopped bothering to keep track a long time ago.

There was a problem for me dealing with her. She has a bit of a double edged personality dealing with me. She's fiercely loyal to me and when I needed her professionally her personality was that of someone who has people killed on a regular basis as part of doing business. However when no one else is around she acts like a teenage girl with a massive crush. It's irritating to say the least. I see her as my little sister, much in the same way as I see Sarah, but the line has blurred on occasion, much to my lessening regret. The blurring had led to a sometimes strained relationship, in which when I ask her for favors she asks for romantic vacations in return. Truthfully things were getting to a point where a long lasting relationship was becoming a possibility.

Yvette took up a position in the room opposite from Sarah and simply glared at her. I would settle for that for now. The best I could hope from the two of them in their actions towards each other was strained civility. Anything beyond that was only possible in a pipe dream. At least they would never openly act against each other.

Shadow sidled up to Sarah. He always sided with her over Yvette for reasons I had never figured out. It was almost as if the crow had decided that it was up to him to force me to protect the new private dick, and he did have a point to some extent. Of course back when I had saved Sarah from a serial killer named The Necktie Killer when she had pulled him over for a busted tail light, he had been uncharacteristically brave and attacked the guy. He had been enough of a distraction to give me a clean shot. After that he had formed an odd attraction to her.

Shortly after Yvette arrived Detective Wallace of St. Paul PD arrived. I had met him when he worked in homicide and he had come to me with a need for help on a case. He had heard of me through the grape vine as one of those people who could help, just try not to ask or it feels like you've given up. I have many detractors in the various police agencies in the area, and more than a few people have commented on my supposed agelessness. I've been here for over a century and I've seen them come and go. I remember a time back when the Mob ran St. Paul with Police Chief John O'Connor taking kickbacks from illegal enterprises and hiding notorious gangsters from the feds. Memories of that day always remind me of the good old Green Lantern. I was there New Year's Eve of thirty-two and Alvin Karpis was right when he talked about it being the biggest gathering of criminals in US history. It was a different day back then, and a fun one at that. However Wallace is a modern cop. He traces his family line of cops back to the late eighteen hundreds, and proudly says that none of them were corrupt, though personally I doubt it. Still Wallace is a good cop and I had use for him right now, though mostly what I could do at this point was get him off my ass for withholding evidence.

Wallace didn't approve of my relationship with the Countess. To be fair he didn't approve of her period, and with valid reasons. However he knew that I was the only one who could keep her from running an empire that every other crime leader could only dream of. What he doesn't realize is that there are members of the Court in most police departments of major cities throughout the country, and St. Paul's was no different. Here one her agents is in Internal Affairs. If she got annoyed with him he'd quickly find himself looking for a new job.

"So what has us all here tonight?" Wallace asked.

"I have a case that I need help with and I need help from Yvette and Sarah. As for you Detective? Here." I handed him a file of everything I had on the case at the moment. At least everything an official cop could use, much of what I had would be useless for him.

"This for the Odinsdottir case?" Wallace asked. "You could have gotten this to me earlier."

I shrugged. "I had to figure out what would be useable for you. Much of what I have is useless for the regular cops."

"Let me be the judge of that."

Wallace flipped through the file for a few minutes during which time my client walked in, having been dropped off by Jamie. Taking her natural form she pulled her wings in tight so as not to hit anyone in the tight confines of the outer office. "Hello Sasha, thanks for joining us," I said motioning her to take a seat.

"So what is the scam Jason?" Yvette asked. "I take it she's the reason you called us all here."

"She's my client. Now I'm fairly certain that you've seen Sasha at the Mystic before." When they nodded I kept going. "Then let me get down to brass tacks. Someone's kidnapped a Valkyrie who is a good friend of my client and I need your help finding her."

"I take it that you've already talked to Odin?" Sarah asked. I gave her a withering look. "Sorry."

"Odin doesn't know what happened to his daughter, Kara. He told me that she can't be dead or he'd already know about it. However she's not in any realm directly connected to Yggdrasil so he can't see her himself. However I do have some theories." I was about to continue when Wallace interrupted me.

"What are these theories of yours?" he asked sharply. "That place was destroyed, we couldn't find anything that would point anywhere."

"I take it that you didn't take a very close look at the cut marks in the furniture?" It may have been a question, but the fact that I had to ask it was evidence that he hadn't.

"What was there to see?" Wallace asked. "They were made by a heavy sword and or ax. The fact that no one heard anything was more worrying."

I shook my head sadly. Wallace should have realized right away that Kara was a Valkyrie based purely on her name, but apparently he hadn't thought much about it. "So you didn't notice that most of those marks were made by bronze weapons?"

Wallace gave me a blank look for a second and looked like he was about to say something but Yvette got there first. "So you're saying that this Valkyrie, Kara, was taken by Fey?"

"They're insane if they think that Odin would stand for it," Sasha yelped. "Why would they attack and kidnap a Valkyrie?" Her confusion was blatantly obvious, and with good reason. Everybody else's faces asked the same question.

"I'm fairly certain that they weren't after Kara," I said calmly. "I think that the intended target was you."

"Me?" The sound of confusion was replaced by one of fear. No Succubus could put up anywhere near the kind of fight that a Valkyrie could. If the group that had taken Kara had found my client unprotected it would have been Kara coming to seek my help. Well her and Brisbane.

"Unfortunately yes." There was no point beating about the bush on the issue, it was important for my client to know all the facts in a case like this one. I only keep clients in the dark regarding their cases when their knowing certain things could hurt the investigation. This time my client needed to know what happened and why. This case was going to be like the one that my secretary had gone through earlier in the year. Sasha was potentially in danger and not only was I going to have to figure out where her friend was, but I also had to keep her safe at the same time, so I needed help.

"Let me get this straight. You're saying you need an army to help rescue a Valkyrie from who knows how many Fey?" Yvette asked.

"In time I will. However I do need other help than just storming the castle with an army and killing a mess of Fey. I'll also need help figuring out who is after my client." I turned my attention from Yvette to Sasha.

"How brave are you?" I was again reminded of my case with Jamie. I had asked her the exact same question, except in her case it was someone trying to kill her, not kidnap her.

"Brave enough to fight to get Kara back safely," Sasha sad calmly, almost too calmly. "I'll do anything that needs doing, including picking up a blade."

"That's good, because we are going to need your help to crack this case." I didn't usually want to scare my clients, or put them in danger, but in this case there was nothing I could do to help that. However the fact that she wanted to fight was a bit strange, for the most part Succubi scare pretty easily. I chalked it up to her working at the Mystic Wolf. The waitresses have, apparently, gotten used to slapping rowdy customers around.

Sasha's eyes began to glow red, she was pissed. "What do I need to do?" Her voice was a growl, and she sounded almost eager to kill someone.

"You just have to keep to your regular routine. I want you to act as if nothing has happened that has you overly concerned." I wasn't going to have her do anything complicated, especially since she now knew she was in danger.

"But what if they try to kidnap me again. Are you going to be with me?"

I ignored her question for a second to ask Yvette for a favor. "Okay Yvette what is it going to cost me to borrow a few of your best trackers? I'll also need a few fully human hangers on if you can manage it."

"I'll figure out something." I did not like the sound of that answer. "But the real question is how many do you need?"

"Give me a second." I pulled out a map of the U of M Twin Cities campus. "Sasha can you show me your normal routine around the campus?"

"Sure, but why?"

"I'm going to have you tailed, I also plan on having look outs stationed around the campus near areas you normally pass by." The plan was simple but it required a lot more man power than I could muster on my own.

"Okay that should be easy." I handed Sasha several highlighters and let her trace her typical routes using different colors for different days of the week.

"Well seeing as you're busy with this I'm going to head back to the precinct with this file and hand it over to homicide," Wallace said as he grabbed the file and headed out the door.

"Have a good one Wallace and tell your friends that even though they're treating it as a homicide I don't think it is and to stay out of my way." I knew I was going to step on toes with this one but that was just the way of things.

"They're not going to like hearing that." Wallace warned.

"I'll worry about them later. If they want to arrest me let them, they'll have nothing to charge me with." With Yvette's Court member in IA whoever tried to arrest me would be in serious trouble.

"They could try to nail you for obstruction."

"I don't give a shit about that. Just tell them to stay the hell out of my case."

"Your funeral." Wallace's voice was dry and humorless.

"Theirs," Yvette said without going further.

I looked at her and guessed that she had a new agent in the St. Paul PD that she hadn't told me about yet. She was in the process of tightening her grip all over the place. I was beginning to wonder how tight her grip now was. She had the ability to provide services that no one else could so she had something to offer that many people would die for, and some of them had done just that.

"Who do you have in your pocket now?" Wallace asked Yvette.

"That is Court of Night business, and as long as you do your job properly you'll never have to worry about it." Yvette's voice was cold, and her stare equally so, which was offset with an almost kind smile.

I saw Wallace put his hand around his throat as if to protect it from her fangs and swallow hard. I was relieved to see that he wasn't going to push the matter. Sometimes people just disappear, it can happen to anyone, and cops are no exception to the rule. I liked Wallace, he was a good cop and I respected him as a friend, however he knew that I wouldn't stick my neck out very far for him. However I would always do him the favor of warning him off a trail that was going to mix him up in the business of the Court of Night. I have Yvette's ear but I'm not a part of the Court and she protected it from outside interference, but she was always willing to give me just enough information to keep my friends from getting in too deep.

"I guess I'll be leaving now," Wallace said trying to recover some of dignity that he had just lost in front of the Countess.

"Have a good night Detective." Yvette's voice sounded like a venomous syrup.

"I think you made your point a little more thoroughly than you really needed to," I told Yvette after the detective left. "Do you have new Court members in the St. Paul PD?" I asked.

She sighed and gave me an uncomfortably loving look. "I love you Jason, but that is strictly Court business. However it would be fairly safe to assume that you are now shielded from the worst that the state can dish out as long as you don't cross the bounds too far."

The thought that she had that much power scared the hell out of me. She had become a major power in the country and I wasn't even going to bother to think about how much power she actually wielded. As long as we stayed loyal to each other I was in good shape. I didn't care to think about what would happen to me if we had a serious falling out. Of course something major would have to happen for that to be an issue.

My thoughts were interrupted when Sarah tapped me on the shoulder. "So what do you want me to do?"

"You're going to tail Sasha." The job was simple and Sarah had the necessary skills for the job. "You don't have the same face recognition that I do and aren't as noticeable to people familiar with magick as I, or any of the Vampire or Werewolf members of the court are. I'm also not about to trust a Human hanger on of the court to get the job done right."

"That works for me." Sarah looked like she was about to say more when Sasha spoke up.

"Okay that's all of it including the timeline for when I'll be on these routes," the Daemon said.

I turned to look at the map of the campus which was uncomfortably large. Thankfully most of the classes she took were located in buildings that were fairly close to each other. "Thank you. Now let me figure out where we can position a few troops," I said.

Yvette slid up next to me and pointed out look out spots for where her followers would do the most good. Having been a soldier herself in the Knights' War, which had been a covert war, the Countess had a keen sense of positioning agents for information gathering. At several points Sarah tried to interject with a suggestion but her knowledge was from a book and I politely told her that we could do without her help. The poor girl looked crushed but she needed to realize that while she may be a private dick herself she still had a lot to learn. After fifteen minutes we picked out key locations for fifteen spotters to keep an eye out for my client. We decided to rotate look outs so that who was stalking my client wouldn't be able to spot them.

"That should do it," I said. "So Yvette what do I owe you?"

"Three nights in the Bahamas come this summer," she said, which made me nervous as to what Sarah was going to ask for. "More if I lose any soldiers in the battle." Crap!

I could hear Sarah make a low throated growling noise, which I ignored. Unfortunately Yvette didn't ignore it and gave her the kind of smug and wicked smile reserved for a high school cheerleader who got the date with quarter-back instead of the goody two shoes. May the Gods above and below save me from these two.

I sighed; there was nothing I could do about the rivalry between my two friends. I've been alive for over three hundred years and I still have no more clue about women than a twelve year old boy that just figured out the joy of being part of a species with two sexes. "And what do I owe you Sarah? Keep in mind I have a fairly good idea of where your finances stand." The last thing I needed was her to try to get into a pissing contest with the Countess.

The private dick closed her eyes tight and eventually gave a resigned sighed. I had been bluffing about knowing where her finances stood but I was always willing to bet that she was close to desperate for cash. "Three-hundred a day, plus expenses with a five day retainer," she finally said. I was thankful that she was playing sensible. "I also want a dinner date at Buca's." Damn it!

Yvette gave a smug 'humph' which irritated me to no end. Those two...

"Okay here's the plan." I was going to get this done come hell or high water and just deal with the fall out with the two of these girls as it came. "Sarah you are going to go to the Mystic Wolf an hour before Sasha leaves there for school. Give her five minutes out of the bar and follow her."

"What happens if someone tries to make a move on me as soon as I leave the bar?" Sasha asked, which was a reasonable question on her part.

"I doubt anyone would be stupid enough to grab you right outside the bar. However just to make sure that they don't I'll take up a parking spot directly across from the bar," I explained.

"Okay that sounds reasonable I guess." The Succubus sounded justifiably worried about the situation.

"Now back to what happens during the tail. I want you to head straight to your school. When you reach the college you're going to this parking lot in separate cars," I indicated the parking lot closest to the part of the school her classes were, "make sure to park as close to each other as you can.

"After that I want you to go to your classes as normal, no deviation from your normal routine." I didn't want her breaking routine since it might tip whomever was stalking her. "Remember I don't want you acting as if you've been to Kara's house. You are not supposed to know that anything happened to your friend."

I then turned my attention to Sarah. "I want you between 50 and a 100 feet from Sasha at all times. I'm sure I don't need to tell you to keep an eye out for anyone who seems especially interested in our client, and make sure they're giving off a magickal aura."

"This isn't the first time I've tailed a client Jason. I know what I'm looking for," she said in a cool, level voice.

I nodded and gave her points for the remark, she was starting to learn the trade properly. I just hope she isn't going to start getting cocky on me. "Good to hear," I said.

"My people of course will be stationed at their look out points looking for people who seem overly interested as well, and later we'll compare notes to see if we can find a pattern," Yvette said. I hadn't even needed to explain that part of the plan to her. The two of us had done stuff like this before and knew how each other thought. Of course I had been the one to teach her how to do this.

"Where will you be during all of this?" Sasha asked. It was a fair question since I was the one she had hired, not the people I was employing to help.

"I'll be here." I pointed to a point in the middle of the area where her classes were. "I'll be looking around through Shadow's eyes to see what is going on from above."

I was beginning to think you had forgotten about me, the crow said from behind me.

I simply nodded in reply to him. It creeped Sarah out to no end when I replied to Shadow since she was unable to hear what he said, and while neither could my client or the Countess they were used to that kind of stuff.

"So we all know the plan?" I asked. Each of the girls nodded as I turned my attention to them. "Okay everyone get some rest. And Yvette get your troops ready."

"I just have one question." Sasha said. I nodded for her to continue. "What happens once we figure out who is responsible?"

"I will lead a force of Yvette's enforcers into battle against an army of fey," I said leaving the loan of Valkyries a secret. "We'll get Kara back, and the people responsible will face Odin's justice which will be messy, and deadly."

"Then I'm coming too," my client said in a voice that seemed to have no intention of being swayed, but I was going to try anyway.

"Be reasonable," I said. "We're talking about an army of the Fey. You're a succubus. What good do you think you can do?" She may have shown a real interest in fighting but I doubted she could really be of help.

"I drained the life energy of more than a few warriors from Sumer. I gained more than a little insight on the use of weapons from that draining. Trust me, I know how to use a Sumerian sword. I may not be as good as a Valkyrie with a blade but I want to fight. I plan to spill blood, lots of it." Her voice was a low, threatening growl, with her eyes still glowing blood red. She really wanted to dip her hands in the blood of those who had attacked her friend, that much was obvious. I relented.

"Okay you can have your revenge. Just remember that you're my client and you hired me to find Kara, but that also means I'm going to protect you." I was not going to let her die in the process of saving the Valkyrie she loved. If that happened it would be a tragedy worthy of a proper Skaldic Saga.

"Fine, as long as we understand each other."

I nodded. I could understand her wish to save her friend from who knew what torture and I could respect that. If it had been Sarah, Yvette, or Jamie I knew that no matter what I'd go into the fight all guns blazing. "Okay everyone, tomorrow we start this up."

CHAPTER 5

I was in the Mystic Wolf as zero hour approached. In thirty minutes Yvette and I would head out to the U of M to get into our positions. Yvette was going to patrol her people, and I was going to be stationed in the middle of all of it ready for a take down.

"Everyone know their roles?" I asked Yvette who had just walked into the Mystic Wolf after phoning her team of court members to make sure everyone was in position.

"They're ready," she confirmed. "Are 'Scarface' and Sasha ready?"

"Sarah is ready and keeping an eye on my client." I called Sasha over to make it look like she was bringing me the check. However it was really a code we had arrived at to let her know that all was ready.

She came over dressed in very tight shorts and a low cut tank top, the uniform of the sports bar theme that the bar had taken for the night. She put the bill envelope in front of me. "Everything ready?" she asked quietly.

I was surprised to find that she was carrying a spatial fold with her when she was close enough for me to sense it. "What are you carrying with you?" I asked her.

"A couple of sickle swords and a recurve bow with a dozen or so arrows," she replied with a nasty smile. "If things go to shit I want to be ready for a fight."

I returned the smile. I had to give her credit for being ready. I too was ready for things to turn sour. My Tommy gun and whippet shotgun were in my car, both loaded with enchanted iron rounds. My sword was also in my car. It had been a few years since I had fought with a blade but I was hoping that it was like riding a bike. Yvette was ready as well, along with all of her soldiers. She had pulled together all of the Werewolf enforcers she could and had them nearby ready for a fight. I had stopped by the Court of Night's headquarters earlier that day and had seen a shit load of Werewolves preparing for a fight with the efficiency of a military Special Forces unit. Yvette had trained her enforcers to fight as an efficient unit and this was going to be a massive test. Due to the time of day the vampires would not be used in this fight, Vampires are good soldiers at night but this operation was taking place in the mid-afternoon.

Sarah gave me the sign that she was ready from across the room. Unlike most of us she wasn't going into the fight. As a mere human she wouldn't stand a chance in this fight. Had she been honed for a magick fight like my old unit from the Knight's War it would have been a different matter, but she wasn't. When things went south, which would hopefully be sooner than later, I had ordered her to bug out.

Sarah had put up a massive stink about it but I had given her a flat order. I was going to have enough trouble hunting down Kara, fighting Fey, and organizing a battle of my allied forces, without having to keep an eye out for her. A few months ago she had killed one of the Ladies of the River when they had been after Jamie. But popping a few rounds into a magick whore like one of those bitches was nothing compared to what we were going to do now. I just had to hope that she wouldn't do something stupid.

Sasha gave me a warm smile. "Was everything to your liking?" she asked in a voice that was loud enough to be heard, but not too out of the normal to attract attention. If she was nervous it didn't show.

"It was indeed," I replied. I place a 'C' note with the check. "We're just going to finish our drinks. So have a good afternoon."

"Well, have a good day." She left with her normal bounce. This was going well.

Both Yvette and I had been keeping an eye on everyone in the bar to see if we could spot anyone who was paying extra close attention to my client. Unfortunately neither of us had spotted anyone particularly interesting. Everyone from a couple college students to a minor God out of the Hindu Pantheon had been ogling my client. There had been a couple of Fey eyeing her as well, but they were far from being powerful enough in their own right to have orchestrated the attack.

"Well shall we go?" I asked Yvette as I stood up.

The Countess stood up and pulled her beat up field jacket off the back of the chair. She gave me a hug and a kiss on the cheek, which was more to piss off Sarah who was sitting not thirty feet away than to show me affection. "I'll see you later," she said.

I let her lead me out of the bar and once outside we split up and headed to our separate cars. Thankfully she was driving one of her more inconspicuous vehicles, a blue Ford pickup. She had much fancier cars but they would have been far too noticeable on a college campus to really be effective.

I drove my Buick which I planned to put an illusion on when I got to the campus. A classic like a Forty-one Buick Special would be hard to miss anywhere in St. Paul, but no one would look twice at the VW Bug that I was going to make it look like.

Twenty minutes later I was pulling into a parking lot on the U of M campus. I took Shadow from his perch in the back of the car. "You ready boy?"

'Always am,' he replied.

"Know the plan?"

My familiar gave me a withering look. 'How many times have I done this sort of work before?' he asked sounding more than a little annoyed with the question.

I gave his head a quick scratch. "Just making sure. Now off you go." I gave a quick boost of the back of my hand.

Less than ten minutes later my phone rang. It was Sarah's ringtone so I didn't bother saying hello. "Has she left?"

"She just got to her car. I'll call you as soon as I park." Sarah may have sounded calm and relaxed, but I knew she was on edge. She may have tailed people before but this was big. This was the kind of the thing that the FBI pulled off. Sarah hadn't even been out of the academy two years when fate had brought her into this world. Now she was in the middle of something fairly big. This would scare anyone, but she sounded like she was coping well.

The next call I got was from Yvette. "Everyone's in position," she said as soon as I answered my phone.

"Okay Sasha is on her way, so we are hot," I replied.

"I hope they show today. I don't want my people getting bored." Both Yvette and I knew that the worst thing was a bored soldier, they get sloppy and right now we needed them at the top of their game.

After twenty minutes I got another call from Sarah. "We're on campus and heading for her first class of the day," she said then hung up.

I called up Yvette to relay the information and made myself as comfortable as I could manage on a stakeout. I looked through Shadow's eyes and clearly saw that everyone was where they were supposed to be. When Sasha got to her first class hall, Sarah waited outside and we sat on our thumbs for the next two-and-a-half hours. When Sasha left the hall she made a straight line for the next class. She only had a half hour to get to her next class. As planned Sarah stayed a decent distance back.

We were scheduled for a nearly three hour wait until the end of this second class. However we didn't have to wait that long for something to pop.

A couple of Fey trackers showed up on my sight through Shadow's eyes. One was standing directly across from the entrance to the hall. They didn't need much of a glamour to hide from the humans on campus. They were a bit taller than average, thin, and androgynous in ways that every non-binary person I had met would kill for. The main thing they hid were their tall and sharply pointed ears. A body modification specialist probably couldn't get that look with out massively expensive surgery.

Sarah called me almost at the same moment that I spotted the two of them. "I've spotted a Fey across the walkway from the college," she said as soon as I answered the phone. "There's a second one..."

"Yeah I just spotted him," I said interrupting her. The other was off to the side trying to blend into the bushes and doing a half way decent job.

"What do you want me to do?" she asked.

"Keep the one in the bushes in your sight until he gets grabbed by Yvette's soldiers," I told her. "If he makes a break for it I'll need you to follow him, but I doubt he'll do that. As soon as they stuff him in a sack I want you to bug out because that's when things are going to start jumping."

"You sure you don't need me to come along?" she asked and I could hear a hopeful tone in her voice.

"Not a chance, you're not trained for that kind of stuff." I hoped I wouldn't have to worry about her following me into an Arcadian court. "So as soon as the Werewolves grab that guy I want you to bug out." I then thought about it for another second. "Cancel that last order. Keep up with Sasha and call me if anything happens. Once she's out of class bring her back to my place."

"Got it."

I took out my cell and called Yvette. "I've got two targets," I said as soon as she answered.

"Where?" she asked.

"One is directly across from the front entrance of the hall. The other is blending into the shrubs behind them," I replied.

"Who's taking which?"

"Have your enforcers take out the guy in the bushes and keep it quiet. I want you to meet up with me coming from the guy's other side," I said.

"Just like when we took out the Baron in New Orleans," she replied.

"What was that bastard's name again?" I asked as we got into position.

"That was 57 years ago. I don't remember," she replied. "Right now he's just a body we threw into the river. The cops never did find his left arm."

"Good times that," I said when she got into position. "See you in a second."

I eased 'Ace of Spades' out of her holster and put her into my coat pocket, my finger on the trigger guard. In thirty seconds we were on top of him.

I jammed 'Ace of Spades' into the Fey's ribs while Yvette blocked any passerby's sight of the gun. I immediately recognized the guy as being one of the customers Yvette and I had seen at the Mystic Wolf. "Well, well, well. Isn't it nice to see that even Fey are thinking about taking classes at a Human college," I said in a jovial voice to the Countess.

"Oh I don't know. Considering that he was at the Mystic Wolf just a few hours ago he might be too much of a partier for class work," Yvette replied, her voice sounding almost amused.

"That's true I guess." From the tone in my voice, you would never have guessed that I would have been more than happy to put a round into the guy's back.

"Who are you?" The Fey said with sweat dripping from his brow even though it was fairly cold. Then there was a slight rustling of bushes across the walkway and a couple of pairs of furry arms wrapped around the Fey and yanked him out of sight. That was when our man started to seriously sweat.

"Well my name is Jason Black and the young lady on your right is the Countess Bloodwolf." His reaction was almost comically Loony Tunes which caused me to smile. "Judging by your reaction, I'd hazard a guess and say you've heard our names?" He nodded. "Is it safe to assume that you know our reputations?" Another nod.

I turned my attention to Yvette. "You know I do believe that we might be able to get information without too much blood being spilt?" I said happily, not for a second loosening my grip on the fey.

"Pity," Yvette said giving me a melodramatic pout. "Oh well I'm sure we'll able to find some fun today."

"Shall we take this to a more secluded place?" I said happily. "It might get awkward if we were to question this guy out in public."

"Well how about we take him and his friend to your trophy room?" She was referring to the room in my house that I often used when interrogating subjects. The sight of the stuff I've collected over the years tends to scare the hell out of people and they often assume that the type of person who would collect that sort of stuff can be rather unpleasant at times. In my case that is perfectly true, as I am often paid to be highly unpleasant to people.

"Capital idea!" We had worked together so long that this came off as almost being rehearsed. "Now how does that sound mister... mister... I say what is your name anyways?" I asked patting the fey on the cheek.

"Um." He hesitated then mumbled something.

"Do speak up lad. You see this gun is loaded with iron bullets and we would hate to see what happens when Fey get shot by that sort of thing." The tone in my voice was the kind of happy one usually reserved for talking about how great the weather is. "So please don't be shy, I'm sure we can get along smashingly." I dug my heater a little deeper into his back.

He mumbled again, still not giving his name.

"Well since you don't want to give me your name I'm just going to call you Bunny," I said happily. I smiled at the Countess. "Doesn't that sound like a fine name dear?"

"Oh yes Bunny does sound like a good and proper name for a Fairy."

"My name is Frost Wing!" our prisoner yelped.

"Too late we're just going to call you Bunny, and since I named you I get to keep you," I said in a happily smug tone. "Aren't those the rules?"

"I should think so Jason."

"But my name is Frost Wing, damn it," Bunny yelled.

"No, no, no your name is Bunny. Well then Bunny we're just going to go home now and I'm going to give you some delicious tea and crumpets. And if you're a good boy I may even be persuaded not to poke you with a piece of iron too much. Now move before I get tempted to ventilate you." The last part drew down into a snarl as I jammed 'Ace of Spades' so deep into his back that he had no choice but to move away from it.

Bunny seemed resigned to his fate and let me push him to my car where Shadow already was waiting to meet us. I tossed Yvette the keys. "Why don't you drive dear Countess and I'll ride in the back with Bunny."

So who is this? Shadow asked cocking his head to one side.

"Shadow this is Bunny. Bunny this is Shadow," I said politely introducing my prisoner to my familiar.

Shadow cawed and nodded his head. When Bunny didn't react I poked him in the ribs. "Well just don't stand there Bunny. Say hi."

Bunny mumbled a 'hi', which is a bit more than I had expected out of him. "Well Shadow you're going to sit up front while Yvette drives and I sit back here with Bunny and we go back to the trophy room."

CHAPTER

When we arrived at my house we were met by Yvette's Werewolf enforcers, led by the infamous Black Hat, with their own prisoner. The guy was scratched up quite a bit but otherwise unharmed. I handed Bunny over to one of the other Werewolves and led the group into my house. Once inside, Yvette set guards at each door in case these guys had back up who were going to force a fight in the mortal realm.

"Well let's get on with this," I said to Yvette. "Time to have a polite conversation with these two." I turned my attention to Black Hat and the other Werewolf, a big SOB named Terrance Red-Heart. "This way."

I led them to the trophy room and had the Werewolves, who had taken their full Lycanthropic form, firmly plant the Fey into a couple of plush chairs. Black Hat had been in the trophy room before and didn't give it a second look. Terrance on the other hand hadn't and gave a quiet shiver of disgust as he looked around. My two prisoners looked terrified. I wasn't quite sure what they were looking at that got them so upset. Probably most of it. The jar with an infant with a Devil's backbone fermenting in alcohol. The child had died at birth of course, having your backbone exposed to the elements sort of does that to a child. In some cultures they stick a kid like that into a large vat of alcohol and the shit turns into a cure for impotency. Thoroughly disgusting and absolute nonsense of course. However it makes for an interesting addition to the room. I keep the jar next to my pair of shrunken heads. On the other side is a Hand of Glory, much like the one in the Whitby Museum in Yorkshire, only mine's not in as good of condition since I've had to use it a couple of times. There are many more horrors and the mere sight of them helped me interrogate scum.

"Nice collection I have here isn't it," I said proudly to Bunny and the other Fey. "Now let's have a nice chat." I sat down in a chair directly across from my subjects.

Their attention was still roving the shelves so I snapped a couple times in their faces. "Bunny. Bunny, look at me." I then looked at the other prisoner. "Well since I don't know your name I'm going to give you one just like I gave Bunny."

"He looks like a Squeaker," Yvette said cheerfully.

"You know I think you're right," I said. "Now let's have a nice little chat," I repeated.

When the two Fey didn't look at me I snapped my fingers right in their faces. "Come on Bunny, you too Squeaker, pay attention."

Squeaker looked around. "Who? Me?"

I gave an exaggerated sigh. "Yes, you Squeaker." I gave him a tone of long suffering patience.

"My name is Autumn Rain," Squeaker said refusing his new name.

"No. I named you Squeaker," I said slowly and deliberately. "So I'm going to call you Squeaker because until I choose to let you go you are my property."

"We are no one's property," Squeaker said defiantly.

"Actually you are," Yvette said as she sat down on the arm of my chair. "In case you have forgotten the rules to which your kin are beholden, when you are captured you must trade either goods or services in exchange for your release. Now since we have captured you, you must make a trade for your release."

"Um, err." Both Bunny and Squeaker looked nervous.

Black Hat dug his claws into Squeaker's shoulder, and ground them in. The Fey screamed. "What do you want?" He asked, crying from the pain, blood oozing from his shoulder. Bunny looked terrified.

"I just want a couple questions answered. You answer me nicely, without lying and I let you go simple as that. Don't and well," I nodded to Red-Heart and he followed Black Hat's example, which caused Bunny to scream, "You get the idea."

"What do you want to know?" Squeaker whimpered, tears of pain rolling down his face.

"I want to know where Kara Odinsdottir is," I said calmly.

"What makes you think we know anything about a Valkyrie?" Squeaker asked. He was ballsy I'd give him that but apparently he was also suicidal.

"Well let's see. We caught the two of you stalking my client Sasha Sumer. She had been spending a lot of time with Kara, and it was by pure chance that she hadn't been there when a group of Fey attacked." My tone of voice sounded as if I was musing the words to myself but it was obvious that what I was saying was directed at my two prisoners.

"I'm serious," Bunny pleaded, "We've never heard of Kara Odinsdottir."

"Red-Heart," Yvette said lightly.

The Werewolf worked his claws further into Bunny's shoulder. "I don't know who you're talking about!" Bunny screamed.

"How about you Squeaker?" I asked. "Do you feel like being more cooperative?"

The Fey looked at his fellow stalker. "Please don't, we've never heard of her. We were just told to follow the Succubus. I never heard of any mention of any Valkyrie."

"Black Hat, would you be so kind?" I said.

The Werewolf squeezed again. Squeaker screamed. "Please we don't know anything." Tears were streaming down Squeaker's face.

Bunny looked at me, his face was almost ashen at this point. "I'd be more than happy to tell you what you wanted to know to make this stop but I don't know anything." His voice was desperate and I was beginning to think he was telling me the truth.

"Should I get a hammer?" Yvette asked obviously hungry for tasting another's pain. I may be a professional bastard some times, often more than I really need to be, but Yvette was on a different level. This time I was going to reign her in.

"No. I think he's telling me the truth."

"Pity." The Countess sounded genuinely disappointed. As I said, she's an absolute psycho at times.

"So who do you answer to?" I asked patiently. "And remember, I'm all that stands between you and The Countess right now."

"King Tormisican," Bunny said. I had never heard of the guy, but with Fey that didn't mean much. There are so many Fey kings, almost all of whom are self-appointed, that not hearing of the guy wasn't surprising. "He told us to follow the Succubus. He didn't tell us why. All we were told to do was let him know when she was alone. He said that there had been a massive fuck up a few days back. That was all he said. Please don't hurt me anymore." At that point Bunny simply broke down in tears.

I was looking at both Bunny and Squeaker who was nodding his head. "Do you have something add Squeaker?"

"I overheard that the King wants to make some sort of power grab..." Squeaker was interrupted in his line of thinking when a pissed off Sasha stormed into the room. She had taken on her true form, only far taller than normal and had her swords hanging from her belt in their sheaths.

"Let me guess. He wants me to be by his side while he rules a decent part of Arcadia?" She grabbed Squeaker bodily out his chair with one hand around his neck and squeezed hard.

"Gerk... keck... yes..." The fairy clawed at Sasha's arms trying to get her to loosen her grip enough to breathe properly. "Plea... kerck... let... me... dow... keck."

Sasha threw him back into his seat with enough for it to fall back against Black Hat who didn't even flinch. As Squeaker scrambled back to his feet I saw blood flowing freely from puncture wounds left by the Succubus's claws.

"Well I think your would be king is a fool if he thinks he has any chance of ruling any part of Arcadia with Sasha. She's seems a little pissed." My tone was easy as I'd let her actions speak for her.

"He won't take 'no' for an answer," Bunny said, obviously terrified of my client. "He is used to getting his way..." Now it was Bunny's turn to face Sasha's wrath.

Sasha had her clawed hand wrapped around Bunny's throat. "You can tell your king, or whatever he is, that I'll rip his eyes out and force feed them to him so he can watch as I eviscerate him if he doesn't return Kara to me. Am I being perfectly clear?" Her voice was a full throated growl. She meant every word of what she had just said.

Bunny didn't even try to say anything, he struggled a nod before Sasha slammed him back into his chair. Unlike when she threw Squeaker into a chair, this time Sasha didn't let go and the chair died in an explosion of wood and upholstery. "Bill me for it," Sasha snarled before I said anything.

"Okay you two have one chance to save your lives before I let Sasha work you over, and I'm willing to bet she'll be more creative than I could possibly imagine." Sasha rubbed the knuckles of her right hand, her eyes glowing red. "So what I want is for you to lead us to your kingdom. You do that, you are free to go. If you don't, well, I'm fairly certain that you will learn what true pain means. So if I were you I'd cooperate."

"You won't be able to defeat his army," Squeaker said panicking at the sight of Sasha.

"As you may have noticed I have an army of Werewolves to back me up," I said calmly. "What does he have?"

"He has hundreds of Fey, including Goblins, Trolls, and Giants. You simply don't have enough werewolves to fight them." Bunny stammered. His voice showed the same fear as Squeaker's. "Plus he has Sir Lamorak of Arthur's court in his service." That was worrying.

"I thought Lamorak was killed by Morgana's son Mordred," I said.

"No Mordred made a deal with King Tormisican's late wife for her to take him, after he drugged him with a poisoned dagger," Squeaker said.

"Who's Lamorak?" Yvette asked.

"He was a knight of the round table, and a really nasty piece of work. According to the legends he fought and defeated twenty knights in one battle. However I don't know how much of that to believe. However with the evidence that was at Kara's house he was one of the combatants." He would have spent years in Arcadia so only the Gods know what that had done to him. More than likely he would be far more dangerous now.

"I don't care who you have you miserable scum. Anyone that stands between me and Kara will find themselves on a direct route to Kur-nu-gi-a!" Sasha snarled. I was beginning to think that the Succubus would be one of my most dangerous weapons. She had at first been scared at the thought she was in danger. Now she had evolved into someone who was in love and was going to fight for her love with everything at her disposal.

"Kur-nu-gi-a?" Yvette asked me in a whisper.

"Sumerian land of no return," I replied at the same low tone.

"Ah..."

I walked over to where the two Fey lay on the floor. "Now you are going to lead us to your section of Arcadia and once there you're going to tell your king that we have come for him and the Valkyrie. Any resistance will be met with extreme force."

"And if he refuses?" Bunny asked worriedly.

"Your realm will be razed to the ground. There will be a scorched Earth policy held by my troops and I."

"And if we refuse to tell you?" Squeaker asked trying to seem brave.

"Well I'll let Sasha work both of you over for a while. After that I'll get down to the serious torture. And so you know I've gotten Daemons, tougher than you two wastes, to break contracts before." As I said this I went over to a cabinet and got out some rather nasty instruments that dated back to the Spanish Inquisition and made sure they saw it.

"You're insane!" Bunny yelped.

"No, just ruthless," I said calmly. "Now before Sasha and I start becoming highly unpleasant would you like to lead us back to your part of Arcadia? You see it really makes no difference to me how much you suffer, I'm being paid to find someone that your king has. I just want to earn my check and get the Valkyrie back and if you make it more difficult than it has to be, well..."

"I'll talk! I'll talk!" Squeaker yelped, obviously aware that I wasn't bluffing.

CHAPTER 7

When we got to the realm where Kara was being held the ring immediately started to vibrate. The whole group of us were armed to the teeth. The Werewolves carried assault shotguns that had been retooled to be belt fed weapons where the belts were 10 gauge, blessed, iron slugs. No Fey was going to stand up to that kind of power. They also had mortars and RPGs with them for some long range power to soften the bastards up. The Fey still didn't understand more modern weapons very well. They had been driven from the Isles by steel swords and very few traveled back to the mortal world long enough to see what new toys we had.

As for the rest of us Yvette was in her 'working clothes' which meant that the short, nonagenarian teenager looked like the biggest badass that wasn't an actual God, and there was even some debate on that matter. For her part Sasha was armed with her sickle swords and a recurve bow. As for myself, my Tommy and whippet were loaded with iron rounds, my little girl, 'Ace of Spades', was resting in her holster. On my hip was my sword.

I could see the castle from where we stood. It was a palace that, had it been built by humans, a three year old armed with a water pistol could have taken. However this was a Fey castle which made it dangerous.

I grabbed Squeaker by the throat and looked him dead in the eye. "Tell your king that we are here for the Valkyrie and that he is to bring her himself. If he doesn't wish his kingdom to be destroyed then he had better come. If he refuses the destruction will be thorough. You have one hour to return with his response." To make things clear I grabbed 'Ace of Spades' and forced Bunny to the ground with the gun pressed against his skull. "And be quick about it or your friend is a dead man. Got it?"

"Of course. I'll be back with his answer as quickly as I can." Squeaker yelped, and then disappeared.

"So what now?" Yvette asked.

"I get ready to call in the cavalry," I said with a smile.

"You think we're not going to be enough?" Yvette asked.

"I'm not sure. Besides you know me, I always stack the deck as heavily as I can."

"How heavily?"

"This heavily." I took out Huginn's feather and wrote a note on a piece of parchment, and burned it to summon the rest of Odin's Valkyries.

Within a minute nearly forty black winged, golden haired, armor clad beauties appeared. Each one bore a shield emblazoned with the symbol of Odin's ravens, and a golden sword. One of them approached me. "I am Hildr, I take it that you are the infamous Jason Black, whose very name has come to mean the Bringer of Justice." That was a new one on me.

"I am the one known as Jason Black," I replied, I was going to have to wing this one. "The king of this realm will face justice and if possible I will bring him to Odin to face the All Father's wrath."

Then Hildr turned to face the rest of the Valkyries. "My sisters, today we go into battle with The Bringer of Justice as our leader! We fight to save our sister Kara 'The Wild Storm'!" The Valkyries screamed a battle cry that shook the very earth.

Yvette leaned up against me. "I think you just stacked the deck plenty," she whispered in awe.

It was at this point that Squeaker returned. "The king refuses to return Kara unless Sasha agrees to become his queen. He is sending his army to destroy you." Then his eyes caught site of the Valkyries and he just about fainted.

I slapped Squeaker back to reality. "You and Bunny can run now. You have served my purpose well so I'll let you save yourselves. So run and run fast." I was feeling a little generous for the first time in quite a while.

I started seeing large forms moving in the distance, giants. I turned to look at Black Hat. "Are your men ready?"

"We're ready, Black," the Werewolf replied as he patted the RPG he was holding. Behind him were several mortar crews that had just finished setting up four medium weight mortars.

"Good man." I looked at Hildr. "Give us an idea of how far out these guys are and we'll know what to shoot at."

"Of course." The Valkyrie jumped high into the air and with several beats of her wings had achieved a decent elevation. In a minute she was back. "They're about a mile out, and we are heavily outnumbered." She then grinned. "Just the way I like it."

"Time to soften this scum up a bit." I turned to look at Black Hat and his crew of Werewolves. "Okay boys. Light 'em up!"

A forward spotter for the crews set the range and called the strike. I heard four muffled 'fumphs' and saw the mortars arcing through the sky. Not too long after came the explosions, then the screaming.

"Shadow, take to the air and give me the news. I want to know everything that is going on." I head another volley of mortars being fired off.

Yes master. Then Shadow was off into the sky.

"Just like the good old days, isn't it?" Yvette said to me with a grin.

"Just like 'em," I said returning the grin.

After a few minutes the mortar crews ran out of ammunition. "What do we have coming our way Shadow?"

Okay they're still coming but we really thinned them out. Problem is, is that these guys are damn near suicidal. You'd swear that they're World War

Two Japanese soldiers the way they're ignoring the casualties. It's almost like their king has the whole lot of them under some sort of geas. Shadow reported.

"More likely they're just severely pissed that anyone from our side of the veil dares to cross over to fight them on their soil," I replied. "All we've done is stirred up the hornets' nest."

Well whatever we've done they're just about here.

I turned to Hildr. "Okay little lady. You and your girls are up. We'll provide ground support."

"Thank you, Bringer of Justice, our blades wish to taste the blood of those who stand between us and our sister." She turned her back on me. "My sisters! For the honor of Odin we fly!!!" The host of Valkyries pulled their swords from their sheaths and with a deafening battle cry jumped into the air.

"My turn?" Yvette asked. I simply nodded. I watched her body twist and listened to her bones break and reassemble themselves as the color fled from her skin until it was the pale bluish gray of a corpse. As horrifying as she was, a skeleton of a Werewolf as designed by a fever induced mind, with skin stretched over it as if the monster hadn't eaten in months, I was beginning to think of it as cute in her own way. She turned to look at her small army. "Okay boys let's show these Fey pansies how real soldiers fight!"

Yvette's army didn't have time to cheer when the opposing force fell upon us. The sound was deafening as the machine guns roared to life, and the Fey who were hit by the iron screamed in agony beyond agony if they weren't outright killed. Our allied army was still heavily outnumbered but between the werewolves' machine guns and the Valkyries swooping in from above to deal mortal blows with their magickal swords, the enemy forces were quickly diminishing. Yvette simply ignored any attack and would kill any idiot dumb enough to attack her. Between her Vampiric and Lycanthropic natures she was damn near untouchable, she just kept moving and killing.

Sasha had to jump into the fray to get close enough to attack anyone. Apparently the Fey army had been ordered not to attack her directly since she was the prize that the king wanted. Still she had taken some injuries as elven archers let fly arrows at me that went wild and grazed her. Still nothing serious had happened to injure her too severely but she was, however, covered in the blood of the slain.

The Fey that came close to me took a volley from my Tommy, though after a while I had to let him drop for lack of ammo. The second weapon to run out was the whippet which I had used on anything that flew that wasn't Shadow or a Valkyrie. From then on out I just popped off rounds from 'Ace of Spades' every time I got a decent shot.

Twenty minutes into the battle the Fey started retreating, obviously aware that they were literally out gunned by my allied forces. The Werewolves kept firing at the backs of the retreating fey. As the fey retreated out of range of the guns, we ran after them towards the castle, and that's when things went Antarcticly bad it was so far south.

As we followed the castle simply stayed put, never getting closer, we had run for what seemed like hours. The ring's buzz had stayed consistent so I knew we were still going nowhere. "Shadow what the fuck is going on, can you see me?"

Master can you hear me?

"I can what's going on?"

Thank the Gods above and below I've been trying to reach you for the last two hours. You've been running in circles for awhile now. They must have gotten you trapped in some kind of ring I can't find the edges of so I can't break it. You need to force your way out. And when you do it's going to get ugly real quick.

"Fuck! Where are the Valkyries?"

They've got their hands full at the moment.

"What's going on? I can't see through your eyes, whatever has us trapped is blocking most of our connection."

A flight of wyvern riders just showed up and are trying to roast or shoot the Valkyries out of the sky. They're holding their own right now, but could really use some help.

It took me a solid two minutes to remember a trick for breaking out of a fairy circle. I pulled off my trench coat, turned it inside out, and put it back on. That yanked me off my feet and I landed hard on my ass outside of the circle of running Werewolves. We were in the middle of a trampled field, no castle in sight but where there had been now lay a twisted, dark woods. This was going to shit.

"Shadow can you hear me?"

There was only static. I couldn't hear him, whatever had us trapped now had gained another layer of defensive energies. I saw the circle of runners returning and as Yvette passed me I grabbed her, and with a loud bang I had her out.

"What the hell is going on Jason?!" She screamed as she shook her head.

"Fairies had us trapped in a circle chasing our fucking tails. I don't know where we are at the moment though. I have no idea where the castle is, but first we need to grab the others." We waited for another go round of our army. As they came into view I yanked Sasha out and Yvette grabbed her top lieutenant, Red-Heart out.

As Sasha snapped out of the effects of the circle I heard her screaming a loud string of profanities in more than a few languages. "… bastards!!! You will all fucking pay for this!!!" She looked around confused and was getting ready for another long screaming fit.

"No time for that," I said quickly. I looked over at Yvette who was bringing Black Hat up to speed. "Yvette have your lieutenant start pulling everyone else out, we need to find that castle."

Yvette spoke a few quick words to her soldier before running up to me. "Can Shadow guide us out of here, that woods doesn't look very inviting."

"I can't hear him, and last I heard the Valkyries were having their own issues, so we can't wait for help from them either."

"Woods it is then," Sasha said with a snarl.

By this time we had about a dozen Werewolves with us with the number quickly growing. "Okay everyone were going into the woods. Last I heard from Shadow there have been some major changes in what we're facing, but I haven't heard from him since we got out of the circle. We're going in slow. We don't know what's in there yet so Yvette and I are taking point."

"I'm coming with you." Sasha stated simply and I knew there was no point trying to dissuade her.

"Of course you are. Everyone be careful."

As we approached the woods distances stopped meaning anything once again. As we had taken ten steps forward, and suddenly we were deep in the woods and were barely able to see the clearing we had just been in. The woods had the deep, earthy smell of wet, rotting timber. What I did notice though was the vibrations of the ring were getting stronger so I knew we were heading in the right direction.

There was a sudden yell as Black Hat dropped midstride, and as he fell he returned to a human form. "Everyone kiss the dirt and find cover!" Yvette yelled as quickly as she could, but not fast enough as there suddenly five more humans stretched out flat amongst us. "What the fuck is happening?"

I wriggled snake like to the nearest human and did a quick examination of him. First checked to make sure he was still breathing, thankfully he was. Next I checked his pupils and saw that his pupils were relaxed and dilated, no one was home. Last I checked for injuries, and quickly found a small needle with a piece of nearly invisible thread trailing from it. Fuck this was going to suck. "Elven soul stealers!" I yelled out.

"Are they going to make it?"

"We'll need to find a shaman or witch doctor and hope, but first we have to get out of here."

I looked around using my magickal sight, trying to see if I could spot an elven sniper or more. I couldn't see any but I wasn't taking chances that where ever we were wasn't playing more tricks.

"Can anyone smell any of these bastards," I called out.

I heard a lot of Werewolves sniffing, making it sound like they all had colds, would've been funny if not for the circumstances we were currently in. There was a lot of shaking heads. Fuck time to slow down everything around me. Not something I wanted to do in a circle because of how easy it would be to get lost plus it took a hell of a lot out of me, but I needed to cover a large area and stay relatively safe. "Yvette, I'm going to take a quick peek around."

"Are you sure that's a good idea here?"

"It's a terrible idea but it's also the only one I have at this moment." I took a coin out of my pocket and put it on my fist ready to flip, and got into a crouch. "If I'm not back in time to catch this before it lands you can worry."

"Just like scouting around Eagle's Nest. Be care..." Yvette said as I flipped the coin. I slowed down everything around me and ran like hell over an area about the size of four football fields. I found two elves, snapped their necks, did another quick check, and returned as she finished "...l."

I snatched the coin out the air and dropped down next to Yvette breathing hard. "I hate that," I said, gulping air. "Two dead elves 40 yards up. After that we should be clear for a while."

"Takes a lot doesn't it." It wasn't a question, she knew I could go longer but right now I didn't have enough time for the luxury of a recovery period.

"Sound off! Who's still fuzzy and ready for a fight?" Yvette yelled, giving me a couple precious minutes.

Sasha snuck up next to me. "You okay?" She sounded genuinely concerned.

"Nothing to worry about, just need a second." Which was all I got as our army informed Yvette we were down seven troops. Yvette ordered three more to gather the fallen and stand guard but to keep quiet as possible until they received new orders directly from her.

"Let's saddle up," I called as I got up and started moving out again.

"Hold up Captain, I want to try something out," Yvette said. I wasn't sure what she was about to do, but she was always learning new tricks that I'd never seen before.

She stood up tall; her eyes began to glow blood moon red. I didn't know what to expect when an icy wind whipped up sending the temperature into a nosedive, and an eerie howl started echoing off of nothing. I looked around and saw the skeletal ghosts of a pack of wolves charging through the woods. I had the feeling of a parade walking across my grave as three ran through me.

Up ahead I heard some screaming and then waited a few minutes for the pack to return. They stopped in front of Yvette and bowed their heads. She bent down, "What is your report?" There was a howl and the pack disappeared. "Ahead the trees are alive," she said.

"What's that mean?"

"Unsure, I didn't even know I could do that until just now. I'll have to work on it more before I fully know."

"Great," I muttered. "Okay everyone stay sharp and keep an eye out for your mates."

We started moving again. We reached a nearly full wall of densely packed trees. I approached them and was suddenly grabbed by a branch and thrown back 30 feet into another tree. Then all the trees started moving with a motion similar to a jerky marionette and started grabbing Werewolves and tossing them. My soldiers didn't take well to that and raged as they fought back, but they were making very little progress.

"Time to burn trees!" Sasha screamed next to me, as she cloaked herself in Hellfire, and with her sickle swords burning like the sword of the Arch-Angel Michael went on rampage of slash and burn deforestation. Soon the woods dissolved around us and we were a mere hundred yards from the castle.

The castle appeared to be made of pink spun sugar, with no real door. The crenellations were barely there, but I knew looks were usually deceiving in this realm. This was going to be all sorts of nightmares.

Hey boss can you hear me?

"Good to hear from you buddy. What's going on up there?"

Look up and you'll see.

I aimed my eyes skyward and saw the remaining four Wyverns in full retreat, then turning my attention to the ground I saw the plain littered with probably a dozen or so broken bodies of the Draconic creatures, their blood liberally painting the grass red. About 30 Valkyries landed next to them with Hildr in the lead. She was bleeding from a couple arrow wounds and looked bloody well pissed about the matter.

"How are you ladies doing?"

"Two of our sisters have been forcefully returned to Valhalla, and five others badly wounded and are going back now before a forced return. Right now the rest of us just want to slaughter these cowards."

"Works for me." I looked over at where Yvette was talking with White-Face. "How are we doing on artillery?"

"Not well. We have a only about a dozen or so shells for the RPGs, and most of my men have less than hundred shells for their guns. After that it's tooth and claw time. Though after what happened to their comrades they're looking forward to the taste of blood."

"Got it, let's get locked and loaded. You've got five minutes."

"Then what?" Sasha asked.

"I give them an opportunity to surrender. Which isn't bloody likely but I'm still going to give them the choice."

In five minutes our remaining forces were ready to unleash another wave of Hell in Arcadia. I approached the castle, staying what was most likely out of long bow range. "Shadow."

Yes master? He asked landing on my shoulder.

"I want you to fly around the castle far enough to not be a target but close enough to make sure we don't get flanked."

Got it boss, be careful. He took off and I waited for a couple of minutes and using an illusion to amplify my voice, I gave them their chance. "King Tormisican I am giving you a chance to surrender and hand over the Valkyrie and give yourself up. If you do we will spare the rest of your people, defy us and you and your people will die."

There was no movement for a while. Then I saw archers pop up from behind the crenellation and had my demands answered by a volley of arrows that landed mere feet from me. "Countess we have their answer, let's light 'em up."

"You heard him boys, blow the fucking roof off the place." In seconds the twisting trails of six RPGs signaled our counter offer. The explosions sent great chunks of sugar like stonework crashing to the ground turning to nothing more than dust as they hit, as bodies flew high into the sky.

"I want you to hit the base of the building with your next set of rounds. Let's see if we can make a door."

Six more RPGs blasted into the base of the castle, and I could see a cracking that showed a large gate just barely visible. This was just the opportunity we needed. "My dear," I addressed the Countess, "the door is cracked open; I think that's our invitation to open it the rest of the way."

Yvette gave me a look that was almost cute in childlike eagerness to wreak unimaginable havoc, even taking into account the skeletal wolf face. Her eyes were just so full of unearthly light. "My pleasure."

Yvette simply ignored the defenders attempt to dissuade her entry; boiling oil and dropped rocks only managed to piss her off even further. She simply ripped the gate of its hinges with sheer dumb strength. I'd seen her toss tanks in the Knights War, a simple gate was nothing to her.

We met little resistance once inside the castle but just to be safe I had the Valkyries keep watch on the ramparts for any reinforcements as the Werewolves with Yvette in charge ran throughout castle to find any remaining enemy force. This left me and Sasha to do our own search.

I followed the vibrations of the ring and we made our way deeper and deeper into the castle. What worried me was that we had yet to run into Sir Lamorak. I was guessing that he was going to be closer to King Tormisican. I had put 'Ace of Spades' back in her holster having run out of bullets on the way through the gate and now had my sword in hand. I turned down the hall and saw the throne room with a bloated Elf that I assumed to be the king sitting on the throne looking suicidally smug.

"Give me Kara you smug, bloated bastard!" Sasha screamed, pointing at him with the blood coated, sickle sword held in her right hand.

"Ah you've brought me my prize," the Elf king said. This guy was completely mad as the proverbial hatter.

"Hardly," I said calmly. "You must be insane to think that a pissed off Succubus would willingly be your queen."

"No one gains entry to my castle without my permission so you must have brought her to me." There was something off about the king's eyes. They weren't focused properly.

"Come out Lamorak, I know you have the king under some sort of control." I yelled. Only a human so long in Arcadia could pull off a stunt like this.

"Well you have caught me out," Sir Lamorak said in an almost amused tone as he stepped out from behind the king who simply fell to the ground. The back of the king had been hollowed out as if to make him into some sort of grotesque parody of a ventriloquist dummy. The sight would have made me wretch if I hadn't seen worse. Truthfully I was half tempted to take it back with me and put it in my trophy room. It would make a great addition if I put it next to the electric chair that was used to execute William Kemmler back in 1890. The museum's display houses a great copy, even they don't know that it's a fake. The remains of the king would be nice and disturbing for the next person I questioned.

"How long have you been in control of this kingdom?" I asked.

"Completely?" Lamorak looked up at the ceiling in a musing moment. "Ever since the queen died. You see I made this puppet soon after I came here. It was of course the queen that directed me to do it. She wanted complete control of the kingdom so she had me kill the fool since his followers were devoted to him and would never have done it."

"You are sick and insane if you think I would even consider committing to a Human as vile as you." Sasha raised her swords and leapt at the corrupted knight. Her wings forced her into a head on rush that took Lamorak off guard and sent him smashing into a wall.

However the Arcadian strengthened knight wasn't about to take the hit and stay down. "I will have you as my queen," he roared as he pulled himself to his feet and sent her sprawling with a well-placed punch to the jaw.

With Sasha out of the way I could launch my own attack. I rushed him with both my hands wrapped around the hilt of my sword. The knight blocked the attack easily and came back round with his own. Every strike I attempted he blocked easily and I barely managed to parry his own. Quickly he smashed my sword from my hands and slammed his knee into my gut and then smashed a tooth loosening punch straight to my jaw. I could feel blood drooling from my mouth but I had no time to worry about it.

I was obviously no match for the knight in physical combat, so time to switch up the game. I jumped into the nearest shadow to hopefully regain some advantage. I scaled the walls of the castle hoping to get the literal drop on him. Unfortunately the Knight had his own magick, and with a blast of light threw me out of the shadow dropping me 20 feet to the ground. With the breath knocked out of me I didn't have a chance to recover for he rolled me on to my back.

"Time to die, half breed," he snarled as he placed his foot on my chest and was about to drop his blade straight through my neck. This was it, I knew I was dead and ready to regret some of the last 70 plus years worth of life choices. Then he suddenly jerked, once, twice and his sword dropped. On the third jerk he turned; I saw the arrows that had found their way from Sasha's bow into his back. He started walking towards her, his arms stretched out.

"Nobody can claim me and steal my friends away," Sasha growled and let loose a fourth arrow that found its mark in the knight's throat. The knight finally dropped to the floor, his sightless eyes staring at the ventriloquist dummy made of the real king. I picked myself up and for good measure kicked him hard to make sure he was dead.

"Well Odin can bring him back to life and torture him to death again if he wants," I said hazily, as colors danced in front of my eyes.

"Now we just have to find Kara and rid ourselves of this place," Sasha said and grabbed me by the wrist to look deeper into the castle.

I let my eyes unfocus to talk to Shadow. "Hey feathers, how are things going up there."

We hold the castle and there is no longer any resistance, he replied.

"Okay find Yvette and send her down to me."

How will she find you? My familiar asked.

"She's got a hell of a good nose for tracking remember,"

It wasn't long before the vibrations of the ring on my finger were so fast that the ring was audibly humming. "We're getting close," I said unnecessarily.

A couple minutes later we found ourselves in what I guessed was the dungeon. The humming from the ring was getting a bit too loud for my taste so I took it off which immediately quieted it. Looking down the row of cells we saw one that had weapons dropped around it. I guessed that the Fey guarding her had realized what was going on and had done a runner to try and save themselves. Most likely a Werewolf or two had killed them anyways. I opened the door to the cell and was horrified with what I saw. It was Kara pinned to the ground by her own sword. My guess was that she had healed too fast from any other weapon so they had eventually used her own sword to hold her.

Sasha ran over to the Valkyrie and wrenched the sword from her chest and cast it aside. Kneeling down, she propped the warrior woman's head in her lap. She reached over and grabbed Kara's hand with her right hand and gently caressed her cheek with her left. I heard the Infernal whisper to her Angel that she loved her and not to leave her. I stepped back through the door not knowing what to do.

I'm well over three-hundred years old but relationships still confuse the hell out of me. The relationships I have become used to over the years are with me being the one pursued. I would have no idea what I would do in such a situation. I turned back around in time to see Kara reach up with her own hand to touch Sasha and I felt a great sense relief wash through me. We hadn't been too late. It was about this time that Yvette showed up.

"I just saw a guy in armor used as a pin cushion on my way down here," the Countess said.

"Yeah Sasha saved my life." I looked at Yvette, who had returned to her Human form and noticed that her clothing was shredded. "Need my jacket?"

"Why?"

"With all the damage your clothing took you're not too far off from being indecent," I commented.

"Like anyone but you would say anything about it."

"True enough. So what's the news?"

"You tell me. We hold the castle, and there has been no attempt by the Fey to take it back." Yvette should have looked smug about it and when she didn't I knew something was wrong. She just sounded tired, which meant bad news.

"Who did we lose?" I asked knowing I didn't want to hear the answer.

"Red-Heart's dead, along with White-Face and Shadow-Dancer. Plus we have to find the victims of those Soul Stealers, we didn't go back to check on them after the woods disappeared," Yvette said slowly. "And before you blame yourself, I was the one who brought them in. They're my soldiers and even Werewolves die. This was a war and in war even the good guys die. Just like the Knight's War, we lost good people too early." She slumped into me and simply started crying.

I wasn't sure how to react. I was just glad that no one else was around to witness this, especially none of her people. I put an arm around her. There was nothing else I could do.

After a few minutes she pulled herself together and her face took on its usual hardened features that accompanied her working clothes. "What is going on down here?"

"The king of this realm has been dead for quite a while, and Sir Lamorak, that was the pin cushion you just saw, had hollowed him out and turned him into a magickal ventriloquist dummy," I explained to my old friend.

"Going to keep it? It would make a nice addition to your trophy room." She knew me almost too well, and the joke was going to help her from cracking again.

"Already trying to figure out a good place to put it," I replied. "Can you send Hildr down to talk to me?"

"That Valkyrie that did the talking with you?"

"Yeah her."

"Sure I'll bring her down to you," Yvette said.

"Thanks."

Fifteen minutes later Hildr arrived following the Countess. "How is my sister?"

"She'll live, but it would help if we got her to Eir or Odin. She had a sword run through her chest for a while, and I don't have the skill to patch her up," I said.

"Was it one of those bastard Fey's swords?" Hildr asked.

"No it was one of your own."

"Then you're right, it will take Eir or Odin to patch her up. One of Idun's apples would do it as well." I've met Eir once or twice, nice lady. Idun doesn't get out very often because of tending her orchard. The perpetual teenager had a lot on her plate tending the apples that grant immortality to the Gods and it kept her as busy as her fellow teenager Hel who had to deal with the dead down in Niflheim.

"Can we get to Asgard from here?"

"Once we get out of this wretched castle it won't be a problem," Hildr replied.

I turned expecting to see Sasha still holding Kara in her arms in the cell but instead she was standing just behind me cradling the Valkyrie in her arms. Kara's head was nuzzled against the Succubus's shoulder, seemingly asleep. "Let's get out of here, I want to take her home."

"We first need to get to Asgard to patch her up. Then we can go back to the mortal plane."

"Fine let's get out of here."

"Let me grab Lamorak and we'll take our leave of this place."

On our way out of the castle I stopped in the throne room and threw the lifeless body of the corrupt knight over my shoulder. "Why are you bringing his body with us?" Yvette asked.

"Odin wants to perform a Blood Eagle on him. So he'll probably resurrect this guy, perform the Blood Eagle and then keep him alive with his lungs ripped out of his back in eternal pain," I replied. "And before you ask I doubt Odin will resurrect your soldiers."

Yvette nodded. "Would you mind if I come with you to see that?" she asked.

"It's pretty gruesome."

"Jason, this is me we're talking about. I'm always looking for new ways to kill those who would get in my way," the girl said as she picked up the magickal ventriloquist dummy.

"Even for you it may be a little..." I stopped when she simply scowled at me. "Fine you can come with."

As we walked through the castle Yvette whistled and her Werewolves left through respective parts of the castle to join us on our way out. As we headed back to the hill from which we had started the battle we came across Yvette's men who had stayed to look after their comrades and the now Human bodies were picked up and brought with us, as were those of our soldiers killed in battle. I looked around and picked up my Thompson and we got ready to shift to Asgard.

I surveyed this small chunk of Arcadia and really wasn't pleased. We had retrieved Kara which was something but it had been at the cost of thousands of lives of Fey. They had died because one bastard decided that he wanted my client for his own and kidnapped her friend as a means to an end. It had just been like the Trojan War except one side had been completely out gunned. The Fey only had been able to fight with bronze swords and arrows. We had shown up with nasty modern weapons and been able to mow them down en masse. When Humans had pushed the Fey from the Isles thousands of years ago with iron swords there had been tens of thousands of dead on both sides. Today we had probably killed a few thousand, and we had only lost ten people, seven of which I hoped we could save. Sure I had led an army of Werewolves and Valkyries, but the battle had been one-sided to say the least. This was going to haunt me. At least there weren't children. At least I hoped not.

You're right. This will haunt you. I heard Shadow say. I merely nodded in reply.

"Not as clean as we would have liked," Yvette said. "Still it could have been worse. While you were busy I talked to my guys. No kids, only soldiers."

"Thanks." There were times I swore that girl could read my mind as easily as Shadow. "Let's get the fuck out of here." With that a doorway to Asgard opened up and we left that shit hole realm of Arcadia behind us. Hopefully never to return.

CHAPTER

Before we headed to Asgard we dropped off Yvette's soldiers at the headquarters of the Court of Night. There was no need for the army, and I didn't want to make too big of a scene. From there it was a quick skip and a jump to Asgard.

The lag you get from crossing dimensions is worse than any jet lag, and right now I was feeling it, three dimensions in one day is hard on the system. The Mystic Wolf is a sub-dimension that touches all of the others so you just never feel it because you aren't traveling that far. However if you jump between dimensions using the Mystic as a go between you still hit the lag factor because of fully moving from one place to another.

One of the Valkyries left us and summoned Odin from his hall, leaving myself, still carrying the pin-cushioned body of Lamorak, with Yvette and Sasha, who was still cradling Kara in her arms with the rest of the host of Angels. As the All Father came out he looked regal in his armor and helmet with spear in hand resting on his shoulder. Yvette drew herself up to her full height, which wasn't very tall, and did her best to look unimpressed. Amazingly enough Yvette, who was still in her blood soaked and tattered battle clothes, looked almost as dangerous as the God.

"Well, I see that you have done what I asked and brought back my Valkyrie. I see that you were unable to bring back this criminal back to me alive," Odin said. "Though I must ask where the arrows came from since I know that you mostly use a gun."

"Those are my arrows," Sasha said. "No one steals my friends away from me and lives to tell about it."

"Well, well, well a Succubus who can fight. In that case I make you an honorary Valkyrie," the God said with a loud laugh. Then he took Kara from Sasha, who was staring blankly at Odin. "Now let me see how my daughter is doing."

Kara made a whimpering sound as she left Sasha's arms. "Hm, this is a nasty wound. Made worse that she was unable to heal properly from it as it was kept open by her own blade. Oh well, easily taken care of." He lay Kara out on the ground and ran his hand over her chest. As his hand moved over the wound the hole sealed up.

Once the wound was healed Kara took a deep breath and started coughing up blood. Looking around she spotted Sasha. "Thanks for coming for me, Sasha."

Sasha dropped down next to her. "I had to know what happened to you. I… I…" Sasha cut off her last words, but everyone knew what they were going to be.

Odin laughed again. "Come on daughter, you know what you want to say. And so you know I have decided to adopt her as one of my own."

Kara grabbed Sasha around the neck. "I love you too." So saying she gave her a deep kiss.

Yay warm fuzzies all around was my only thought until I caught the Countess's eye. If she had her way there would be too many warm fuzzies, and truthfully maybe that wouldn't be a bad thing. I had had a few days in the Bahamas to think about it. Disney had been fun, not always romantic, and often silly but fun because of the distractions. The Bahamas though lacked all distractions, there would probably be some romance, and maybe that wouldn't be a bad thing. I'm normally used to giving out good news at the end of a case, or at least news that was both good and bad, this mushy stuff isn't normal for me.

"Well, this is a reason to celebrate," Odin said, "but first there is a certain matter that needs to be attended to. It's time to resurrect this fool and perform a constant Blood Eagle." Odin took Lamorak from me. "Who is this fool anyway?"

"He's Sir Lamorak, formerly of King Arthur's Court. He was driven insane after spending too much time in Arcadia," I answered.

"Hmmm an Arthurian knight had done this. Never would have guessed it. Never mind that now." He brought the dead knight over to a set of wood pillars and suspended him between them by chains. He wrenched off the corpse's armor which fell away like so much tissue paper. He slapped the knight's cheek and Lamorak woke up, his eyes glowing from the process of resurrection.

"Who are y..." Lamorak choked off his sentence seeing the one eyed God. "What are you going to do to me? I've already been killed so I guess that you want to kill me yourself."

"Kill you? Hardly." Odin's smile could have frozen Muspellsheim. "I'm going to perform a Blood Eagle upon you, however you aren't going to die from it, but I assure you, you will wish I had from here until Ragnarok." So saying Odin produced an ax from thin air.

He looked over at Sasha, Yvette, and myself. "You may want to turn away. This is going to be pretty messy." None of us looked away. "Suit yourself."

Lamorak screamed when the axe bit through his back twice. Then all that was left was a bubbling, sucking sound as his lungs were ripped from his body and chained to the posts he was bound to, which could not be described. None of us flinched to see his blood fall unceasingly from his back, the soundless screaming was given voice by the sound of his thrashing body. He deserved his fate and maybe it would serve as a warning to others. To quote the Chinese 'Shā yī jǐng bǎ'i' 'Kill one enemy to warn a hundred'. Or in this case rather 'Víg eins óvinar varar hina hundrað við' as would be said by a Viking. I just find the Chinese easier to pronounce, I just can't wrap my tongue around Icelandic.

The Valkyries left us and returned with a feast the likes of which was rarely seen even in Valhalla. We began our festivities with the silent screams of Lamorak providing the background music.

"This is a great day," Sasha whispered into my ear. "I've got my love back, and now we are having a great feast while listening to someone in torment. Almost makes me miss my home realm."

Kara turned to the succubus. "Do they really torment people like this in your home realm?"

"Well the Blood Eagle is probably a purely Viking thing, but every infernal realm has its own way of torture." Sasha turned to me. "What do they do to people in your own realm, Jason? I mean I know you are partially infernal. So what do they do to the people that end up there?"

I shrugged. "Couldn't tell you what my dad's place is like, I never go there to look around. I've seen just about every torment that humans have thought about using in the last 350 plus years. Humans aren't as creative as we used to be. I can't think of anything quite as nasty as the Sicilian Bull having been produced any time recently. Would love to get my hands on that thing." That sucker, if I could get a hold of it, would be the coup de grace of the trophy room. I'd also have to move to a bigger house to get a trophy room big enough.

Both Sasha and Kara gave me a puzzled look. "What was the Sicilian Bull?" Kara asked me.

"A truly nasty piece of work. Probably the most gruesome way you can torture or kill a person," I said. "This guy named Perillos invented this bronze bull that you would open up and stuff some poor soul into. Then you'd build a fire under it and let them cook..."

"That's disgusting." Kara said with a shudder.

I gave her a sick smile. "Oh it was worse than that. The guy put in this weird system in the head of the thing that converted the screams of the poor bastard into the sound of a bellowing bull. Story is that Perillos was stuffed in the bull himself by the guy he sold it to, Phalaris, the tyrant leader of Akragas, Sicily, just to test the sound system. After that there are two stories, one was that Phalaris took him out and shoved him off a cliff. The other is that he let Perillos cook all the way through and that when they opened up the bull his bones shone like jewels. Truthfully I'd love to get it to add to my collection. Would make the US's first electric chair look comfortable by comparison."

Sasha gave me an odd smile. "Are you sure you weren't born in an infernal realm? You certainly seem to have the taste for it."

I shook my head. "The first time I was in an infernal realm for anything other than paperwork, was when I came with Brisbane to look for waitresses for the Mystic Wolf."

Yvette kicked me under the table. "Do you know the plans for that Sicilian Bull thing?" she asked.

"Let me guess, you want to have one built for you?"

"Got it in one. Can't think of anything more suitable to get someone to cooperate than that," the Countess said.

"I swear you would take life lessons from the Spanish Inquisitors as long as they would teach you everything they knew on the subject of torture."

"Coming from you that's rich Mister 'I break Daemon contracts by cutting on them'. I'm sure you had fun doing that," Yvette said.

"So I enjoy my work." I was glad that I was sitting among my fellow Daemons, assorted war Gods, and Yvette. Most Daemons don't shy away from brutality and Yvette is a dyed in the wool psycho. "So what do I owe you for the help Yvette?"

"Original deal was for three nights in the Bahamas. However, with the deaths of White-Face, Shadow-Dancer and Red-Heart I'm going to extend it to seven nights. And don't book two rooms. One room with one bed."

I still wasn't sure this was a good idea. Truthfully she is good in bed, it's just that I'm still not sure I want to make a habit out of it. I have a feeling that even though she's well into her 90s because of what was done to her when she was a teenager that caused her to become immortal, it left her with the same raging hormones of any teenager.

"Something wrong Jason?" Sasha asked. "The Countess is a good looking young lady. Is there something wrong about the situation?"

More than you can possibly imagine, lady. "No, not really. It's just complicated."

Sasha then turned her attention to Yvette. "I'm sure Jason is like any other man. Just grab him and don't let go, and he'll quickly turn into mush."

"Don't worry, he will." Yvette said giving me a lecherous smile.

Odin stood up at the head of the table and banged the butt end of his spear on the ground. "Attention. I declare a toast to the rescuers of my daughter Kara. Jason Black who found her and led an army to retrieve her. The Countess Bloodwolf for lending Jason her army to bring the fight to Arcadia. And last but far from least Sasha Sumer, a succubus that fought beside them to rescue Kara and carried her to me. For that I have chosen for her to become a Valkyrie. From now on she is to be known among our people as Sasha Odinsdottir." The cheers of the Valkyries were deafening, I'm not sure they know the meaning of the word quiet. Of course when they are serving the fallen warriors at Valhalla they have to be loud.

From that point on the party began to degenerate into loud conversation aided by way too much mead, ale, and roast meats of all sorts. Thankfully no one thought to serve lutefisk. I've had it, there's a lot of other stuff I'd try just to avoid eating it again.

CHAPTER 9

The return to the mortal realm was by comparison painful. The first thing Yvette had to do was find a shaman with the right skills to help the werewolves hit by soul stealers in Arcadia. That had taken a bit longer than I had expected, but after a few days we found the right person for the job. Had to fly them up from Jamaica and pay a ton of money, but it was worth it. After that the Countess had to make arrangements for funerals for the three soldiers who had died. There weren't as many to plan and write eulogies for as after the incident with Lady K, but it still sucked for her. Say what you want about the little psycho, she may be evil, but she wasn't Bezos evil. She cared deeply about each of her employees, she may not know all of them by name immediately if introduced, but that didn't mean she didn't care.

While she was busy doing that I had a vacation to plan, and I decided that I wasn't going to skimp. Most expensive resort I could find, we'd simply take Yvette's private jet there so didn't need to worry about booking a flight. I set our arrival date for two weeks before Christmas. We'd have plenty of time to enjoy ourselves and be able to avoid most of the holiday rush. If we ever got out of the bedroom there were plenty of fun things to do, and truthfully I was beginning to more and more enjoy our bedroom hijinx, I just wasn't about to tell Yvette that… Yet.

I also had a date with Sarah to worry about. Yvette would complain. She always did but we weren't an actual couple yet, which I had to keep reminding her of. I'd plan the date for the first weekend in November. There really wasn't much to plan, Buca's didn't require a reservation so I mostly just had to set a pickup time for my date and to tell Yvette that unless bodies were filling the street that I was unreachable for a certain time. I had learned that after the second date with Sarah. Yvette had figured out a way to keep me busy and away from Sarah for a good portion of that time so I had rescheduled and once I had picked the right time and place, set my phone on mute. I had also learned to keep an eye out for a tail, by date four. That girl was jealous and possessive in the extreme. She had already had Sarah and myself arrested once to break up a date.

Unlike that date though I had now had leverage. I had told Yvette that if she tried to ruin my date with Sarah I'd make certain I couldn't make it to the Bahamas because I'd specifically find a complex case that would have me chasing my tail for a month. Yvette would know the threat was a load of bullshit but it should give her a big enough hint.

There was a knock at my office door. I hadn't heard the outer door open or close so I could only assume it was Jamie. "Come on in sweetheart."

The door opened a crack and the first thing through was a leg with a purple pump and not much else. I wasn't really sure what was going on until the leg was followed by a hand in a purple opera glove. Oh dear, Jamie had found her costume. "Come on in Mrs. Rabbit."

"I'm not bad. I'm just drawn that way." Jamie said as she came through the door. And damn could she pull that off. "Oh Mr. Valiant I need you to find my poor hubby wubby."

"I'll take you to The Wolf for the party and you can find your own rabbit to play patty cake with," I said smiling. "You look great dear."

"Thanks," she gave me a bit of a flushed smile. "I was going through some of your detective stories for inspiration."

"And you settled on the Toontown series for inspiration."

"Everything else was a bit depressing, and I loved the movie. So here I am."

"Well you look absolutely amazing. Let me know if you find a rabbit though so I can make sure they're no looney toon."

"Oh but that would be the fun part." Jamie smiled leaned over and kissed me on the forehead. "Come on boss the party is probably starting to warm up, and this outfit was designed for flirting in."

I stood up and got my coat on. "Put on your mink and I'll get you to the party. Apparently Sasha has an announcement she wants to make, and wants to get hammered with the rest of us."

"I bet they're already engaged and that's the announcement." Jamie replied as we went to the outer office so she could retrieve her fall coat. It wasn't particularly cold, and it wasn't snowing. So we I doubted we were in for a repeat of the Halloween of '91. Still this was Minnesota and anything could happen, but by the time it dropped that kind of snow on us, we'd all be too drunk to drive home from the Wolf so we'd just have to camp out there and keep the party going for a few more days.

CHAPTER 10

"To the ladies!" I said, raising a glass and trying to be heard over the Samhain revelers at the Mystic Wolf, most of whom were smashed beyond belief. "Without whom I would never have had a case or would have been able to solve it and bring it to a happy conclusion." I was in the company of Sasha, Kara, Jamie, Yvette, and Sarah, who had played a small but important part of this whole mess.

The five women raised their glasses as well. "To us!" They cheered drunkenly. The Mystic Wolf is about the only place you can get a Daemon blind, stinking drunk unless they had some particular alcohols designed with immortals in mind.

I had ended up with sitting between Yvette and Sarah which was fairly uncomfortable, knowing that both of them would be happier if the other simply dropped dead. Still everyone had a right to be there and I was the only person of the six who was relatively sober. I had to keep my wits about me to handle 'Scar Face' and The Countess.... so that the young private dick didn't end up in the river.

I saw Sasha motion Lori over to her. "Well, you certainly seem to be enjoying yourself." The succubus said acidly.

"So I got a new honorary title. So what?" Sasha said with a smile.

"Just as long as you don't get stuck up about it," Lori commented.

"Well anyway, can you give this to Brisbane?" Sasha asked handing the waitress a note.

"Certainly, little Miss Odinsdottir," Lori said sticking her tongue out at her coworker as she stalked off.

"So, what's the note say?" Asked Yvette.

"You'll see."

After a few minutes Brisbane rang a gong asking for everybody's silence. "To all friends and family of the Mystic Wolf," Brisbane called in his booming voice. "I have an announcement to make. Or rather one of my waitresses, Sasha Sumer, has an announcement."

Sasha stood up on the table so that people could see her. I watched as hundreds of drunken eyes turned to look at the succubus. "Dear friends and family. As some of you may have heard I recently ventured forth into an Arcadian realm with the help of Jason Black and the Court of Night to find the kidnapped Valkyrie, Kara Odinsdottir. Having successfully rescued her, I was able to ask her to marry me..." At this point you could have heard a pin drop. Even Eris in the back corner juggling Apples of Discord had stopped to listen.

Then Kara stood up next to her. "And I have said yes," Kara continued.

Then the two of them said in unison. "So to announce our engagement this round's on us!" The cheers were deafening, though I was unsure if it was because of the announcement of the two Daemons engagement, or the free round of drinks. I was encouraged to say the latter.

"So, when do we get to make an announcement like that?" I heard from both sides of me which caused me to sweat bullets. Women, can't live with 'em, can't live without 'em.

THE HALF BREED CAPER

CHAPTER

The strains of Caravan Palace's *Lone Digger* playing on my phone broke through my dreams and woke me up to a dark room. I didn't bother to look at the caller ID on my phone to know it was the Countess Bloodwolf calling me. I took a few seconds to decide whether or not it was worth answering the phone. I decided that since Yvette never calls me at this horrid hour unless it was important I should probably answer.

"Good morning, evening, something in between the two whatever." I wasn't much on hellos at this time of day. "This had better be important."

"I wouldn't have called you at three in the morning if it wasn't important. A problem has come up between some major players, and before all hell breaks out I need your help."

"Who are the players?" I asked as I started to move.

"The Department of Daemonic Affairs is at its own throats. The tensions between the Divines and Infernals is running high and I don't need to tell you of all people how bad it could get."

That was the last thing I, or anyone else needed. If the Department was to fracture things would go to immediate shit. Divines and Infernals don't need much of a reason to go to war at times, which was the point of the Department. It was meant to keep some idiot from lighting a fuse to a possible powder keg. Individually Infernals and Divines get along fine; in large groups though, not so much. There are two other factions controlled by the department, the Elemental and the Fey, and I wouldn't be surprised if either division was behind this.

"What's got them so riled up this time?"

"It's kind of hard to explain, but outside players including myself, and the Kitsune Court have decided that you are probably the only one who can settle matters before blood spills."

"Who came up with this idea from the Kitsune Court?"

"A nine tail named Kukiko. Why?"

Shit, an ex-girlfriend, not what I needed. Once she had discovered cellphones she had gotten in the habit of drunk dialing me way too often. I've just been lucky that I was never with Yvette when she has called. "It's nothing. Okay where are they meeting, and please tell me it's not at the Court."

"Are you crazy? I don't want those idiots near my home if they decided to really go after each other."

"So where are they meeting?" It really wasn't much of a question, if they were meeting as a group and had brought in Yvette to mediate there was only one place they could be.

"They're meeting at the Mystic Wolf. Brisbane has already prepped the place for a fight. Every employee is there right now, and he's got Complaints Department in hand."

Just what I didn't need. In the Mystic Wolf every employee is ranked as either Arch-Angel or Deity on the power scale, and all other people in the bar are brought down a few notches. The original point is to keep Gods from getting too rowdy, and pounding on the mere Mortals. It has also proved advantageous in situations such as dealing with powerhouses. I'm ranked Minor Deity there since I'm technically part owner, and I often need to make certain people play by the rules during the negotiations that take place there. If everybody was there it meant real trouble, and everyone was going to be acting like they were dancing on a floor covered in razor blades. "Do you have anyone there yourself."

"Are you insane? I'm not taking any of my enforcers into the bar. They're outside making sure no one else comes into the place to set off the proverbial bomb. Besides I just found myself hired."

"Wait that God hired you?!?!?! As what?"

"Emergency bouncer." By the Gods above and below Brisbane is going to kill me with that move.

"Just wait for me to get there before you kill anyone."

"Not a problem, this is going to be enough of a headache for me as it is."

"I'll be there in a few minutes, I just need to get dressed and I'll be on my way." I started going through my closet looking for something that was suitable for the occasion. Shadow opened one eye and looked at me from his perch, seeming slightly annoyed.

What are you doing? Or should I ask what are we doing? He asked grumpily; he was quite likely at the beginning stages of a hangover after his date with Muninn. Which is odd since he only drinks once a year, though with him dating that particular raven things may have changed.

"The Department of Daemonic Affairs is having some issues, and I need to make sure things don't blow up."

If you don't mind I'll sit this one out. Truthfully I couldn't say I blamed him.

"I'll let you know if I do need you later. Hopefully though it'll be easily settled and I won't even have to wake you up."

Shadow told me not to get myself killed then tucked his head back under his wing, and went back to sleep. I had dressed and was ready to head out; all I needed was my gun and jacket. Before I left I loaded up the gun with banishing rounds. If need be I was going to send some of these bastards back to where they had come from as a warning to the others.

I threw on my jacket and trench coat as I headed for the door. The last thing I grabbed was my trusty fedora. I had to look the part of noir detective. For some reason the feel of the prohibition heyday of

St. Paul had become ingrained in the feel of the Magickal community, so I always dressed for success. Even the weather was fitting for a case that already had the makings for a nightmare, as a heavy thunderstorm had rolled in on the city. I drove the ten blocks to the Mystic Wolf and circled it to see what kind of enforcements had been put up. I spotted twelve strategically placed Vampire and Werewolf snipers courtesy of the Court of Night. There were also more than a few Daemons of different types all over the area, placed with little sense of strategy.

I parked my car and lit up a cigarette, which was enough to cue up a loud clap of thunder. If things were going to go to hell I was going to make damn sure that it was going to at least happen with style. I walked through the door head down collar up. The blaze of a deafening light hit me as I walked through the door, but I was used to that. It came with the territory of transferring to a different plane of reality. I was met at the door by Brisbane who was dressed in a three-piece suit, and carrying the infamous 'Complaints Department', a broadsword sized to fit a giant, made by the same smith that had forged Excalibur. Truthfully he looked like a character out of that one show about immortals, can't remember the name of it though. "Wet out there?"

I gave a dry laugh. "I'm drenched and you ask if it's wet. Very funny Brisbane."

"The case is going to be a different one for you." He sounded almost sad.

"What's wrong?" I asked, I never got normal cases, which means business as usual.

"The Department is starting to fracture because of a little girl."

Crap! I hate working cases for kids, especially if it's a little kid. "Who's in there?"

"Let me put it this way. If it was a mob meeting everyone in there would have the middle name 'the'. This is a serious issue. I literally think that it's the heads of the Department in there and their top aides." Double crap.

"Okay, I guess it's time for me to set things straight."

"I hope you can do it, because you may be the only one who can solve this. As crazy as this may sound, I think the Infernals hold the moral high ground right now."

If that was true, something truly horrid must have happened. Infernals rarely hold moral high ground on anything, and when they did life was never pleasant. "Let's not keep them waiting." I fixed the collar of my coat and entered the back room with a crooked, and hopefully cocky grin. Never show fear among these people, it's best for them to think that you have them exactly where you wanted them and were more than willing to make them pay dearly for whatever they may do.

As soon as I entered the room I saw the girl they were talking about. The girl, who if she was Human I would have guessed at being about five, had black feathered wings each tinged blood red at the tips, with hair to match, was sitting in a corner with Sam happily coloring. She had a halo of dark energy, so dark it warped the light around it, which sat almost directly on top of her horns. Like the Succubi who worked at the bar, she had a whip-like barbed tail that seemed to be twitching in concentration as she colored. She was definitely a half breed Daemon. The room its self was filled with cigarette smoke and just as I suspected the Daemons from the Department were wearing well cut business suits styled as if they were out of the thirties. Also represented was the Court of Night, represented by the Countess Blood Wolf, the Kitsune Court represent by Kukiko who had several bodyguards with her, and a representative from the Dragon Court whom I didn't know. Brisbane was playing host and therefore represented the Mystic Wolf. Meaning most of the non-Pantheon players were represented. Yvette and Kukiko both waved slightly at me.

"Ladies and gentleman I'm here to settle this matter so let's get down to the business at hand. Who's the kid?"

"That's why we've decided to hire you," the chief of the Infernal division said. "We have no clue as to who she is, who her parents are, or even where she came from. With one exception we would like you to find out who her parents are so we can give her back to them, and find a place for them to stay away from the rest of us."

"I still say we should just get rid of her and her deranged parents to preserve the status quo of the Department. It's obviously the fault of the two Daemons that couldn't follow the ancient laws. If we want to preserve law and order, we need to eliminate the girl and her parents." The chief of the Divines practically shouted. Brisbane was right, the Infernals did hold the moral high ground right now.

"No one is killing anyone, especially a little girl right now," Brisbane roared. "If need be I'll keep her here until her parents or a suitable family can be found."

"You stay out of this," the Divine said. "That thing is an abomination and doesn't belong anywhere but..."

I cut the Divine's putrid, verbal thought short by slamming his head into the table and putting my gun to the back of his head. In a flash there was the sound of energies crackling around me. I ignored it, everyone was willing to kill someone and I didn't have to worry about being one of them. "I'd think very carefully about what you say around me at this moment," I snarled in his ear.

"You thing that a puny gun will work on..."

I thumbed off the safety. "This gun has banishing rounds in it and I know for a fact these will banish you to where ever you came from and it will be a far from pleasant trip."

"You wouldn't dare."

"Bet your life? Trust me this will hurt more than you'd care to think about." There are times I really hate dealing with Divines

The Chief of the Infernals started clapping. "I see that you do indeed live down to your reputation, Black."

I simply nodded in acknowledgment. "Now would anyone else like to say something to seriously piss me off?" I let go of the Divine's head. People were smart and stayed quiet. "First off I want a safe place for this girl to stay until her parents can be found or more permanent arrangements can be set up."

"I have an idea of a couple who might love to have her," Brisbane said. "And unless people want to piss off some other major players no one will risk touching her."

Brisbane left the room to talk to most likely an employee and her partner. "We can always take her back to the Kitsune Court," Kukiko offered.

"Sorry sweetie I trust you about as far as I can throw the entire Court of Night." The Kitsune looked a bit hurt. As racist as it may sound, it was never a good idea to trust them.

"I can't take her," Yvette said. "I don't want to inflict my place on a kid."

"Don't worry I think I know who Brisbane is talking to, and she'll be fine."

Brisbane stepped back into the room with a pair of female Daemons. One was a Valkyrie with large black feathered wings named Kara. The other was a Succubus named Sasha with horns, bat like wings and a barbed tail. They were a sweet couple whom I had helped a while back. They were both dressed in armor carrying their own swords. Like everyone else they were ready for a fight.

"Who are these *foster parents*?" The Divine spat out. I so wanted to plug the guy.

"Sasha Sumer and Kara Odinsdottir," Brisbane said by way of introduction.

The Infernal laughed. "Well, that is a master stroke. Now you have no reason to complain, Gerald." So that was the Divine's name, I'll have to remember to put his name on a bullet. "Two Daemons, both unattached to the Department, one of Divine origin, the other of Infernal. I must ask you a question Brisbane, are you certain they will make acceptable parents for the child?"

"They are a loving couple who have already made blood oaths to each other. On top of that Sasha is completing her student teaching to become an elementary school teacher," I said. "They are the best option she has at a relatively normal life if her parents can't be found.

"One more thing to be clear I represent the girl's interests from this point out. Any interference on this case and I will rain brutality from above and below, and you should know my reputation for that kind of thing. I'm sure if you didn't I wouldn't be here."

"I would also like to make something clear," Yvette said. "From this point on forward this girl is under the protection of the Court of Night. I have declared her safety as a top priority."

The Dragon rumbled that as far as he was concerned the meeting was over, but that he wouldn't leave until the members of the Department left. Kukiko seconded the motion to end the meeting. I was thankful for that, I didn't want these bastards being around if Sasha and Kara found out what the Divine had said should be done with the girl; blood would have been shed by Sasha, who was still technically an employee. The Department heads left quickly, I didn't think any of them really wanted to be there any longer than need be.

"Thanks Yvette," I said after the Department heads and the Dragon left. "I'm always happy I have you for support."

"You trust her but not me?" Kukiko asked.

"You are constantly drunk dialing me, plus you're a Kitsune. So no, I don't trust you."

"Wait a second she drunk dials you. Why does she have your number?" Yvette was starting to get pissy, not good.

"She's my ex and she's a Kitsune so her getting my number was inevitable. Now if she's smart she'll leave."

"We could have made a great couple Jason," Kukiko sulked.

"Blame your father for siding with Japan during World War Two. I fought for the Allies and was not about to betray my country for a rocky romance."

"Sure blame the war, jerk." Kukiko left in a huff.

"Why did you date her?"

"At the time I was stupid and she was fun to party and sleep with."

"So nothing serious?"

"Nothing serious." I was beginning to think of a permanent relationship with Yvette, still it was only a thought. She wanted it. I just wasn't sure if I did yet. Emphasis on the 'yet' part.

"Well time to interview my little client," I said to no one in particular.

I approached the girl who had started yawning by this point. "Hello there little lady." She turned to look at me and I could immediately tell that at best I was going to get a name out of her. "My name is Jason and I want to be your friend like Sam here. So what's your name?"

The girl yawned and blinked at me a bit. "Mom called me her Red Raven," she said.

"How about I call you Red then. Would you like that?"

"Okay," Red said with another yawn.

"These are my friends, Kara and Sasha, they're going to take you back to their place where you can stay for a few days while I find you parents. Okay?"

"Are they nice?"

"Yes, they are very nice, and they will make certain that nothing bad happens to you."

"Okay."

"Can we take her home now?" Sasha asked.

I looked at Red. "Are you ready to go little one?"

"They're going to keep me safe?" The little half breed asked.

"Yes you'll be perfectly safe with them. And I'll come see you in the morning to talk to you. Would that be okay?"

Red nodded and yawned, her eyes watering from how tired she was. Sasha knelt down next to her. "Shall we get you home and tuck you in for the night?"

"Okay." Red reached up and Sasha scooped the girl into her arms. As soon as she was pressed against Sasha the little one was asleep.

"Her name is Red Raven," I told her new foster parents in a whisper.

"The guestroom is always ready, so we can put her to bed as soon as we get home." Kara told me as she stroked the little girl's hair.

"I'm glad the two of you could do this for her."

Sasha smiled. "Well, I must admit we didn't think we'd be parents before we got married, but how could we resist."

"Well why don't the three of you go home. I'll see you sometime this afternoon."

"We'll see you then," Kara said giving me a hug.

"I'm heading out with you," Yvette said. "I need to make a phone call."

I was fairly sure I knew what Yvette was planning. She didn't trust the Divines so she would probably send a couple teams of enforcers to keep an eye on the girl. Say what you want about that little psychopath, she has a big soft spot for people who can't defend themselves.

"Okay everyone," I heard Brisbane call out to his employees, "let's wrap it up for the night. The kid's on her way to a home and is going to be safe, and there is a bonus for everyone for sticking around tonight or for coming in on your night off. You helped a little kid stay safe from a bunch of Divine assholes so thanks for taking time out of your night to help. Now everyone, go home and go to bed."

"Round on the house!" One of the bartenders cheered, jumping behind the bar.

"Fine! Then go home." Brisbane threw up his hands and headed behind the bar to help pour. I decided to head home instead of sticking around for a drink.

Once I was out of the bar the storm had started to wane. Yvette was still standing outside just putting away her phone. "Hey shorty."

"Hey Jason. All the damn Divines have cleared out along with the Infernals. I've also sent several teams of enforcers to keep an eye on her. I trust those bastard Divines as far as I'd trust a Nazi."

"Can't say I blame you. When Infernals hold the moral high ground things are seriously wrong." I looked at her for a while, and thought about... Nah, not tonight. "Goodnight Yvette."

"Goodnight Jason. I know this is going to sound weird and all, but this shit has got me pissed. I'm not even going to bother asking for a nightcap." Truly amazing turn of events. "I'll see you tomorrow. And thanks for helping the kid, I knew I could trust you."

Yvette gave me a hug and let go as a large limo pulled up in front of bar. "Goodnight."

CHAPTER

I headed back home for a few extra hours of sleep. I needed my mind clear for the shitty case that had just been dropped into my lap. In order to do that I'd need all the rest I could get. Once inside the house I headed to my liquor cabinet, grabbed my favorite bourbon, the cheap shit, and poured myself a couple fingers into a lowball glass. After downing it I made my way to bed and dropped on to it still fully dressed. I swore up and down that I'd probably have to kill, or at least banish, someone before this case was over. Depending on who it was, killing them would probably be preferable, or at least make me feel better. If they gave me reason I'd be more than happy to torture someone.

Something wrong master? Shadow asked.

"Ugly case, and I'm hoping to kill at least one person before it's solved."

Shadow cocked his head giving me a quizzical look. *Then it must be bad. Normally you dislike killing people unless necessary. You love torturing people, killing not so much. What's different this time?*

"Head of the Divine Section of the Department wants to kill a little half breed girl to preserve the status quo."

What the hell?! He wants to kill a little kid, for what her parents did?

"Basically. Look I need to grab a couple more hours of sleep before I hit the pavement on this one. So…" I didn't even bother to say more as Shadow cut in.

No problem master. You get sleep, I'll go back to sleep myself and leave you alone.

"Thanks." I closed my eyes and fell asleep before my head hit the pillow.

When I woke up the light was streaming across my face as Shadow had pulled open the blinds. *Good morning.* He sounded cheerful, stupid bird.

"How long have I been asleep?"

Four hours. Snoring through most of it. That explained why my tongue felt cracked.

"Thanks for letting me sleep so long. I needed the rest."

"Also why are you cheerful? I could have sworn you were going to have a hangover after your date."

I managed to keep my beak out of the mead. I had a great time, but I managed to stay sober.

"Good for you."

You should try it some time, it's quite fun after all.

"I don't drink that much."

No, going on a date. You going out with Yvette and getting laid regularly would be preferable to you being mister grumpy every time I get home late after a rendezvous with my girlfriend.

"I thought you didn't like the psycho?"

She's growing on me, and as far as I can tell she's the only person you can tolerate for more than a couple days at a time. Remember that nine tail you dated, Kukiko?

"Please don't bring her up. I ran into her last night, and I don't want to think how badly that could have ended."

Did she hit on you?

"No but she was the one to propose I get hired for this case. Yvette didn't realize that the two of us had a past and when she found out the

Kitsune drunk dials me on occasion I was worried that I was going to have to keep the fur from flying."

Oh nuts I wish I had been there for that.

"Look can we not talk about this. I just want to get this day moving, so I can figure out who I have to kill."

It was Tuesday so I headed to the office to let Jamie know about my case, and to have her screen my calls. Shadow wasn't saying much since nothing really needed to be said about the case itself. He knew I was going to be in a horrid mood until long after this case was over, so no reason to agitate me further. The office was a scene of calm and tranquility right now. My secretary had brewed a fresh pot of coffee, and there was box of donuts on her desk.

"Mornin' boss," she sounded annoyingly chipper, but I couldn't blame her, she hadn't heard about the case yet. Beyond that she hadn't looked at me and I'm sure my sour mood showed. "I need you to sign some bills for me before we get started. So what are your plans for the day?"

She turned to look at me and dropped her paperwork. "What the hell happened to you?"

"I got a nasty case dropped into my lap last night, around three in the morning, and I'm going to go through hell on it. I've got a little kid that needs saving from some major players. And hopefully I can find her parents before someone else does."

"Oh dear. Well, have a couple cups of coffee, since you still look like hell, and don't forget the donuts. I picked them up on my way in this morning so they're still fresh. And forget the paperwork you can take care of it later." She pushed me into the back office where my desk was, then left and came back with a coffee cup, the pot, and couple donuts on a tray. "I can keep myself busy for a while."

Do you need me or should I join Jamie in the office? I couldn't blame Shadow for not wanting to be around me right now. I hated dealing with capers where the victim was a kid or a kid was a client. In this case the victim and the client was a little kid.

"No, go ahead and keep Jamie company. I'm going to be in a crappy mood all day. No reason for you to be here suffering through it."

Thanks master. You're the best there is, and you'll have that girl's problem sorted out in no time.

"Thanks for the vote of confidence buddy. I'm going to need everything I've got to get through this with any shred of humanity left in me, I think. That kid needs me and I'd love to kill someone right now, so I'm probably in the worst mood possible." Shadow left as I tried to think of the best way to approach the case.

My first thought was the safety of Red. I all but knew for a fact that she had made it safely home with Sasha, and Kara. If she hadn't Yvette would have called me and a whole war would have broken out. The Infernals wanted the girl and her family kept safe, which while it may be surprising to some it wouldn't be at all a surprising to someone truly familiar with them. Infernals aren't so much evil as most people think, they are more a representation of natural chaos, which may seem odd, considering they have law enforcement officers in their own realms. Divines represent order in the world and are anal retentive about keeping things on the straight and narrow. An Infernal and a Divine having broken the ancient law was a reason for the Divines to completely flip out. More precisely the fact that there was offspring from such a coupling was the issue. It was common, though highly denied, knowledge that this law was always being broken, but rarely did it result in a child. Such a child was the ultimate show of chaos and that was what the Infernals so desperately wanted to protect.

I picked up the phone and called Yvette. "Hey Countess is everyone safe?" I asked when she picked up.

"Yes, I've got teams rotating around the area, and they are loaded for Daemonic bear. So far they been spotting Divines and Infernals all over the place, but none of them close enough to be of any concern yet. And I emphasize the 'Yet' part." Yvette sounded frustrated, and I couldn't blame her. She had a lot on her plate at all times; this had to be a nightmare for her.

"So what's your next move?"

"I'm going to be heading over there in a little while to talk to the kid, and see what kind of information I can get out of her. I'd like to find out where she was found for one thing, and anything I can about her parents."

"I can tell you about where she was found myself. It was a couple of police officers on my payroll that found her. She was hiding and scared out by the Cathedral near the Wolf."

"Then why didn't you call me right away?"

"There wasn't any time. A couple Divines showed up shortly after and tried to kill the kid. The dispatcher sent them to the Wolf as a way to get them out of the line of fire before something happened to them or the kid. Apparently it was a pretty nasty fire fight that broke out. Thankfully I was able to arrange for damage control on it before it hit the news. Anyways I was then notified and by the time I got there those assholes from the Department had shown up, along with the representatives from the Kitsune and Dragon courts. It's all too neat. Someone tipped them all off; that kid is being used."

"If that's the case then I need to find out as much as I can about this kid as quickly as possible. If that kid is a pawn than she is in more danger than I thought. I'm heading over to Sasha and Kara's right now."

"For now she's as safe as I can keep her without being there myself. Do you want me to head over there?"

"For now she should be good. Sasha and Kara will probably be able to hold off anyone long enough for your back up to arrive. Plus I wouldn't be surprised if there are more Valkyries there already. Maybe even a few Gods."

"We can hope so. I'm ready to start treating Divines like Nazis if they keep this up." Not exactly what I needed to hear but it was the thought that counted. Her idea of a good Nazi was a messily butchered one.

If she was to go to war with the Department's Divine section it would be a bloody mess that would spill out all over. There would be no way to keep it out of the public light. On top of that not only would the Court of Night and the Divines be involved, other players backing either side would show up which would be a nightmare and a half. All of his over an innocent little kid.

"Look keep things low profile for now, we don't need a war right now. It would be a slaughter fest that couldn't be contained, and we both know that sort of thing is bad for business." I was going to appeal to her business side. She liked her money and she made money by keep things running smoothly. The kind of anarchy that would be the result of such a battle would be extremely bad for business.

"I'm still going to keep everyone ready for a fight. I've also been in communication with the head of the Infernal section of the Department. He's being most helpful." Oh crap, that probably meant an arms deal of some sorts. That could mean a total game changer and that was the last thing I wanted at this moment. As much as I didn't want to admit it, sometimes even to myself, one of the reasons I stayed close to Yvette was as a safe guard for the world if she went nuts. I was the Kryptonite bullet to her Superman.

"Okay, keep the talks low key. Don't make any big moves for now."

"What kind of idiot do you think I am?"

"I don't, just keep in mind though Infernals aren't very trustworthy in the long-haul."

"Look, you just find the kids parents, I'll worry about a potential war."

"Not a problem, we'll each do what were good at. I'll call you later." I hung up and started to seriously worry.

My next call was to Sasha. "Hello?" I heard Sasha yawn.

"It's Black, how is the kid doing?"

"Good morning to you too," she replied sarcastically. "Red's fine, she's still tuckered out the poor girl, and is passed out on our bed.

"On your bed? I thought you had a room ready for her?"

"We do. She just came and curled up in bed with us, poor thing was scared of something last night. Kara is still asleep with her right now. She had a rough day at work and was about to hit the bed when Brisbane called us so she just wanted to sleep in and Red's curled up with her."

"Do you mind if I come over now, I'll just hang out with you until Red and Kara wake up? I want to talk with Red as soon as she gets up. Things are getting weird right now."

"That won't be a problem, though it would be great if you could pick up bagels and some cream cheese on your way over."

"Consider it done." I hung up knowing I could probably crash out on her couch for a few minutes. I left my office and saw Jamie reading a reprint of a couple old Shadow pulps, it was nice that they were back in print, since my originals had fallen apart long ago. My Shadow flipped the pages of a bird watcher's magazine and whistled a couple of times.

"Wouldn't Muninn get offended if she knew you were looking at that?" I asked him amusedly.

Museum rules regarding other birds. Of course we always see each other naked so it's really not a big deal. I'm just admiring the plumage. Black is classic, but sometimes I think a splash of color would be nice.

"I'm not sure how to respond to that."

"What's he talking about boss?" Jamie asked looking up.

"He just told me that sometimes he wishes he had a splash of color."

"Come here feather face," Jamie said reaching into one of the desk drawers, "I may just have the perfect thing for you."

Shadow looked at me and I shrugged. I had long stopped keeping track of what Jamie kept in the desk so I had no idea what she was planning. Shadow hopped over and looked at her quizzically. "Now close your eyes and no peeking." Out came a bottle of nail polish, in short order she painted Shadow's talons bright red. "Okay you can look now."

Shadow opened his eyes a looked at his feet. *I've got red nails! This is actually pretty cool.* He jumped up and let out a little caw to show to Jamie he was happy with the change. *Tell her I said thanks.*

"Shadow says thanks," I looked at my watch and decided it was time to leave. "Well Shadow it's time we got going."

"Where are you going boss?" Jamie asked.

"The girl is staying with Sasha and Kara so I'm taking Shadow and heading over there. I want to talk to the kid as soon as possible, because things are starting to get nasty out there. The sooner I can figure this out the better for everyone out there."

"Okay keep me in the loop." Jamie picked up her book again.

"Do me a favor will you?"

"What."

"I'm really worried about everyone at the moment," I walked over to the gun cabinet and grabbed 'Lady Bell', a big .357 and loaded her with banishing rounds. Handing over to Jamie I said. "Please keep her on you. I don't want anything to happen to you."

"Things that bad?"

"Possibly worse." I looked over at my familiar who was still admiring his talons. "Time to go bud."

CHAPTER

I stopped by a bagel shop and picked up a baker's dozen and a couple tubs of cream cheese. Next stop was a café for the biggest cup of coffee they had. I had a distinct feeling that caffeine was going to be a major fuel for this case, along with a heap full of foul mood.

I turned up the street to Kara and Sasha's place and realized I would probably have to call Jamie to bring a lot more bagels. There were four extra cars jammed in the drive way, and there were more cars parked up and down the block than there should have been for any normal occasion. I drove to the end of the block and found a parking spot on the cross street. As I walked back to the house. I checked all the cars and immediately confirmed my suspicions, each car had either a Raven Banner, or Mystic Wolf sticker on the windshield. That meant there were both Valkyries and Succubi here and apparently a lot of them. This kid didn't need Court of Night protection though I knew Yvette still had her people out there. She'd never let her guard down like that. Still it would be insane for anything but a mass of highly trained Divines to even think of making a move on the kid right now.

Prepare for insanity, master, Shadow said.

"Probably right."

The door opened before I had a chance to knock and I was face to face with Sasha, who seemed to be mighty busy at the moment and in need of some relief. She was so stressed out that I wasn't sure if she realized that her horns and wings were showing. "Thank the Gods you're here. These girls insist on sticking around for a while and I need help."

So much for crashing on the couch. "What can I do?"

"We're pretty much out of everything in the way of food. Can you do a grocery run?"

"Sasha, don't you have any more beer?" I heard a voice call up from the basement.

"What do you mean we ran out of beer?!" I heard another horrified voice ask.

"Just that! I can't find a single one in here!"

"Please, I need help." Sasha practically begged.

"Hold on." I handed Sasha the now completely inadequate bag of bagels and took out my phone and dialed the office.

"Black Shadow Detective Agency, how may I help you?" Jamie answered.

"Do you even look at the caller ID?"

"What do you want boss?"

"I need food for a massive party of Valkyries and Succubi. Think Super Bowl party for sixty frat boys for the amount of food then quadruple that. Everything unhealthy, including 100 pounds of hamburger meat, check that make that 200 pounds, the same for steaks, and plenty of stuff to go with them, and don't forget the hot dogs I'm sure we'll need plenty of them too. I'll also need a at least 50 cases of cold beer, or a few of large kegs, whichever is easier." I covered the phone with my hand. "Gas or charcoal grill?" I asked Sasha.

"Charcoal."

"And ten large bags of charcoal." I told Jamie to finish the order.

"That's a lot of money boss."

"Just use the company credit card and keep the receipt as a business expense." I wasn't about to blow a few grand on food and booze and not get paid back for it.

"Okay boss, where am I bringing it all?"

I gave her the address and she told me she'd arrive as quickly as possible. "There you go, the food is on its way. Is Red still asleep?"

"Thank you so much for that," Sasha said wiping her brow. "Last I checked she was still out cold, I'm not even sure if Odin himself could tell us how long she had been out there before she was found. At some point in the night she had a horrid dream and crawled into bed with us. She was quivering so bad that the bed was practically shaking."

"Poor kid. Can I come in now?"

"Oh sorry, please do. As you can see we're a little crowded at the moment. I swear it's like at least half the girls from the Wolf, and easily as many, if not more, Valkyries are here."

"I'll find a quiet corner then and wait for Red to be ready to talk."

"Do you see a quiet corner around here? I used a charm to dampen the noise in the bedrooms but I'm not sure how long it can handle the sheer volume before it fractures. As I'm sure you can tell Valkyries aren't exactly the quietest of people." There was a crash in the background. "Who broke what?!" She yelled over her shoulder.

"I didn't do it!"

"Yes you did!"

"Shut up! You were the one who broke it!"

"Can someone please just tell me what broke?"

"That horrid vase of yours! I didn't break it!"

"Please excuse me for a minute Jason. I'll be right back." As Sasha stalked into the dining room I could see storm clouds literally forming over her head as she muttered a long stream of ancient curses. I was going to happily sit out this little mystery. Mostly because I wasn't being paid for it. Besides knowing Sasha and Kara's tastes when it came to decorating their home that vase was probably better off dead anyway.

I'm so glad you don't host these kinds of parties, master. My head is going to start killing me soon if the volume doesn't drop bellow a hundred decibels soon.

"At least you didn't go out drinking with Muninn last night."

Very funny, very funny.

Eventually Shadow found me a corner of the couch to sit on next to a couple of Valkyries. Almost immediately my lap became residence to a Succubus. Thank every God imaginable that Yvette wasn't around. The Countess would have blown a power station worth of fuses if she saw this. "How are you doing, sweetie?" Tammy hissed in my ear.

"Just waiting for the kid to wake up," I said, squirming slightly. Succubi are hot as sin and the one in my lap was no exception. Almost on cue to save me from any physical embarrassment there was a knock on the door. I plucked off my lap's current resident and rushed over to the door. Thankfully it was Jamie with the food.

"Come into the madhouse," I said.

Jamie popped her head inside and looked around. "I think it might be safer if I stay out here."

"You're probably right." I looked over my shoulder and yelled back into the house. "Food's here so grab what you can and get outside for a cook out."

I grabbed Jamie and pulled her ten feet away from the door, still pressed against the house to protector her from the hoard of Daemons that came dashing out swarming over the car like piranhas. "How many girls are in there?" she asked.

"Probably way more than allowed by fire code," I grinned. "Want to stick around?"

"Sure, I'm kind of hungry, especially after buying all of that." Jamie headed towards the back and now that most of the girls had cleared out it had gotten a reasonable volume again.

Thank the Gods I can hear myself think again!

I didn't have long to wait until Kara came out of the bedroom dressed in workout shorts and a tank top. "Hey Jason, have people left?"

"They're in the backyard grilling up food."

"Who's here?"

"Succubi and Valkyries. A flock of both." I smiled at her. Her hair was a mess, and it looked good that way. I could easily see why Sasha had fallen in love with her.

"Can't say I'm surprised." Kara yawned. "Not very often that either side gets a niece. For the most part Valkyries don't have time to get pregnant and Succubi apparently can't have kids of their own, at least not normally. So this is huge."

"Is Red awake?"

"That's why I'm out here to make sure things had quieted down enough out here to get her out to talk to you without being swarmed. So I'll be right back."

In a couple minutes Red came into the living room wearing one of Kara's shirts. At least I assumed it was Kara's since I doubted that Sasha would have a shirt with her own Holy Symbol on it. "Hey Red," I called out.

"Jason!" Red said running into me at full tilt. I knelt down and picked her up. She still had all her non-Human characteristics so either she wasn't bothering to look Human since no one in the house was either, or she didn't know how. Either way she looked adorable.

"So do you want to talk to me so I can find your parents?"

"Yes, I miss my mommy," she said quietly. "I really miss her."

"What about your daddy?"

"He hurt mommy, I don't want to see him anymore. I just want my mommy back." I closed my eyes tight this was another tick on the list of people I want to kill. More than likely the scum sucker had crawled back to his home realm so banishing rounds wouldn't do shit, I'd just have to kill him out right when I had the chance. "Who's the pretty birdy?"

I hadn't noticed that Shadow had flown onto my shoulder to get a good look at Red. "This is my familiar, his name is Shadow."

"What's a familiar?" Oh right not at all Human.

"He's an animal assistant. He also happens to be a big pain in the tail." Shadow nipped my ear. "Well it's true feather brain."

Oh shut up, master.

"Don't sulk."

"He's funny," Red said with a little squeal. Shadow danced as much as he could on my shoulder and cawed happily to show he appreciated the compliment.

"Enough about this twit. Let's talk about you for a bit. Well more about your mother to be exact." I sat down on the couch and patted the cushion next to me.

"Okay, she is incredibly beautiful. She has these beautiful wings, sort of like Sasha's but hers were red not black, her horns were the same. She also had red hair like mine, and she always kept it in different braids. She also had a tail like mine but the end was a different shape." Interesting, that meant that more than likely the girl's mother was a Succubus which made little sense, as Kara said Succubi are, for the most part, unable have kids. At least I was fairly sure that most of them couldn't but this did explain a few things. I wasn't ready to go to the Department yet to answer that question.

"What's her name?"

"Zackia."

Interesting name and from a language that I couldn't place. Though that may not mean much. I may be old, but I'm nowhere near old enough to know all the languages out there, especially not ancient languages or most daemonic ones. "What did your dad look like?"

"He was tall I guess, maybe as tall as that really tall guy I met last night."

"Do you mean Brisbane?" At seven foot plus, not many people were as tall as the chief God of the Mystic Wolf. Save for a few proto-Daemons, who had little to do with Humans these days, most Daemons who did a lot of business on the Mortal realm weren't that tall. That narrowed things down considerably.

"Yeah, that's him. He was about that tall. He also had wings, they looked like Kara's except his were yellow. He also had a halo like mine except his was bright yellow not black." That explained the look of her wings, as well as the fact that she had a halo. There is no real concept of dominant genes when it came to Daemons, but certain traits were common.

"Did he wear any clothes?"

"Yeah, sort of like yours, but without the long jacket, or the hat." So he was a businessman or at least some professional. "He complained a lot when he got blood on his clothes."

"When he got blood on his clothes? Whose blood?"

"Mommy's," she whimpered. Someone better be ready to be tortured to death, because I wasn't about to let an abuser off easily. Kara gave off a bestial growl, and I knew she too wanted to kill the bastard.

"Don't worry Red, I'll make sure that he won't hurt anyone ever again, especially your mom." By the Gods I hoped for the kid's sake that the woman was still alive. No matter what, the dad, once I found him, was as good as dead. There would be a line to have a crack at him, and I had a distinct feeling he'd be trussed up and hung from a tree for a fun game of 'use the Divine scum as a Piñata'.

"Can you find mommy?"

"I'll do my best Red, I'll do my absolute best." I gave the girl a hug. She wrapped her arms around my neck and began to cry. "I'll do everything I can for you."

I heard someone walk into the house and looked up to see it was Sasha. "Red, some friends of ours are here, they want to meet you. Why don't you let Jason go so he can start looking for your mom."

"Okay." Red let go of me, and was led back into yard by Sasha.

"Can you help her, Jason?" Kara asked.

"I think I can. I'm going to head out now, so take care of the poor kid." I headed out the door and towards my car, my thoughts stuck on what I had learned.

"What do you think Shadow?" I asked my Crow.

I think you are in the mood to kill someone.

"That obvious?"

I've known you since before you were born. Of course it's obvious.

"Where do you think I should start with trying to figure out what's going on?"

Your office, so you can clear your head. You need to figure out why everyone was waiting for that girl. The Countess said that kid is being used by someone, and we need to know who that is and why they're doing it.

"Good enough start. I'm going to call Yvette to meet me there so we can talk about what's going on around here."

CHAPTER 4

Do you need me, master? Shadow asked when we got back to the office.

"No need to stay here. How about you wait until Jamie gets back and keep her company. If you want you can bring her up to speed, I have things I need to do." That was one of the best ideas Jamie ever had. Shadow's computer allowed him to talk to Jamie, as long as she didn't mind having to wait long periods of time for questions to be answered. Being a Crow and having to use only his beak Shadow wasn't exactly the fastest typist out there.

I headed back into my office and thought about my next move. Yvette was obviously a good choice to talk to. She had men and women stationed out all around the area so she would immediately know what was happening outside of the house.

The call was picked up on the second ring. "Hey Jason how's the kid?"

"Hello to you too. The kid's going to be fine. Her mother I'm not as sure about."

"That bad?"

"Worse. I think the creature, and I use creature, because the guy was an abuser, and apparently had a habit of using the girl's mother as a punching bag."

"As soon as you find out who was responsible for that I demand first crack at them," Yvette snarled.

"Sorry, I think that you're going to have to get in line behind a shit ton of Valkyries and Succubi. And I'm in front of them." I gave a half smile at the thought of what Yvette would do to the people who were behind this. She had found interesting ways to slaughter Nazis for fun as a way of dealing with anger management issues and besides they had deserved it. She was beginning to view Divines with the same disdain. Anyone who used a significant other as a punching bag was just as bad as a Nazi as far as she was concerned. "Look, what's going on over there?"

"My teams are reporting Daemons of various sorts all over the place. Especially Divines, though I think they're the most angry about what's going on at the house right now. There is virtually no one out there who would be dumb enough to make a move on the girl at this point. But the Valkyries and Succubi can't stay there forever. At some point I'm going to make an appearance and stay for a while."

"I wouldn't be surprised if you met with a God or two while there. Still I'll rest a lot easier if I know you're there." No one with even a vague sense of self-preservation would go anywhere near Yvette when she's pissed, she is a literal force of nature. "Has anything else popped on your end?"

"The Infernals have made another proposition at an arms deal. With all these Divine dickheads running around I'm not sure I have enough fire power to handle them."

"What do the Infernals want?" I didn't trust them, it was never a good idea to trust them.

"They want the souls of the corrupt expedited on their ways to one of the Infernal realms for one of their arms dealers, what else?" Yvette paused for a second. "Truthfully I'm beginning to consider it. Especially since they have provided a list of A-list scum bags that they want."

"What kind of scum?"

"Mostly child molesters, and serial rapists. There are also a few others that I would love to see die on principle, such as hate group leaders, and televangelists who preach hate. People that would generally be better off dead for the sake of the country."

"No drug users?" I asked.

"Their souls aren't worth a whole lot apparently. Besides a lot of them really haven't done much to warrant killing."

"Look do me a favor. I need to find out what's going on, I have some serious questions about what else is going on. As you said that girl is being used as a pawn in this and I have no clue as to why she was created. For all I know she's in her position to make such a big arms sale needed."

"Are you saying that I'm getting played?" Yvette sounded pissed.

"The Divines are assholes that outnumber Infernals, and I wouldn't put it past the leaders to give the rest a reason to go to war. They may not have realized you'd get involved. At the same time, the Infernals may have expected you to get involved and the arms deal would be a great way for a company to make a killing on an arms deal."

"Someone is going to eat their own arm without the benefits of salt and pepper. No one uses me, or a kid, for something like this. What else can you tell me?"

"I'm not sure yet. But I do have a few ideas. Do you have any idea who the arms dealer willing to make the deal is?"

"Alistor of Hell Bringer Enterprises." Oh fucking hell!!! "Does that mean anything to you?"

"Unfortunately it does. Alistor was the Executioner of Hell; he is also my father. Things may have just taken another turn for the worst."

"Your dad's an arms dealer?"

"Among other things, yes." This is going to be a nightmare. "I need you to stall until after I talk to dear old dad. Things aren't lining up properly here, and I need more answers. That being said be ready to make the deal."

"Are you sure?" Yvette sounded concerned and I was fairly sure she had every right to be.

"No but do it anyways. Right now I've got to go bash some heads together and get some answers from people. Hopefully without too much blood being shed."

"Be careful."

I hung up the phone and looked at the wall. Trying to piece it all together. A lot of things weren't adding up. I needed to know if Hell Bringer Enterprises was responsible for all of this, and truthfully I could believe them getting a child involved. As I've said before, never trust an Infernal. I decided to sum up everything I knew from what little I had to go on.

First, Red's mother was a Succubus and her father was some sort of Divine. Second her dad had been using her mother as a punching bag, more than enough reason for me to kill the bastard. The fact that the mother hadn't left before hand was an indication that this was a long-term Stockholm Syndrome type relationship. One thing I wanted to know was why a Divine had risked it, the fact that he left the kid alive at all was insane. He had to have serious connections to not worry about it. The chief of the Divine Department made it clear that he wanted to kill Red's parents if he had the chance. From what I could infer from what Red had told me about her father it sounded he dressed in expensive suits which meant he was probably of some importance.

So the guess was that Zackia had finally gotten the guts to run. Most likely she had been planning to meet someone in the Mortal realm; because of travel restrictions it would've immediately tipped off her abuser. Unfortunately it looked like he had gotten wind of it before she had been able to meet up with someone. Now I needed to find out who she was supposed to be meeting and where she had gone. My guess as to why she had disappeared was that she had dropped Red off somewhere to hide, then run off to draw away anyone who would hurt her daughter. That meant that there was a chance that she was still alive, at least I could hope so for Red's sake.

This led me to a theory as to how the Chiefs of the Department had been able to meet up at the Wolf before Yvette had gotten there. Someone had tipped off at least one part of the Department. Which one was of interest, but considering that it was Divines that had found her and had ended up in a battle with the cops it was most likely that the Divines had been tipped off first. Possibly hoping that they would eliminate the evidence of the Angelic asshole's indiscretions before he could be pointed out. If that was the case, he had to know that Red was still alive and that put her in some real danger; thankfully she had more protection than that scum had expected. She was being watched over by two Daemons plus their families. Along with them were groups of heavily armed Court of Night enforcers patrolling the area. Soon Yvette would be there and I was one of the best detectives out there with a reputation to live down to.

Now to call dear old dad. I picked up an interdimensional phone and called him up. The phone was answered on the first ring. "Hell Bringer Enterprises, you have reached the secretary of Alistor Black," said a female voice

"Hello Tracy, it's Jason, I need to talk to my dad."

"Well, that was quick." She sounded cheerful which was never good.

"What do you mean?"

"Your dad told me to expect your call sooner or later. I just wasn't expecting it to be this early."

"Can I speak to the old man?"

"He's in the middle of a meeting but if you want to you can come down to the office and I'll clear his schedule for you."

"Fine I'll be down soon enough." I asked her for the proper summoning circle since I had never been down to his office before.

After I hung up with the secretary I stuck my head into the outer office. "Hey Shadow I need to go see dad. Want to come?"

Do I have a choice?

"No, not really."

"Where are you going boss?" Jamie asked. I hadn't heard her come in.

"Down to an Infernal realm to meet with dad at his office. His secretary said she'll clear his schedule if I come down in person."

"Oh fun," Jamie clapped her hands together with glee. "Mind if I come along?"

"Definitely no. You are staying here, where I don't have to worry about you."

"You never take me anywhere fun."

CHAPTER 5

To set the record straight I absolutely loathe traveling by Circle, but it was either that or spend the Gods only know how long in a cab. Most likely in what was probably rush hour traffic, with an insane Infernal behind the wheel. So going by Circle was preferable, but only just.

I wouldn't normally do this. In fact I tried very hard to stay out of the Infernal realms entirely except when I have to go back to do highly irritating paperwork every few years. The problem with being half Human and half Infernal, was that I had to do a shit ton of paperwork no matter where I lived, and I had zero say in political matters. Not that I wanted any. I was effectively a second class citizen and I had no real pull there and didn't have much of a reputation to speak of. All I did have was access to some high priced lawyers. Thank you dad.

When I arrived I found myself in the main lobby of what I guessed to be Hell Bringer Enterprises. These guys were major players as far as I could tell from reading the several Infernal newspapers that I had subscriptions for. I exited the summoning Circle inbound platform and walked over to the company's reception area. I found one harried young man looking in distress at a bank of phones that wouldn't stop ringing. I could tell from the bags under his eyes and the shaking of his hands, that he had probably hadn't slept in days and was running on pure caffeine, enough to give any Mortal a heart attack. He was the most inviting receptionist to push around as the others all looked competent.

"No Mrs. Jacklyn is on vacation with her husband. No I don't know when she'll be back. No I did not know that you were her husband. No I don't know where she's gone. Would you like to talk to her secretary?" The man pushed a couple buttons to transfer the call. As he reached to grab another phone I grabbed him by the wrist.

"Which way to Alistor Black's office?" I asked.

"Who do you think you are, you stinking half breed?"

I lazily pulled Ace of Spades out of her holster and placed her under the guy's jaw. The receptionist swallowed hard as no else behind the desk made a move. "I'm the one asking questions here bucko. Which way to Alistor's office? If you want, call his secretary and tell her that Jason Black is here. She is clearing his schedule for me."

"I very much doubt…" He cut himself off as I pulled back the hammer of my Colt.

I gave him a disturbed smile. "Which way?"

Um master, the locals are getting antsy. I looked over my shoulder. The guards started heading my way but keeping their distance. Only someone completely bat shit crazy, or with one hell of a card to play would pull a stunt as stupid as the one I was currently doing.

The receptionist pointed to the main elevator. "Top floor office on the right." He sighed in relief as I thumbed off the hammer.

I tapped him a couple times on the cheek with the barrel. "Very good. That wasn't so hard was it?" I gave him a quick laugh as I tucked Ace of Spades away. His return laugh was cut short when I grabbed him by the back of the head and bounced his face off the counter. He dropped unconscious to the ground.

I looked at the guards who were backing off and shrugged off the whole unpleasantness. "He desperately needed a nap." I straightened the collar of my jacket and headed towards the elevators.

I rode the elevator to the top floor. Once I exited, I headed right and saw Tracy sitting neatly at her desk, her hair was done up in a severe braid, yet on her it came off more as dominating than prudish. Even by Succubus standards she was incredibly easy on the eyes. I had met her on several occasions when dad had come up for our annual get together. She looked at me with one raised eyebrow. "I hear from one of the receptionists down in the lobby that you pulled a gun on someone and then did some damage to his face."

I simply shrugged, not much needed to be said on the matter. "Is my dad in?"

"He's waiting for you right now. Go on in."

"Thank you."

I walked in on a scene of my dad practicing his putt. His jacket was hanging from the back of his chair. You could buy a Ferrari for the cost of one of his jackets and I knew for the fact that he had dozens of them. "Hello dad."

"Jason my boy!" He sounded to be in a good mood. "Heard about what you did downstairs. You do your old man proud."

"Thanks dad."

"So what can I do for you?" He said after he sank a putt at ten feet. "You've been causing a stall in a deal with that psychopathic little friend of yours. Sweet kid, you'll have to introduce the two of us sometime."

"I'll talk to her about it." I could see the two of them getting along swimmingly. "I have questions regarding a case of mine that brought this deal into a possibility."

"I know, and this is going to turn very, very personal for you, and by the end of it you're going to be begging me to make the deal."

"How can this possibly get any more personal. Cases involving kids are always personal for me. And what makes you think I'll have Yvette make the deal based on what you're about to tell me."

"It's about Red Raven's mother." He walked over to his desk and picked up a picture frame and came back to me with it. "This is Zackia and you of course recognize the other two."

I nearly choked on nothing in shock at who the other two were. One was Red, younger than she was now, but the child was obviously Red, the other was my own father. "You mean...

"Yes, Red's mother was family."

"Her father is going to be begging me to kill him by the time I'm done with him. As soon as he starts begging I'll know I have made a good start." I knew my eyes had turned blood red in pure rage.

"I'm glad you're like that, it makes me proud to call you my son. I could tell that Zackia was wearing a lot of makeup that day. Her abusive lover had been using her as a punching bag, she would never tell me who it was. All I ever knew was that he was Divine scum, and that I only knew by looking at little Red there."

When I found that bastard to hell with everyone else who wanted a shot at him. I was going to cut that bastard's wings off with the rustiest saw I could find. I would do to him what Yvette did to Nazis and hang him from a tree tied up with razor wire and then gut him, and leave him to the Crows. Better still, I'd tie him to a cross outside the biggest damn church I can find just to send a message. I handed the picture back to my dad. "Is there anything else you can tell me?"

"On the day your people found Red, her mother had called me to tell me she had run to the Mortal Realm and was hoping I could send someone to pick her up. I'm sorry to say that apparently some Divine law enforcement agents found her before any of my men could, and by all accounts they killed her. Red got lucky that those Human cops found her when they did. I'm fairly sure that whoever Zackia was running from is close to the Department, otherwise she would have gotten away cleanly."

"You're probably right." This was beyond the level of personal I take with most cases involving kids. This was family, and as dad taught me, nobody fucks with family and lives. It brought back the smell of smoke as the town that had killed my mother burned at my father's hands. I had been seventeen when that had happened but right now the memory was as clear as if it had been yesterday. No one had lived. They all deserved their deaths. The person who had done this to Red's mother was going to die just like the people of that town only more painfully. "Whoever is responsible better be prepared to die." My voice was a guttural growl.

"What's going to happen to Red Raven? I'm not parent material, and neither are her grandparents. We're busy business people, we wouldn't have time to raise her." My father's question snapped me out of my rage, and I could tell from the tone of his voice that dad was indeed truly concerned for her.

"She's currently with a Daemonic couple who I'm sure would love to be permanent parents for her. They have fought and killed for each other, and I'm sure they'll do the same for Red."

"That takes a load off my mind. I would be worried about what would happen to her but if you trust them…"

"I've fought beside one of them, when she was on a mission to rescue the other." I put my hand on my dad's shoulder and looked him square in the eye. "They will make excellent parents."

"Thank you son, if your mother was still alive she'd be so proud of you right now."

"That means a lot dad. Especially now." The anniversary of my mother's death was fast approaching, five weeks out now. "Shadow keeps giving me the 'If your mother was alive today,' treatment."

Dad shook his finger at Shadow. "He's a good boy so ease up on him, bird brain."

Shadow cawed both loudly and indignantly. "You don't want to know what he just said."

"I probably don't. Now son take this picture with you. I don't know where Red Raven had been living and this is one of the few I have of her mother. I want her to have it." He looked at the picture one last time and handed it back to me. "Her mother had been such a beautiful care free child, now all of this ugliness. Do me proud Jason."

"I will dad, I will." I gave my dad a long hug. "Can I use your phone?"

"Sure. Who are you going to call?"

"That little psychopathic friend of mine. I want her to make the deal."

CHAPTER

I had returned to the office in a puff of sulfur and brimstone. "Is that you boss?" I heard Jamie ask from the outer office.

"Yes it's me sweet heart. I'm in a really pissy mood right now, so please bear with me for a while. If you want you can go home, I don't think I'll need you. Just take the phone off the hook when you leave."

"Sounds like you're planning on killing someone. Things must be worse than usual," she said walking into my office.

"I just found out that my victim was a family member. So yes, things are personal now and that means people are going to die."

"Understood Jason. Is there anything I can do?"

"No, not at the moment. Just keep Lady Bell on you, it'll make me feel better." It really would. Jamie knew how to use that bitch of a gun, I had made sure of that. If something happened to her I'd be beyond enraged and heads would roll. As far as I was concerned Jamie wasn't just an employee, she was family.

Jamie put on her shoulder holster and tucked Lady Bell neatly under her left arm. Then putting on her jacket she headed out the door. *She's going to be okay master*, Shadow said soothingly.

"I know but I'm still allowed to worry about her, aren't I?"

I guess so, she's family after all, and family means everything. Especially to you.

"I'm going to have another crack at talking to Red. Maybe I can get some more information on who her dad is. The sooner I find the bastard the sooner I can relieve some tension by doing some body work on the Hell bound Divine."

I slid into my trench coat and hat and grabbed my keys off my desk. "Come on Shadow, we have work to do."

Shadow hopped up on my shoulder and got ready for what I knew was going to be a hell of a ride. I had places to go and people to kill. Now I was going to start with helping a little girl find justice for the loss of her mother. After that I was going to get down to the serious business of making examples of people, Countess Bloodwolf style. Translation, by leaving an unsettling number of butchered corpses in my wake. I may only be a half breed, but I had been called to do this job because I knew how to do my job, and how to do it well.

CHAPTER 7

I parked in front of what I was sure was going to become Red's home. The Succubi and Valkyries were gone, but I did see some other cars I would have recognized without even needing to blink. Thor was here, along with Sif I was certain. Freya was also here, along with her brother Freyr. Thank the Gods I had been right, no idiot Divine would attack this place currently. With Gods of War around, this place was safer than the strongest U.S. military base.

I knocked on the door and was met by Kara who seemed to be in a relatively decent mood, which wasn't surprising since one of her bosses was here, helping out. "Hey Jason come on in. What's the news?" she asked beckoning me inside.

"Not much good, but I do have some questions to ask little Red. And I do need to have a sit-down chat with you and your other half."

"Sounds serious."

"It is, it really is." I put my hand on the picture frame knowing that it was going to make Red cry but it couldn't be helped. "Where is everyone?"

"Out back playing with the kitten, well everyone except Thor of course. Freya thinks he'd be too rough, and he probably would be."

"Who got Red a kitten? That's a little early isn't it?"

"Hey wasn't my idea, or Sasha's either. It was Freya who brought the little fluff ball here. Apparently one of the cats that pulls her chariot had kittens recently, so she decided to bring one down for Red. The girl has been playing with the homicidal fluff muffin for a while with a laser pointer." All the time we had been talking Kara had led me to the back of the house and out into the back yard.

The 'homicidal fluff muffin', as Kara had put it, was passed out on Red's lap. Sif and Freya were down talking to Red who was openly staring at Sif's golden hair. Thor was talking with Freyr and Sasha was playing hostess to the group. I walked up and tapped Sasha on the shoulder. "Hey, I need to talk to you and Kara for a few minutes," I said instead of saying 'hello' when she turned to face me.

"What is it about?"

"The kid."

Sasha nodded. "Do you want me to get her?"

"No that's okay, I just need the two of you right now."

Sasha twisted her head over her shoulder. "Okay everyone I'll be right back, help yourselves to whatever you want." She then followed me back into the house.

"Okay Black, what do you have for us?" Kara asked.

"Let's sit down first."

"We can talk just fine standing up," Sasha replied.

"Okay then I have to ask you a question. How would the two of you feel about adopting Red as your daughter. I know this is a big question but I have found out some particularly upsetting news."

"You mean?" Both Sasha and Kara and asked me at the same time.

"Red's mother is dead. Her uncle confirmed it."

"Who's her uncle? And are they sure."

"Red's great uncle is my dad, making her some sort of niece to me I think. Red's grandparents and my father by their own admission wouldn't make good parents for her. I would be lousy at the job, for obvious reasons. So I thought maybe the two of you would take the job. If you're worried about money and the like, don't be, the family will definitely help with that. Please, I'm asking as the girl's uncle and your friend to please take care of her."

"I think we need a moment," Kara said looking at me and holding up one finger. The two Daemons turned towards each on and had a brief discussion.

"The main thing we'll need help with will be getting paperwork since we know so little about her, and there is simply no paper trail for the girl," Sasha said. "Can the Countess help with that?"

"Are you kidding me? I can have all that stuff done in about an hour." Now that was a load off my mind.

"Good we'll get everything ready, buy her a brand new wardrobe. Of course, and help her decorate…" Sasha started getting carried away, and I just let her and Kara plan away to their hearts content.

While they were babbling I went back outside. "Hey Red."

Red Raven looked up at me and grabbing the kitten off her lap ran up to me. "Have you found my mommy?" The excitement in her voice immediately faded when she saw the look in my eyes. She could already tell, and that look of pain was physical for both of us. "Mommy's dead, isn't she?"

I simply nodded. Red began to cry and continued to cry, like no one I had ever seen cry before. I had so wished that I could tell her differently. That I could tell her that her mom was simply a cavalry charge full of blood and gore away, but I couldn't. After about ten or fifteen minutes, quite possibly more, I didn't know, she finally calmed down to loud sniffling.

"I found something that I think your mom would want you to have." I took out the picture my dad had given me and now past it on to Red.

Red looked at it a ran an arm across her eyes, wiping away her tears. "Do you know that man?"

"He's my father."

"I liked him, he was so nice to us. He didn't like dad, he even said that all mom had to do was ask and he'd kill him."

"Sounds like my dad alright."

"Are you going to?" I saw the girl's eyes start to glow red with rage.

"Am I going to do what?" I knew what the girl was going to say I just wanted to hear her to say it.

"Are you going to kill my dad for me?"

"Of course. First I'm going to make him suffer for what he did to your mom, and for what he would have done to you. Then after I let him suffer I'm going to end his miserable life."

"You're my hero Jason. Can I watch?"

"No little lady. I don't want you to see what I'm going to do to him. He maybe evil, but what I'm going to do to him will only corrupt you beyond reach. I want you to stay innocent, I want you to stay a happy care free child. What I'm going to do to this scum will turn you into monster like him and that's the last thing I want for you."

"Okay Jason, as long as you kill him, so he can't hurt anyone else. Will you at least please do that for me?"

"I will. Now why don't you take your picture to show to Sasha and Kara. They want to take care of you from now on, and I think they'd love to find a special place for your picture so that you will always remember your mom."

"I hope they will." Red squeezed the picture tighter against herself, as if trying to press what remained of her mother deeper into herself.

"Before you go over there I'd like it we could talk little one," I said, bringing her over to a couch.

"Okay."

"What can you tell me about your dad? What did he look like other than what you told me earlier today? What was his name? That kind of stuff." Please may she be able to give me some good answers.

"His name was Azerath, he was always getting drunk, or at least that's what mom said. Mom used to say he had been nice before me, but he had gotten mean just before she had gotten pregnant. She said it wasn't my fault that he got mean, she said it was something about his job."

Job! Now that would be a good lead. "Do you know what kind of job your dad had?"

"Mom said he worked for some important people who kept an eye on people, or something. She said I was too young to understand. She also said we had to stay a secret or he would lose his job, and that I'd lose her too."

A job keeping an eye on people could definitely mean he worked for the Department or some contractor associated with it. I wasn't about to go to the Divine section but the Infernal section would still be able to get me all the information I needed. It would also explain how he had gotten tipped off to Zackia pulling a runner when he did. He may have come across the information second hand, or through the grapevine and gone after Red's mother to keep her quiet. That would make him a cop or detective for the Department.

"Mommy told me that she had heard dad talking to someone about having to kill me. She was going to take me here so we could escape. When we got to this realm, she found a place for me to hide. She said she had seen someone coming and was sure it was dad, and that I had to hide or I'd get hurt. That was where those nice men found me. Then some people like my dad tried to take me from them. I remember shooting and people yelling, then the car ride over to that place where I met you."

That explained quite a bit. Red's dad was probably a Divine cop scum bag, from the way she had described him, most likely a detective. The night of the escape everything had gone straight to shit for everyone. Zackia had run to the Mortal Realm and called my dad hoping for a pick up. He would have known something about her boyfriend and what a massive dick he was and what he was. Knowing that, he had called up the Chief of the Infernal section for help; dad had those kinds of connections. Azerath had panicked; he had gone after Red's mother and had called for backup, probably from his best buddies, the ones who wouldn't sell him out. They had come here, he had gone after Zackia, leaving his friends to hunt down Red. Most likely someone had gotten wind of this and had decided to make a move based on department politics and had called up the chief of the Divine section. Either chief had called the other two, along with the Kitsune and Dragon courts.

Court of Night cops had been a mere chance of good fortune for Red. Luckily the dispatcher had gotten the cops to the Mystic Wolf before it had closed for the night. From there forward I had become involved and we now found ourselves here.

"Jason? Do you think other people are going to try to hurt me?"

I looked at her knowing that this was an answer I could give a fairly sound answer that was at least somewhat encouraging to the little girl who currently had her tail wrapped around my leg. "There are plenty of people, including myself who will make sure that no one will harm you. Sasha and Kara have a lot of powerful friends, and as far as their friends are concerned you are already family. Plus I have a good friend myself, who has decided that she is going to have her people keep an eye out for you. As long as we're around you'll be safe." I gave the girl a hug which she curled into. I hated giving kids bad news about their parents but I always tried to do what I could for them. In this case I had done very well. The girl already had a family. I knew that as hard as Sasha and Kara tried, nothing they could do would replace Red's mom, but they'd make damn good parents.

"Okay." I didn't try to shift the girl off of me; I knew that what she needed was a friend, and someone who would make everything okay. I ran a hand through her hair, between her horns and under her halo. I was getting paid for this case, but right now the money meant nothing. The only payment I wanted right now was knowing that this girl was safe, and that those who had hurt her and her mother, were left out for the scavengers to feast upon after I butchered them. Getting repaid for the large cook out I had sponsored earlier in the day would be nice, and I knew I would get that. At the end of the day however I just wanted to see justice done for the sake of this kid. She was family but that really didn't matter, people wanted her dead, and had already killed her mom. The chief of the Divine said that he wanted the mother and father dead along with the girl. He already had one of the three, next he would get the dad, but he would be a dead Daemon if he tried to hurt the girl.

I didn't notice the knock at the door at first until I looked up and saw Yvette talking with Red's new mothers. After a bit she came over to where I was sitting with Red. "Do I have a new rival for your affections?" she asked with a smile.

"Hardly. I'd like to introduce you to my niece." Yvette stopped and looked at me for a bit.

"So that is why you called and had me make the deal so soon, isn't it?" She sat down next to me and looked and Red whose head came up to look at the Countess.

"Yes, her mother was killed by Red's father, an extremely abusive Divine."

"Daddy used to hurt mom a lot," Red said. "Are you going to help Jason kill daddy?"

Yvette gave an appropriately wolfish grin. "If he lets me. We've killed a lot of people together over the years. I'd love to help Jason kill the man who hurt your mom." Sitting down next to me, Yvette soon found Red emigrating over to her lap.

"I like you."

"Now that you've introduced me to your family I think we're going to have to start dating." She winked at me with a low laugh.

"You've only met my niece in person, and just talked to my dad over the phone," I reminded her with a returned laugh and slight smile. The idea of introducing Yvette to my dad wasn't far off though. He already wanted to meet her, and as I have been thinking of a relationship with her anyway it did make sense. "However maybe it'll happen at some point."

"I can't wait..." She was cut off from continuing her thought by her phone ringing. "Hold on."

"What have you got for me." She answered her phone and had a brief discussion with someone on the other end. "Got it. Keep an eye on them." There was a beeping from her phone as another line came into play. "Go ahead." There was another brief discussion. "Keep an eye on them, and coordinate with the other teams and find the closest one. I want you to separate them out and box 'em in. Do not use deadly force unless absolutely necessary, and I repeat the 'absolutely necessary' part. I need a couple of them captured and brought to Black's interrogation room. But we'll meet you on scene first as back up. I don't want these bastards to get away on us."

"What do we have?"

"A group of Divines are coming closer. I don't think they know who is here right now, but I'm having my men capture a couple of them for interrogation purposes."

"Good. Red, we have to get going, but don't worry I'll come back when I can." I picked Red up and handed her over to Sasha and Kara. "Yvette's enforcers are following some Divines who are headed this way. We're on our way to intercept them and then torture the ever-loving hell out of them."

"Don't worry we got her," Sasha said taking Red out of my arms. "You just find out who did this to the girl's mother. She'll be fine here."

"Come on Yvette there are people to torture and Daemons to kill."

"Can I play interrogate the Nazi's on them?" she asked delightedly.

"Depends on how many we can grab. If we can pick up at least two I'll let you have fun on one of them before I get to work on the other." I led her out the door and into my car. "Hey Shadow."

Yes master?

"Why don't you stay here and play with the kitten."

Thank you, no. I like my feathers right where they are. I'm coming with you.

"Can't say I didn't offer, things are going to be messy."

Things always get messy when you're working.

CHAPTER

When we got to the squad car where a couple of Yvette's hitters were waiting for us, they had found a group of Divines camped out only a couple of blocks from the house. I counted four in the van, and apparently the idiots only had their eyes out for the girl. I was guessing that they were too used to being near everyone at the Department to notice just another Infernal, even one like me.

Yvette got out of my car and tapped on the glass of her men's car. "What's the news?"

"We've got these scum suckers in line of sight, there are two other groups that are apparently moving in closer as well." He pointed towards the van. "These guys aren't too bright are they? They have no real sense of tactics."

"No, Daemons aren't used to dealing with our kind," Yvette said. A smug look plastered on her face. "They're too busy thinking they're going to trick Infernals that they're walking right into a meat grinder."

"What do you want us to do?"

"Have the other two teams kill every Divine they come in contact with. I want it kept as quiet as possible. This is a safe neighborhood, and I don't want anyone getting suspicious or have property values to drop because of this event because people are scared for their safety."

"Keeping it quiet is going to be difficult," the second hitter said. "We just have some noisy tools."

"Don't worry I have a shipment of the fun stuff that just came in that will allow us to kill Divines nice and quietly." Ah yes, Divine nerve gas. It was harmless to anyone who wasn't a Divine and was fairly quiet, the scum would barely make a noise when they dropped. "Now I want you to join one of the other groups. We're going to take some of these guys in for questioning, I want the rest of you to make sure the other Divines don't go anywhere."

"And if they shoot first?"

"Don't give them the chance."

"Got it." The squad car drove off and I saw one of the hitters pick up the radio and call in instructions to the other groups.

"They're not all cops are they?"

"Of course not. I wouldn't waste that much money on a city this small. But I do have a lot of fake squad cars, and enough uniforms to make it look real."

"How many cops do you have on your payroll?"

"Enough. More importantly I have the right people on my payroll. Other than that you know the rules."

"Court business stays in the Court unless I want to get myself killed." The incident with Lady K still haunted me. I had interfered with Court business, and Yvette had nearly killed me, or forced me to kill her. Either way that whole case had changed our relationship, oddly enough it had brought us closer, despite the fact that had we nearly killed each other.

"Well do you want to go kick some Divine ass?" I asked the little monster.

"By the Gods above and Below I am so looking forward to this. How do you want to do this? I count four in there, that's two more than we need."

"Here's my idea. I walk up to the driver side of the van, knock on the window. As soon as that scum bag rolls down the window I put a round in his head and that of the Divine sitting next to him. The other two are going to make a break for it. You grab the one coming from the passenger side, I'll grab the one coming out my side, if need be I'll shoot him in the leg or something. Shift as soon as you hear the first shot, for maximum surprise. Don't worry I have an extra set of clothing for you in my car."

"Great to know." Yvette smiled at me, though leered may be a better word for the look on her face. "I'm going to call for a limo so we can ride in peace with them. That way we can make sure that they aren't dumb enough to try to run from the car."

"Good idea."

Yvette took out her cellphone and called her private limo service. The kind with an expensive bar and hardcore armor plating. "They'll be here in five minutes."

"That's all?"

"I had them drop me off at the house so they're still in the area, just not in plain view."

"Well shall we go make some people's lives miserable?" I checked Ace of Spades to make sure she was loaded with Daemon killers. I had kept her loaded with those since this case had started, but it never hurt to double check. When the clip showed true I slapped it back in and chambered a round.

We approached the van quietly like wolves flanking their prey. We may be outnumbered, but we had surprise on our side, plus we had been doing this sort of thing for seventy plus years now. I came up to the driver's window, these punks were truly stupid. How they managed to be on any law enforcement force was hard to imagine. Well I guess some good ol' boys from some hick town trying to play city cops would be just as useless. It was also possible that these guys weren't department people and just good friends of the dad, even more pathetic.

I tapped on the window, the driver rolled it down. "What the fuck do you want asshole?"

"To send a message." His face didn't even have time to show surprise when my gun came into view and with a violent recoil and a loud crack splattered his buddy with his brains. I yanked the corpse to me and smashed what was left of his head into the steering wheel to get line of sight on his gore covered friend and snapped off three rounds, two into his back and the third into the back of his head. I had already heard Yvette scream in rage as she shifted hard. Apparently it hurts her to shift so she usually takes her time doing it, though there are times I think that it's more for dramatic effect than comfort. When she goes through the transformation fast she screams in pain and rage, at least that's what she tells me. I have heard her make similar noises while sharing a bed with her so who knows. Just as I thought, the side doors were frantically opened and the two remaining Daemons made an utter failure of an attempt to escape. Yvette had grabbed one and I heard bones break when she got her claws on him. Mine I let run about twenty feet and he was just about to sprout wings when I shot him in the shoulder spinning him round like a top crashing to the ground. The report from the gun was muffled by the screaming of Yvette's victim. Whatever she had done to him must have hurt like hell.

I walked up to where my victim was struggling to get back up and dropped on top of him smashing my knee in to the middle of his back and digging the thumb of my left hand into the bullet hole causing him to scream as well. "Try and get away and it only gets worse for you, and if you don't stop screaming it will definitely get worse," I snarled as I pressed Ace of Spades to the base of his skull.

"I've got mine," Yvette called out to me her voice sounding like it was crushing rock, "and I don't think he's going anywhere any time soon, at least not without extreme agony."

"What did you do?"

"Compound fractures to both legs and arms, and fair number of cracked ribs, though I'm guessing on the ribs. The arms and legs are a definite because there's bone coming out of all four."

"Do me a favor and break his larynx to shut him the fuck up. The last thing I want right now is that scum screaming all the way back to my place." I looked at my guy, I heard a thwak and the screaming was cut short. "Now do I need to break your larynx to keep you quiet too, or are you going to come peacefully? I know for a fact it will heal up soon enough for me to start torturing you for information."

The Divine was smart and stayed silent with a shake of his head. "Good boy." To make sure that he actually stayed silent I grabbed him by the back of the head and slammed his face into the pavement so hard that I heard the satisfying sound of breaking bone.

Yvette's limo showed up less than minute later. Out stepped a man in an immaculate tuxedo who was neither Vampire nor Werewolf. "Madame I take it that this is the most esteemed Mr. Black?" The accent was British, so she had really gone and done it. She had actually gone and hired the classic English butler slash chauffer. She was becoming such a snob, of course one look at the bar in her apartment was enough to tell you that.

"Hold on Jasper I need to get dressed." She turned her attention and held out one taloned hand towards me. "The keys?"

I flipped her the keys. "Your clothes are in the trunk. Nothing too fancy of course."

"Thanks Jason you're such a gentleman," Yvette's voice transitioned from rock crushing to normal teenager halfway through the sentence. "Oh Jason you shouldn't have! Just like the old times!" Yvette came out wearing old American military fatigues, circa World War Two, and trying her hardest to pose seductively.

I couldn't help but laugh at her antics. "After what I just saw you looking like I don't think that's going to work. Plus I don't think these two are into your look, or at least any condition to be appreciative of your charm."

"And what does Captain Black have to say to me?"

"Good work soldier, now let's question this scum in the most creatively unpleasant ways we can think of."

"Sir! Yes sir!" Yvette snapped off a quick salute. Part of this was for old times' sake, just to get us into the mood for a good round of torture.

The other part was it was tended to scare the fuck out of our prisoners. The two of us who had been so brutal mere minutes ago were now treating this whole thing like a joke. We were serious about doing our job properly, but who says you can't have a little fun along the way.

CHAPTER 9

The two Divines weren't fully healed up by the time we made it back to my house, where the best torture chamber since, well who knows, was waiting for them. I've seen people break at the mere sight of the horrors lining the walls, and right now this scum was getting an eye full. I was a thoroughly unpleasant person at times and looking around the room you could tell that simply by the décor. In one corner sat the first electric chair used in the US. Sitting in it was the remains of a Fey king who had been turned into a grotesque parody of a ventriloquist dummy. Sasha had been with me when I had found it, and its maker; in fact she had been the one to kill that bastard.

In another corner of the room on a shelf sat a collection of jars containing infants with Devil's Backbones fermenting in alcohol as a means to cure impotency. Thoroughly disgusting and complete nonsense of course. On the shelf above it were a collection of shrunken heads, interesting story about how they came into my possession but that I could save for later. Most of the furniture was made of wood from Aokigahara, the Suicide Forest in Japan. The stuff is expensive because very few people are dumb enough to go in and get it. Of course when you want that kind of stuff you must be willing to pay dearly for it. I won't quote the price, it's enough to say it's expensive.

I could tell that the evil of the furniture was having an effect on my two prisoners, as their halos were starting to smoke. "Well let's get this over with this," I said slapping one of them. I sat down in front of them letting my eyes start glowing red, a testament to my Infernal nature. For her part, Yvette had put on her 'I'm the biggest, scariest bad ass you have ever had the misfortune to meet' outfit. It was a dominatrix outfit made from tanned Werewolf hide and studded with Vampire fangs. They were remains of some of the various people we had put in the ground together as she rose to power. To further scare the fuck out of these bastards she was still in her Human form and was sitting at my desk ignoring them while carefully deseeding a strawberry. I don't know where she had picked up that sort of psychological warfare, all I knew was that it worked. She simply ignored them as if they were so unimportant that she would find something so mind bendingly boring as deseeding a strawberry far more interesting. They had seen her transform from what could only be described as almost Lovecraftian in form, a horror from the deepest, darkest heart of the pit. She looked like a modern special effects Werewolf covered in corpse like skin over a skeletal frame with the cracked nails and fangs of a good old fashioned Nosferatu. She damn near scared the hell out of me when she was like that and my dad is from the pit so when he's in a bad mood he is a thing of nightmares. Yvette is even scarier than my dad when she decides to make a point.

"Now let's come to the reason I have invited you two here as my honored guests," I said putting on a set of Daemon busting knuckle dusters. Normal brass knuckles wouldn't work, these ones however, were enchanted and would hurt like hell when used on this scum.

"We have nothing to say to a half breed like you," one snarled, spitting at me.

"Oh you poor, poor stupid fool." I pulled my fist back and smashed it hard into his face. This bastard had been the one whose face and I crushed with pavement, so that must have hurt like nothing he had felt before. To my amazement he barely let a scream pass his lips.

I looked at his counterpart. "Perhaps you would be willing to be a bit more cooperative. Or are you going to be just as much of a nuisance?"

"Fuck you!"

I turned to Yvette. "What is it with people being so stupid?" I asked. She merely shrugged in response and kept at it with her strawberry. I grabbed the Divine's barely healed arm and broke it again, hard enough to cause another compound fracture. This guy was a screamer. I couldn't help but smile.

"Now would you care to rephrase your answer?"

"What do you want to know?" The Daemon said in a whimper.

"Don't tell him anything," the other hissed at him.

"You shut up!" I walked over to my desk and picked up an enchanted baseball bat, a new toy, sometimes you just have to go with the classics. I pulled back and swung for the fences treating the scum's head as a ball. The force of the hit knocked the chair down and found blood leaking from the Divine's ear, jaw, and eye socket. I set the chair back on its legs then took another swing into his chest; judging from the amount of blood that sprayed out of his mouth I guessed I had shattered his ribcage and punctured both lungs. I shrugged, he'd heal up from that soon enough.

I looked over my shoulder at Yvette. "How much do you think it would cost to get this amount blood out of the rug?"

"I don't know. But there is a reason I keep telling you to dump the rug and go with bare hard wood. It cleans up easier." And then back to her task of deseeding the strawberry.

I turned my attention back to my mostly uninjured victim, okay so he had a compound fracture, I'm sure he felt better than the other idiot. "Where was I?"

"You were going to ask me some questions and let me go?" He whimpered feebly with a smile forced through pain on his lips.

I gave him my best venomous smile. "Now I know that I never said I'd let you go, at least not fully intact. Of course you can improve your chances of getting out this intact if you're willing to be cooperative. You see the girl behind me here, is itching to gut and kill you to make a statement. From the way your friend here has been acting I can almost assure you that he will be the first to die. So, of course, you may find yourself in a good position stay intact if you are willing to answer my questions honestly, and without too much persuasion. Now can I expect your complete cooperation?"

He glanced over at his compatriot who was still hanging limp from the chair and struggling for breath. "Yes sir. No problem sir, I have no problem answering your questions."

"See, that was easy enough. I knew we could make great friends," I said patting his cheek a couple times. "Now my first question is a pretty easy one. Where is Azerath?"

"I don't know." To put it mildly I wasn't exactly pleased with the guys answer I had given him a chance to be my friend, he had agreed to answer my questions and now… "I honestly don't. I really wish I could tell you, but I simply don't know." I looked him dead in the eyes, looking straight into what counted as his soul, and decided that he was indeed telling me the truth.

"Okay. I'll believe you… for now at least. So how do you know him? You were willing to do some nasty work for him. Killing a kid is pretty low for a Divine, even for some scummy ones. There are plenty of people who are usually willing to do more than that, and I can tell you right now that some of the people who have a reputation for it didn't do it. That being said usually Divines are above that sort of thing, or is that also a reputation that you didn't earn?"

"I was told to keep an eye on the house and wait for it to be empty, I had no instructions on killing a kid. I mean I knew there was a half breed there but I didn't know much else. I just work for Azerath I don't kill people, I'm just a look out." I had already frisked him and found that he did carry a gun loaded with Daemon killers, same as the other scum.

I dropped his gun at his feet. "So what's this for?"

My subject looked at the gun and realized he was in for some real pain. "Yvette I'm going to need some help here."

"Whatever you say dear. Has he been lying to you again?" She walked up behind me and leaned her head against my shoulder. "Let me guess he says he doesn't kill people, but we did find that nasty piece of artillery on him, didn't we?"

"Exactly, that. I thought you weren't paying attention."

"I sometimes pay attention to what you're doing but not always." She simply gave me a slow smile. "So what do you need my help with?"

"I need you to hold his wings out, nice and tight."

"Wait what are you going to do to me?" I could see panic spreading across the Divine's face as he wondered what was in store for him this time.

I picked up my bat and gave myself a few passes with it over hand. A sledge hammer would have been a better tool, but for now this would do just fine. "Stretch his wing." Yvette grabbed his left wing and yanked it all the way out and gave me a stomach turning grin. I smashed the bat down on the scum's wing and was happy to see blood oozing through the feathers, his white wings staining a brilliant scarlet. My victim screamed in Earth rendering agony. I hadn't heard anyone scream like that since watching Yvette work over Nazi officers.

"Now would you like to rephrase your answer or do I break your other wing? As you can see I have no real compunction about shedding your blood. I have sworn to protect a little girl, and if that means working people over for fun, that's just a perk. I'm far from being the most pleasant person especially when it comes to protecting children. You can beg for mercy all you want but unless you give me proper answers I have no intention on giving you any. Now why should I believe you about not being there to kill the kid when I found a gun on you loaded with Daemon killers?"

My victim did respond for a while as he sobbed in pain. I was beginning to grow tired of not getting answers when I noticed the other piece of scum was starting to come around. I pointed the bat back at the Divine with the broken wing and looked at Yvette. It was time to send a warning to his friend that I was an unpleasant person to piss off. "Stretch his other wing."

"Gladly." Again the twisted smile. Most people would think that I must be out of my mind to think I could be falling in love with her. But there was just something about that smile that sent my heart a pitter patter.

"No! Please no, not again!!!" I could tell he was about to give me the information I wanted but I had a point to make. I smashed the other wing. His scream this time was, if anything, more full of agony than the one before it.

"As I said you should just tell me the truth, I wouldn't be doing this to you if you would just tell me the truth." I turned to look at his buddy his sat there looking in abject horror at what I had just done to his friend. "Would you like to be a little more forth coming than your friend?

"I ... I don't know what you want."

"Where is Azerath, and what were you going to do to the girl?"

The Divine scum's eyes jumped from me to his friend and back again. He had already learned that I was very well capable of hurting him. After my initial round of batting practice there was no doubt in his mind on that point. "Azerath dropped out on us right after the girl got on to the Mortal realm. We're just here to wait for the girl to be as alone as possible. And with her new foster mothers around, and all of their friends, we weren't going to be getting close any time soon."

"So why are you two little dead men carrying Daemon killers?"

"We're department law enforcement officers you idiot. We have to carry those."

Ah now we were getting somewhere, from the way they had just made it sound Azerath was one of their own. "So you two are just law enforcement shits huh? Of course you're not carrying badges but it doesn't really matter I guess. Azerath didn't want to be caught being called dad by the kid so he had you mooks do the dirty work."

"He didn't want the kid calling him what?!" The Divine sounded legitimately surprised.

"He's the kid's dad, but that's of no concern of yours now. So I take it that you didn't know that Azerath was shacking up with an Infernal?"

"No... Yes... Sort of... Look everyone sort of knew about it vaguely but that kind of thing isn't really news. We've all fucked a few Succubi over the years at parties and the like. A good party always has a few Succubi at it, we get high and want to fuck something, not much different than anyone else. But like most everyone else I ignored the rumors, besides he's a good chief and no one was dumb enough to ask him directly."

"You see you have a very big problem right now. The Succubus your Chief was shacking up with and using as a punching bag was my cousin. My father found her body, so I happen to already know she's dead, and that my client no longer has a real mother, only those two Daemons whose house she's staying at." I paused for a while to let that sink in a bit, the guy's eyes had gone wide in absolute horror as he was probably now coming to terms with what was about to happen to him. I looked at my other prisoner who was now stable enough to understand me. "So here's what I'm going to do: I am going to give you both a chance to call Azerath and tell him where to meet me. If you do that, one of you walks out of here with his breathing rights intact."

"And the other?"

"I'm a professional asshole for a reason. I maybe let you both walk out, but there is no guarantee on that." They both gulped hard knowing that there was a good chance that neither of them would live to see another day. I wondered briefly if they had families, loved ones who would miss them, but I quickly dismissed the thought. Most people had families and friends that would miss them when they didn't come home, but such is life. I was just doing what I was good at, and I didn't care about these two. I mostly worry about those that are close to me, and I worried about those who I am paid to worry about. Other than that, I usually didn't care much. I took out their phones and put them on my desk. I uncuffed the one with the broken wings and brought him over to my chair, Ace of Spades never once leaving the base of his skull. "Now you are going to contact Azerath and tell him to be at the St. Paul Cathedral at one in the morning, that you were able to get the kid but that there were a lot of dead Divines in the process. Do you understand? And put your phone on speaker."

"Understood." The scum picked up his phone and started dialing. We waited for a few seconds while the call went through, that's the problem with calling between dimensions service was sketchy at best. "Hello Azerath it's me Tramdal, look I got the girl liked you asked…"

"Were there any hitches about getting her?" So that was what Azerath sounded like, a booming bass of a voice.

"A ton of them, the Court of Night got involved and we took serious casualties and they're still out looking for me. I'm still on the move right now, can you meet me at the St. Paul Cathedral around one? I want out of this now."

"I'll get you out as long as you don't plan on going to Gerald about this." I was fairly certain that no matter what happened, my prisoner was a dead man.

"Are you crazy? I'm not reporting this to the Department head. I don't want to risk my life any more than necessary."

"You said one? I can do that, just be sure to have her there when I show up."

"Okay it's set," He hung up the phone and looked at me. "Now that?"

"It means you get to live for a little while longer." I turned to his friend. "Which I guess makes you superfluous." With a shrug I put two rounds into his chest and a third into his forehead.

"Wha… wha… what did you do that for?!" The Divine finally got out after staring in horror at the body with the realization that it could have just have easily been him.

"Because as I said, he was superfluous, and I had no intention of keeping both of you alive. You may still get out of this alive, but you have to do exactly what I tell you." I looked over at Yvette. "Are those strawberries any good?"

CHAPTER 10

Yvette was crashed out on my couch flipping through channels on my TV, her feet propped up on the coffee table. Shadow was happily munching on popcorn next to her. As for my prisoner? He was still cuffed to a chair in my trophy room, read interrogation room, and wasn't going to be going anywhere for a while.

When it got close to what I guessed would be Red's bed time I gave Sasha a call. "Hey it's Black," I said as soon as she asked who was calling.

"Hey Jason what can I do for you?"

"I found Red's dad, or more accurately, I've set up a trap for him. I want you and Kara to bring Red to the Mystic Wolf just after close. Can you do that?"

"We should be able to though I can tell you right now, she's in no way going to be very awake for it."

"I really don't need much more than for her to ID her father for the Department heads, after that you can put her back to bed, I'll even have a stuffed animal for her to take home with her."

"You're such a thoughtful uncle, you know that right?"

"Please don't. It's going to take a while to get used to that concept."

"Well doesn't matter you still are?" I could hear Sasha smile.

"Look I'm going to give Brisbane a call and let him know what is going to be happening."

"No problem. Kara's putting Red to bed right now anyway, and then it'll be my turn to read to her. Truthfully being a parent is kind of fun, I'm hoping to never get tired of it."

"I'm sure you won't. Goodnight."

I hung up the phone and flipped through my contact list and called Brisbane. Once he picked up I told him what I was going to need the backroom for. After that I called the chief of the Infernal Division which was a pain having to go through several switchboards at the Department. I wish the bastard had just given me his direct number it would have saved me an hour long headache of, 'how may I direct your calls', oh well once that was done with I could relax for a few minutes. I looked at my watch and saw that I still had a little over an hour to go before I needed everyone to get into position.

I plopped down on to the sofa next to Yvette. "So shall we finish out this plan?"

"Of course. Right now, what we have is still pretty rough, it definitely needs touch ups. So, what do we need?"

"I'm thinking we go classic and use snipers," I said. Snipers in this situation make for excellent cover, and Yvette had some damn good ones. I grabbed my computer and pulled up a map of everything near the meeting point. Unfortunately due to the surrounding geography near the cathedral there weren't many good places to put snipers. I could make their supernatural natures hidden with the use of a little magick, that wasn't the issue. The issue instead was keeping them hidden from normal sight. While most of these guys were ex-military, finding cover was still going to be tough, and apparently Azerath was a half way decent cop so I was worried about him spotting them. We had decided to put the meeting point in the easiest point to stay out of the sight of the public. It wasn't very hard to find if you knew what you were looking for but it was also in an area that most people didn't bother to look at.

"Not many places we can put them." Yvette pointed out.

"Can we place a couple across from the meeting site on the college roof top?"

"I haven't been there but I see no reason we couldn't. They should be able to find perfect cover on the roof. Are you sure that you can hide their signatures as being supernatural? I don't want them to be spotted like that."

"They won't be spotted. I'm more concerned about myself. I'm fairly certain I can suppress my Daemonic side well enough for him to see me as just another person. Of course it will also mean that I'll have to rely on my Human magick and that's nowhere near as strong."

"Don't worry I'll be nearby to act as back up in case things go to south." The girl gave me a slap on the arm. "Come on, let's make some calls and get everyone into position so we can wrap this up and make some people's last few minutes of life very, very miserable. I have the perfect idea for a souvenir you could take from this bastard."

"Let me guess, you think I should rip his wings off and find a place to hang them in my trophy room?" I smiled, I kind of liked the idea. I'd just have to use a little magick to preserve them so they didn't start to smell and fall apart, and I'd have to find a place to put them.

"We also need to get you to a store so you can pick out a plush toy for Red. The question is, what would she want?"

"How should I know?" I honestly didn't know. I hadn't been Red's age in centuries and had no idea what she would like. Besides we were from two completely different periods in time. So I did the only sensible thing I could think of. "What do you think I should get her?"

You could give her a stuffed raven and have her name it Muninn. Shadow suggested.

"You want me to give her a stuffed raven and have her name it after your girlfriend. You are such a suck up. Are you and the little missus having issues?"

Shadow gave me an indignant squawk. *Of course not. It's just she being raised by Valkyries what better name than Muninn?*

"Why not Huginn then?"

Because he's a jerk.

"You stole his girlfriend ..." I was interrupted by another angry squawk.

Muninn is his sister you moron! Shadow had started angrily hopping across the back of the couch.

I threw up my hands in disgust. "Fine, whatever, but I still say you're a suck up."

"You could always go the traditional and get her a simple teddy bear. Or maybe one of those new Pokemon plushies."

"What's a Pokemon? Is that one of those new things that have popped up because of the phone game? They're just stupid." I had no real clue about anything regarding the game, only that it was one of the latest reasons that people would simply stare at their phones for no apparent reason.

"Get with the times Jason." Yvette sounded a little annoyed. She was far more up to date on the current trends, she had been the one to introduce me to the internet thing. Which was great, save for all the cute kitten videos, those things are addictive, howling huskies are a close second. "Pokemon is pretty old, well comparatively. It's just the phone thing that's new. Just track down one of those things and it should make the kid happy. Some of those things are just disgustingly cute."

"You have time for that stuff? I always thought you were too busy."

"Even a massive power broker in the world needs to find a way to relax. Also some of the kids of Court members like the things and I will send them to the kids for birthdays and stuff. Hell even some of the younger court members play the games. I've just picked it up over the years."

"Ye Gods, I thought you were more serious than that."

"Stop being such a stuffed shirt Jason." Yvette put her hand on my leg and gave it a quick squeeze. "Tell you what. We'll grab the idiot up there, throw him in the back of my Limo, drive somewhere to pick up a plushy, I'll run in and pick something out and you can give it to Red. There's no need to tell her that I was the one who picked it out."

I sighed; it sounded like a good idea though. I was clueless on how there was any other way to do it. "Fine we can do it your way. For now though call your men and have them get in position and ready for tonight's party."

"No problem. Let's grab that soon to be corpse up there and get going." She headed towards the stairs with me quickly following her. She then turned to look over her shoulder at me. "He's not going to survive the night is he?"

I shrugged. "Probably not. I'm guessing that Azerath is going to kill him as soon as the guy calls out to him, but that really doesn't matter does it."

"Since when have I cared about scum getting killed?"

"Well let's get going."

CHAPTER

We had gotten everyone into position and had set up the trap around 12:00. Yvette and I were still in the limo with the bait waiting for 12:40 to hit, and sitting in the front passenger seat, with a big bow around its neck, was some sort of yellow mouse thingy. The thing was sickeningly cute, almost to the point where I was thinking of getting one for dad just to see his reaction.

The alarm for the bait went off and I took my prisoner to the meeting spot. I had made it clear to him that if he tried to get away from me I'd make his last few moments of life excruciating. I kept Ace of Spades, jammed into the middle of his back, in my right hand, and in my left I had a mannequin that was about the same size as Red with a little additions to give it the outlines of my niece. Covered with a sheet and at a distance it would be convincing enough, with a little magick I could give it a decent enough copy of a supernatural signature. It should be enough to fool Azerath into getting in range for a decent shot with the rifle slung across my back. One that could keep him Earth bound long enough for me unrepress (is that even I word? I'll ask Jamie) my Daemonic nature, and make sure he stayed down permanently. Yvette was staked out on top of the cathedral itself. She had already her Pit styled Lychanthropic form; she was prepared to help me if I needed help. Once in position I got a signal that one of the sniper teams had my prisoner in their cross hairs.

"Don't even think of running or trying any other stupid move, I've got snipers trained on you and if you want to make it out of this you're going to keep to script. Is that clear?"

The Daemon gulped, and was shaking with fear. "I got it."

"Smart kid." I put the mannequin a few feet away from him and made sure it sat there perfectly. Gods I hope this worked. I ran off about sixty feet and placed myself in between a bush and the cathedral wall. I switched guns from my 1911 to my M1903, which I call Grim Reaper. Like all my other guns I kept training with this bastard, and I could still bullseye at a good five-hundred-yards. I looked at my watch: three minutes to one.

I checked my watch again, five-minutes past. I was beginning to think that Azerath had spotted the trap and was about to be a no show when I suddenly saw a ripple of light about a hundred feet away from the bait. Out walked a damn tall Divine, as Red had said the guy was about Brisbane's height, damn big, but nothing I couldn't handle. His wings and halo cast a golden light upon the ground; I wondered what those wings would look like after I ripped them off of him, I knew that I'd soon find out. I took my finger off the trigger guard and let it rest on the actual trigger.

"I see you found the kid Tramadal, you did good." With that he shot some sort of ray out of his hand that ripped my poor piece of bait into screaming shreds. "And now onto you kiddo."

He screamed when my shot hit him in the stomach, golden lighted blood started pouring out of him. Shit an Arch-Angel, even with my full Infernal power I didn't have it in me to put this guy down without more than a little help. I yanked back the bolt twice both times firing a round into him, the first one to the shoulder the other into his knee. After that I dropped the rifle, and yanked Ace of Spades out of her holster and fired several more rounds into his chest as I slammed into him. "You're not getting away so damn fast Azerath!" I screamed as I smashed my fist repeatedly into his face.

"Get off me you worthless half breed," he snarled easily throwing me off of him. He started getting to his feet when Yvette hit him with a landing from a nearly two-hundred foot drop.

"You're going nowhere scum!" She grabbed him by back of the head, her hand easily big enough to allow her to dig her claws into his temples, and started repeatedly smashing him into the wall of the cathedral. Her other hand ripped through his stomach letting his guts fall out through the gashes.

I grabbed the most powerful pair of Daemon holder cuffs I had out from one of my pockets and smashed them around his wrists as hard as I could. "That should hold you, scum. Yvette let him go, but if tries to run rip his head off."

Azerath dropped to the ground half dead, but that didn't shut his cocky ass mouth. "Who do you think you two are, cause I want to know whose names I should put on the grave markers? I'm going to make sure your deaths are nice and painful."

I dropped down next to him. "I'm Jason Black and the psycho here who ripped your guts out is the Countess Bloodwolf. All that you really need to know is that I'm Zackia's cousin and I plan to do a lot more body work on you before I rip your wings off and hang 'em on my wall. After that I'm going to hand you over to the Chief of the Divines who hopefully will let me blow your brains out."

"You're bluffing." I could tell from his voice that he knew I wasn't, but he still sounded like he was in good shape.

"Who do you think hired me to find and kill you. He wasn't pleased at all to find a full half breed showed up, and wanted to kill everyone. I'm not letting Red Raven get killed, but you already killed her mother and that means he still wants you dead."

"What makes you think he'll even let you kill me? I'm one of his right hand men after all."

"Doesn't matter." I sneered. "Even if says he doesn't want you dead I'm still going to blow your head off for killing my cousin. If he tries to stop me I've got a bullet with his name written on it, and I'm just dying to pull the trigger. Truthfully I think that killing him will probably make my life just that much easier. I doubt anyone would want me hanging around the Department offices if I am known to kill bureaucrats, especially Division Chiefs."

"You don't have the balls." Cocky son of bitch I was getting sick of it.

"Yvette dear."

"Yes sweetie?" The rock crushing voice didn't make my heart go pitter patter, but there was something about it I just loved.

"Get me my bat, a spool of razor wire, and my wire saw. It's time to do a little custom body work on Azerath here."

"You're going to regret …" I kicked the Arch Angel hard in the throat and crushed his larynx. It'd shut him up for a couple minutes.

Yvette pulled out her phone and called her chauffer and had him bring around my tools. I had already found a good beatin' tree to string the bastard up from while I made him as miserable as possible. Once Jasper brought me the requested supplies Yvette picked up Azerath by the hands and gave me enough more to wrap the razor wire around his arms and around a tree branch that would put all his weight on his shredding arms.

"I love to say this," I smirked, "this is going to hurt you a hell of a lot more than me." With that I pulled back my bat and worked out years of pent up frustration on him. I could still remember the death of my mother. This bastard had made Red a motherless child and I needed to work out the frustration. I worked out a century's worth of frustration of not being able to help kids as a detective in so many cases. Thankfully the bastard was a screamer up until the point all that was coming out of his mouth was glowing, gold blood.

"How about you cut his wings off now?" Yvette said as she held out the coiled up saw to me.

I smiled evilly; this was going to be fun. "Let him heal up a bit, I want to hear him scream." Cutting his wings off wouldn't kill him but there would be no healing from it, at least as far as I knew.

Azerath's breathing started to even out and he looked at me. "Is that all you got for me half breed?"

"Countess, stretch his wings. They're coming off."

"You wouldn't," he said, trying to sound defiant but the look showed true fear. He had just experienced some real pain, but that was nothing compared to what was about to happen to him.

"Don't worry sweetie, this isn't going to hurt at all." Yvette smiled sweetly, as sweetly as she could with that distorted mouth. "Okay I'm lying. This is going to hurt like hell. I've used wire saws on people before, the sound of it ripping through flesh and bone, and the accompanying screaming is a lullaby to monsters like Black and myself."

To say the bastard begged for mercy was the understatement of the year. Thankfully Yvette had been smarter than I had, or at least more prepared than I had been aware of. I had just been too wrapped up in thinking what I would do to him, that I hadn't thought of spectators; she had. There was a cordoned off area around the cathedral with what appeared to be fire, ambulance and police officers that looked like something had happened in the area and that they were taking people to the hospital. Yvette had changed back to her human form and had put on a paramedic's uniform and stuffed me into one. We then strapped Azerath to a stretcher and headed off to the Mystic Wolf.

"When did you call those guys in?" I asked her.

"As soon as I got into position on top of the cathedral. I knew we were going to be making a lot of noise in a quiet neighborhood and we were going to need a way to escape without too much notice."

"Thanks. I didn't think that far ahead."

"You got a little obsessive about killing this scum," Yvette smashed a fist into Azerath's jaw as he started moving, "I'm not particularly surprised about it."

"Where am I going Countess?" asked the ambulance driver.

"The Mystic Wolf. After you drop us off go back to the hospital as normal."

CHAPTER

Yvette and I dragged Azerath into the Mystic Wolf. We had bandaged his back while we were in the ambulance so that he didn't make too much of a mess of the floor. To put it mildly it was awkward. Yvette doesn't even rate five-and-half-feet, and I stand at just over six, this soon to be corpse stood at over seven, or would have if he was able to actually stand on his own feet. Once in the Wolf though, he weighed almost nothing, joys of being a Demigod here.

I looked around; the place was hoppin'. Not a single patron, but there were Succubi and Valkyries everywhere. I also saw a decent section of the Norse Pantheon. "Is this the scum?" Brisbane growled.

"Is everyone here?" I asked by way of an answer.

"Everyone is waiting in the backroom. Mostly it's the same characters as there were last night, with a couple additions."

"Let me guess Odin is back there?"

"Along with Freya and Thor. Since Red is now one of their own Odin decided he was going to represent the girl's interest along with you since they are now family as well. Red is also here of course so she can ID her dad so that obviously means that Kara and Sasha are here as well."

"Anyone else."

"No, should there be?"

"Not really, I was just curious." I smiled at Azerath. "Come on Azerath, let's not keep people waiting."

Brisbane led the way, mostly to keep the crowd from killing Azerath before things were settled. He opened the doors to the backroom and we were immediately hit by the smell of cigarette smoke. These guys loved atmosphere if nothing else. "After you Countess," I said, motioning her past me.

Yvette walked past me drawing herself up to her full height. No one was going to mess with her and somehow she could make that known with just a look. She took a position across from Odin and made sure she was looking thoroughly angered at tonight's events. Sitting next to Odin was Red with Freya on her other side and Kara and Sasha standing behind her. Once Yvette was settled I followed her in.

"Ladies and gentlemen I would like to introduce you to some scum, though some of you already know him. Some of you all too well." I threw the soon to be corpse on to the table, his head next to that of the chief of the Divines. "Gerald, this bastard claims to be one of your right hand men and unfortunately Red knows him all too well."

Gerald looked visibly shaken. I wondered what their relationship really was. It could be anything, and right now I was guessing that they may very well be family. I had a backup gun, a Wild Card in my waist band holster behind my back, and it was loaded with banishing rounds. Any of those idiot Divines try anything and they'd find themselves on a painful one way trip to their home realms.

Red simply stared at him, her eyes wide with fright. "That's him Jason. That's my dad," was all she could manage to squeak out.

"That's all I needed from you tonight dear. Kara, Sasha, please take Red out for this, though she'll need to stay in the Wolf for a while, while some other things get settled out."

Sasha and Kara both smiled at me. "Come on Red, we'll get you out of here," Sasha said as she picked the girl up. "I've seen Jason work. It tends to be messy." There was a general murmur of agreement from many others on that account.

"Remember what you promised me uncle," Red said, a low growl escaping her throat.

"Don't worry, he isn't long for this world." I grinned and put my gun to his temple. "He isn't long for any world."

Red smiled. I wasn't sure what she was going to turn into. Hopefully I'd get to see her blossom into a beautiful kid, she already had a good shot at it with who she now had for parents. I sure as hell didn't want her ending up a monster like me, or even worse like the scum I was about to execute. I had no false ideas about what I was, even though so many people tried to make me feel different about myself. No matter how many people told me that I was a good guy, whether it was the people I had helped over the years, or even my own secretary, I knew without a shred of doubt that I was indeed a monster. I just happened to be very good at directing my rage and unpleasantness at people who deserved it.

Kara and Sasha took Red out of the room and I felt the tension in my system ease up. When I sent this guy to wherever Daemons go when they die, my niece wouldn't be around to see it. "Now Gerald, Azerath here claims to work for you. Is this true?"

"He does, he's head of the Criminal Apprehension Division of the Divine Department. He was one of my best men." He turned his attention to the soon to be corpse. "How could you do this to me, you idiot? I trusted you when I gave you that position, I thought I could trust my own son not to fuck this up." So I was right, family relationship.

"You knew the child was your own granddaughter, father. I know I should have killed her when I had the chance. I also know that I should also have killed you at some point. I could have had everything if you weren't around, I would have control of the Division if you hadn't been around." Azerath tried to laugh. Truthfully I found it funny myself. Sick? Maybe, but funny none the less.

"This is your son?" Roared the chief of the Infernals. "This is an outrage. You should know those laws better than anyone. Even I wouldn't break the laws regarding my own children, but you, a self-righteous Divine with the gall to want to kill a child because her parents broke a ridiculous law, when you can't even follow your own laws?"

Gerald looked at his own son in disbelief; I couldn't blame him I guess. The guy had just said that he should have killed him. His son just admitted to having been the father of a true half-breed, and wanting to kill his father for political reasons. The girl was the granddaughter of the chief of the Divines and he had wanted to kill her for no other reason than an outdated, archaic law. This was no longer humorous, it was just vile.

"Shall I kill him now, or do you want to?" I asked. It wasn't really a question since I wasn't going to give him the satisfaction. I was going to kill him anyway.

"No I can't let you kill..." I didn't let him finish the thought, I yanked Ace of Spades trigger and there was a huge hole in his head, then kept pulling the trigger until all that was left of Azerath was a bullet riddled corpse.

"What was that you were about to say?" I asked as I ejected the magazine, and slapped in a replacement. "Kill the bastard, was it? You have to forgive me, I tend to have a hard time hearing people when they ask me to spare the lives of family. The succubus he was using as a punching bag. The one who was Red Raven's mother, was my cousin, so as far as I'm concern Azerath had to die."

"You'll die for that half-breed!" Gerald roared as several other Divines went for the artillery they were hiding under their jackets.

"I think not." I was faster from years of practice. My hand flashed back behind me and grabbed my backup 1911, Wild Card, and shot the Divines that were armed just as they got their guns out of there holsters. The bastards were ripped inside out as banishing rounds sent them on a pain riddled trip back home. I leapt across the table and yanked Gerald out of his seat to look at me and pressed Ace of Spades, still loaded with Daemon killers, under his jaw.

"Here's where you make a monumental decision. One that could affect whether or not you leave here shot full of holes to be hung from the top of a cathedral, or walk out of here with your breathing rights intact."

"What do you want half-breed?" I shot him in the knee on principal for that. He howled in pain, and I loved it.

"You swear to me that you're going to leave Red Raven alone from this point forward, and seeking no repercussions against her or me, or anyone who has helped us, I let you live. If you revoke that I will hunt you down and kill you slowly, including doing what I did to your son there, and cut off your wings. Now swear it."

Gerald looked from me, to Azerath's corpse, and back to me, and I could tell from the look of fear in his eyes that he knew I would be more than happy to kill him right now. "Fine. Let the kid live."

"Good. Now get the fuck out of here you stinking wretch of Divine filth." I threw him back into the chair and held him at gun point until he disappeared in a flash of light.

"I must say that was well done. I see once again how your name has come to mean Bringer of Justice," Odin rumbled. I merely nodded still glaring at the now empty chair.

"Does anyone else have anything to say or can I safely say that this meeting is adjourned?" There was a general murmur of consensus as there were several more flashes of light and the smell of sulfur as the Infernals left. After a while there was another flash of light as Kukiko of the Kitsune court left. The representative of the Dragon court had never shown up in the first place.

Odin, Thor, and Freya left by the door into the main room of the Wolf to meet up with the rest of the Pantheon that had shown up. Brisbane clapped a hand down on my shoulder. "You have one massive set of brass balls for pulling a stunt like that."

"I was pissed off beyond belief. That bastard had wanted to kill my niece, and this scum sucker," I said indicating Azerath, "was using my cousin as a punching bag and wanted to kill a child. I was just helping family."

"Well come on there's a party going on and you are needed for it."

Yvette grabbed me by my hand. "Come on sweetie we need you. You saved the kid, that's what matters."

I slipped Ace of Spades back into her holster. "Looking for this?" Yvette asked handing me Wild Card.

"Thanks." I slipped the Colt back into her holster and headed in to the main room of the bar.

CHAPTER 13

"Happy Adoption Day!!!" I screamed along with everyone else as Red Raven walked into the Mystic Wolf. Her eyes went wide as she saw the heaps of presents and a couple massive cakes.

"Is this all for me?" She whispered to Sasha and Kara. Every single Succubus that worked at the Mystic Wolf, and probably every Valkyrie out there was at the bar, along with damn near the whole rest of the Pantheon. There were some notable exceptions to who was there, mainly Red Raven's actual family, but I couldn't blame them. However they had sent me their present for her.

"Well right here I have all the official paperwork," Yvette said. "Red Raven, your parents are officially Sasha and Kara. There are two things that need to be filled which is her last name? I didn't know how you wanted that to be set. And of course her Birthday?"

"Her name is Red Raven Sumer-Odinsdottir." Kara said. "There is no way to line up her Birthday with the Mortal calendar, so she is five as of last Halloween."

"Then it's official." Yvette said filling the last of the paperwork. She handed over to Kara. "I just need the two of you to sign and I'll have my people run this through."

Red's mothers signed the paperwork, and that started a whole new round of cheering. It was nice to see some happiness at the end of this ugliness. Red Raven would never have her own mother back, but she had two wonderful mothers now who would do everything in their extreme power to protect her. She wouldn't see any domestic abuse now, these two never lay a finger on each other that wasn't affectionate. Plus the Norse Pantheon looked upon domestic abuse as something only done by a true coward. Of course the girls would have to learn to keep down the partying and the like but I'm sure that wouldn't be that hard. At least I hoped it wouldn't.

I walked over to Red. "Look I have a gift that comes from your grandparents and your uncle."

"What is it?"

"Well that's up to you," I smiled. She already had a cat, and now she was about to have a puppy, but …

"What do you mean it's up to me?"

"I think you're confusing the kid, Black," Kara said as she came over with a kick to my shoes.

"It's a puppy, but you have to decide what it looks like." My family had decided to give the girl a Hell Hound puppy.

"Wait you're giving her a Hell Hound?!?!?!" Sasha said looking horrified. "Are you nuts? Those things are so destructive!"

"Oh come now, I had one as a kid," I said trying to be defensive about my family's choice on what counted as a good family pet. "Besides she's a full half-breed, she can handle a little puppy."

"And how little would that be." Kara sounded considerably cross with me, not that I could blame her.

"Why don't you let her decide."

"Kara, Sasha can I have one of those long short wolves with stubby legs?"

"You mean a Swedish Volhund?" Kara asked. "That you can have."

"Are you sure about this, Kara?" Sasha asked.

"They're tiny, they look like what would happen if you were to cross a corgi with a wolf. Though if it's a hell hound it will probably get big. Won't it Jason?"

I shrugged. "How should I know? My own hell hound was a mastiff so he was going to be massive no matter what."

"I'm sure he won't be any trouble mommies, I'll take good care of him, and Rose Flower."

I cocked one eye at my friends. "Rose Flower?"

"That's her kitten," Sasha explained. "If anything goes wrong with this I'm coming down hard on your head."

"Don't blame me?" I turned around and picked up a wiggling box with air holes that had appeared behind me. "Anyways here you go Red. Your very own hell hound. Is it a boy or a girl?"

Red smiled. "She's a girl."

"Okay here she is."

There was a little chirp of a bark, and when Red opened the box she was showered with puppy kisses. "Happy adoption day Red Raven."

"She's perfect," the little girl squealed hugging the heck out of me.

Overall this case had sucked but at least the girl was going to a good home. "Who's ready for cake?" I heard Brisbane yell out, which led to more cheering. So let me rephrase that, the case had really sucked, but someone was giving me cake, which helped.

THE CLOSET CAPER

CHAPTER

I spun my chair around and tossed a crumpled-up piece of paper into the waste paper basket. Well I tried, seeing as how it bounced off the wall and landed in a small pile with a couple dozen other paper balls.

I wouldn't hold out for a career in the NBA. Shadow said dryly. *And I'm fairly sure I heard a tree scream in there somewhere.*

"Very funny bird brain," I muttered. "Maybe if I folded them into paper airplanes?"

Then you'd be wasting even more time and risking a paper cut. Just give it up already. I crumpled up another piece of paper and threw it at Shadow. Much to both of our surprise I actually managed to hit him, which only served to piss him off. *Screw you too master!*

"Sorry moron I didn't think I was actually going to hit you. You could have moved you know."

With as lousy as your aim has been I thought you were going to miss. Now if you don't mind I'm going to keep Jamie company so I don't have to watch you fail at hitting a basket... Dick.

"I heard that asshole. Now watch your thoughts, Shadow or I'll wash your brain out with soap."

Fuck you too master. The crow hopped off his perch and flew through the barely open door into the outer office. I didn't know why but he seemed to be in a worse mood than usual.

To put it mildly I was desperately bored. I needed a case to come along and drop into my lap so I'd have someone to hurt. It's not that I'm a bad guy. Well not always a bad guy. I just like being paid for my vast array of skills at being professionally unpleasant. Just as long as it got results that ended in justice being served. Or at least one asshole ended up dead. If I did it for free I would be so swamped with work I wouldn't be able to keep my head above water for all the cries of those in need. Besides I have a very discreet clientele I work for. Or more to the point I work in a circle of the world that needs to stay discreet. Normal people going about their everyday lives don't need to know that the US is, for all intents and purposes, controlled by a seventeen-year-old who's in her nineties. Or that their neighbor may not even be Human, but has instead been living in this part of the country since well before the landing of Humans on this continent and was here before the ending of the second Ice Age. Your average John and Jane Doe really don't need to know that kind of stuff, and when they did find out they often found themselves getting dragged kicking and screaming into this world and often needed help from people like myself. The problem for most people is that my kind are few and far between, and not all of us are very helpful.

My name is Jason Black, and I'm a hero for hire. By the Gods above and below that sounds cheesy. Maybe I should put that in a book; Jamie has been bugging me to start writing stories of my cases.

I caught myself scribbling that part of it down when I heard a knock at the outer office. Jamie was out there and I knew everything was going to go down well. My secretary had been one such innocent bystander who had gotten dragged into my circle of society against her will, and it had nearly gotten her killed. I had helped her keep her breathing privileges and then hired her. She was a good kid, sharp as a tack, very easy on the eyes, and she had learned quickly how not to scare easily. The only thing she wouldn't do, not that I have ever had the balls to ask her to do anyway, was sit on my lap while I dictated case notes. I had dreamed of doing that back in the thirties, forties, and fifties. I mean if Sam Spade could get his faithful secretary Effie to, I should have been able to get someone to do that for me. Truthfully though it had always been a fantasy. I never would have actually asked someone to do it. I wasn't exactly a feminist at the time, mostly because it was sort of taboo, but I still had some sense of common decency. Besides after the second World War, I became too busy dealing with a lot of other issues to have much time for a secretary. Once I had time to sit down and start up my old business again. I really didn't see the need for a secretary, I just screened my calls. I never thought I'd find the perfect secretary until Jamie's case dropped her in my life. Now my former client could have been a second familiar she was so loyal, and unlike Shadow she could keep my files organized.

I heard someone, sounded like a man, talking to Jamie, and could hear labored breathing. I couldn't make out exactly what was being said, but the man would probably soon be my client. He sounded very upset which wasn't really all that surprising considering he had come here. Since Shadow was out there I decided to take a look at what was going on through his eyes. I let my eyes defocus and saw what was going on.

Do you mind! This is a bit invasive if you don't ask first, Shadow thought at me angrily.

"Oh stuff it. You're a familiar so you'll do your job and stop complaining."

You're still being a jerk.

"You listen in on me all the time so I think that it's only fair."

Whatever I'll sit here all quietly and let you eavesdrop or whatever you feel like doing. Fucking asshole.

I let the fucking asshole deal pass. He was being grumpy with me for some reason lately and wouldn't tell me what was going on. I had a sneaking suspicion as to what was going on, but I wasn't going to press matters. However, that idiot better be careful, dating the familiar of a God is probably more than a little dangerous. I opened my mind up and looked and listened around through Shadow's eyes and ears.

The man had obviously been crying, and was still choking back tears. He was wearing a work shirt that had a company name on it. From where Shadow was perched I could see faded jeans with a couple small holes and pair of high quality boots that had definitely been put through their paces.

"One of the officers told me to look this place up, he said that your firm was the only place I could find someone who could help me. I need to find my daughter, she's all I have." Just what I needed to break the cycle of boredom I was stuck in, a case, too bad it involved a kid.

I hate it when kids get involved in my cases, the end of innocence in a young kid is one thing I hate. It was worse for some kids who had never had innocence at all. Whether it be the Goddess Sam over at the Mystic Wolf, who had been adopted by the Bar's chief God, or there was also my own niece, Red Raven, whose abusive Arch-Angel father had killed her Infernal mother. Bastards who took away the innocence of children needed to be broken to pieces. Even the Countess Blood Wolf, who is arguably the most powerful and sadistic crime lord in the world, had grown up too early because of the Nazi Party. She had been subjected to some of the most horrifying experiments during World War Two as the Nazis tried to create the perfect soldier. They had taken her and pumped her full of the infectious diseases that create Vampires and Werewolves. She had been the only survivor of I don't remember how many victims. I had rescued her in forty-three. She quickly went from scared teenager to rampaging Nazi killer. She wasn't a complete monster though, just mostly one.

"If an officer said that we were the only ones who could help than it's quite possible we are, and that's what Mr. Black is here for." She hit the intercom button and I quickly pulled my consciousness back into my own body and answered intercom.

"Shadow's out there so I heard part of it. Send him back."

Jamie opened the door to the office and ushered the man in. He looked to be about forty, maybe a little younger, however I wouldn't lay money on my guess. He was about average height and of average build. His shirt belonged to some construction company guessing by the name of it. I had never heard of the place, not that it meant anything. There were probably dozens of them out there I had never heard of, since I only take notice if the company is working anywhere that messes up traffic for me, or I come across it during a case. He had thick blond hair that was a bit disheveled. His face was a bit of a mess, his eyes seemed to be burning with the fatigue of looking for his daughter and not getting any sleep.

I stood up and asked him to take a seat, Shadow quickly followed him and took to his perch. "Now let's make introductions. My name is Jason Black, the crow that followed you in is my partner, Shadow."

The man looked obviously confused; as I said he had been brought in kicking and screaming. "What do you mean that he's your partner?"

"Let me put it this way. You have left the world you're used to and entered a completely different section of society, and for that I am sorry. If you were told to come to me for help, things must have gotten very strange for you. So, what would you like to do first? Question me as to what I mean by saying you have fallen into a very different circle of society or do you want to explain to me what has happened to your daughter?"

"You heard what was being said?"

"Only part of it, Shadow over there was being a pain about letting me into his head to listen to you. But I did hear something about your daughter being missing. So how about we get to know each other."

The man looked at Shadow, confused for a bit, but must have decided to drop the matter as currently unimportant. "My name is Adam Johnson, it's my daughter that's missing and more to the point there is a thing that is in my house that is a twisted copy of my daughter. I know that thing isn't my daughter, she looks and sounds like her but I know for a fact that it isn't her."

This immediately brought up the idea of changelings, but I needed more information. "How old is your daughter?"

"She's eight," he told me as he started to shake. "She's the only person I have left in my life, please I need her back."

Ten was too old for a changeling by far. There were still all sorts of possibilities. If the girl had been only a couple months old a changeling would be a good bet, but at ten she was far too old for that sort of thing. "What's your daughter's name?"

"Charlene. I named her after her mother." Adam seemed to deflate even further, if that was even possible.

"Where is her mother then?" I didn't suspect the mother. A doppelganger would be over kill when a straight kidnapping would be easier, and a bad copy would only get someone like me looking into the matter. With a standard kidnapping you find yourself, at worst, dealing with the feds.

"Her mother died while in labor. It's just been my daughter and me for the entire time."

"What about grandparents or aunts and uncles?"

"None on either side that I know of. I don't have any siblings and both of my parents are dead. As far as my wife goes, she never mentioned any family."

This just got interesting, all of a sudden a whole new realm of possibilities opened up to me as to what was going on. "What was your wife like before she passed away?"

"She was kind of quiet, she never liked talking about her life before we met much. I guess you could say she just wanted to live in the present and not worry about her past." Bad sign already.

"So, the question now comes down to money. I will help you, as long as you can pay me, and my rates are reasonable." I stood up and walked over to my filing cabinet and reaching into the top draw pulled out what I refer to as my 'Knight in Shining Armor' Contract. I doubted the guy made a lot of money, and I wasn't going to rob him blind. I use this contract to help those who are desperate and need my help and can't afford to pay me large sums of money. "I charge two-hundred-and-fifty a day with a five-day retainer. If I find your daughter before then I will return the difference. If it goes longer I will expect you to pay, though I am certain it will take you a while so I am more than prepared to let you set up a payment arrangement with my secretary."

The father pulled himself together a bit and took out a check book and wrote out a check for the full amount. "Thank you, mister Black. Thank you."

I gave him as gentle of a smile as I could manage. "You can thank me later, when I reunite you with your daughter."

"Okay," Adam said choking back tears. "What do we need to do?"

"Let's have a seat then and talk. Now what makes you think that thing that's pretending to be your daughter isn't her?"

"Because I saw my daughter get taken by something. And yet there she was." Interesting, it made me wonder.

"What do you mean? And be a specific as you can."

"Well I had just put my daughter to bed an hour earlier, and I heard her screaming for help. I thought she was just having a bad nightmare, she gets them all the time and they've just been getting worse, but anyways. I opened her door and saw her pointing at the closet and she said 'Daddy there's a monster in my closet.' Well, being a good parent I decided to open the closet door to show her there was no monster there. When I opened the door, I saw my little girl, whom I had just seen in her bed, cowering in a corner of the closet under a couple blankets. Then she pointed at the bed and said, 'Daddy there's a monster in my bed.' I had no idea what to make of it; the next thing I know something explodes out of the closet and hits me, throwing me into the foot of the bed. Next thing I know I'm waking up in front of her closet and she's begging me to wake up because she's scared."

Now this is getting interesting. There are few creatures out there that can pull a stunt like this off, and all of them need to be killed as quickly as possible. "How long ago was this?"

"Four days ago. At first I thought I had just dreamed it, but then Charlene started acting weird. It first started with her lashing out at the weirdest things, she was mad at everything and everyone with no reason. Then I got a call from her teacher, apparently she had been using foul language, at least that was my original understanding from the message was…" I accidently cut him off.

"Isn't that kind of normal for kids at some point? Maybe she's just going through hormones early."

"You don't understand she was telling him what she wanted to do to him sexually and, from what her teacher told me, it was incredibly graphic. I don't know where she would have picked up the kind of language she was using, I don't keep porn at home and I have content filters on the internet browsers."

This was starting to get interesting to say the least. I wasn't sure what to make of it yet. "Go on," I said waving him to continue.

"This morning I got up to get her ready for school and get dressed for work. I go into her room and she asks me if I think she's pretty. Well of course I say yes. She smiles, then she did something that caught me completely of guard, she took off her night shirt, she was naked underneath, then jumped at me. While she was on me she tried to stick her tongue down my throat and said, 'Well if I'm pretty why don't you just come and fuck me daddy.' I was so startled that I fell and hit my head and passed out cold. When I woke up she had unbuckled my belt and had pulled my pants half off. I grabbed her, stuffed her into some clothes, then took her to the hospital to have her committed. I called the police but they said there was nothing that could be done. Then one of the officers handed me this card and a note." He handed me a piece of paper.

The note read. 'Detective Black please help this guy. Official channels are currently closed to him.' There was no name on the note but I knew with little doubt that it had to have been a Court of Night controlled officer who wrote the note.

"The last time you saw your daughter, your real daughter, was in her bedroom, right?" I asked standing up and walking to my coat rack.

"Yes."

"Well then," I started slipping into my trench coat and fedora, "it's time to go there and start my investigation."

CHAPTER

Adam's home was in a nice neighborhood of one of St. Paul's inner suburbs. It wasn't anything fancy, a simple rambler with a well-cared for lawn and a work truck in the driveway. I had followed him in my own car, no sense in having him drive me to his place and then bring me back to my office. Shadow had decided to stay home and sulk about something so the ride over had been quiet. I grabbed my satchel off my passenger seat and walked over to where Adam was waiting at the front door. Everything seemed both right and wrong at the same time. I couldn't place my finger on what exactly was wrong but it was pushing at the back of my mind. It was just… I let the thought drop for now.

He unlocked the door and let me in, asking me if there was anything I wanted to drink. I politely declined and told him I wanted to get a feel of his place. The place reeked of the Pit, but an area I was unfamiliar with. Truthfully there is nothing surprising about that, as I tend to not spend too much time down there. When I'm down there I'm a second class citizen at best, and I don't take to that truth very readily. I followed my nose, as it were, and found myself in the girl's room. It was fairly typical as far as I could tell, posters of popstar boy bands next to those of cartoon characters. At least that is how little girls' rooms are always depicted on TV and in the movies.

I opened the door to the closet and the smell was damn near overpowering. How the father been able to resist having sex with it was kind of amazing. Truth be told I'm not sure if I could have. It smelled of pure, unadulterated lust. It wasn't the kind of smell a Succubus gives off. That scent is fairly easy to deal with, as long as you have enough will power, though most people don't, and they're not over doing it. This though, was something totally different. This scent of lust was different. It was pure, raw, evil. I've never come across anything like it before, and I could only guess as to what it was. I would need to bring in a consultant, and I only knew of one person who could tell me what this was.

I reached towards the back of the closet as that seemed to be where the smell was the strongest, though it was hard to say for certain. I could feel something dark from there but I wasn't sure what. All of a sudden, I was sure of one thing and it wasn't pleasant.

I found myself thrown across the room as a blast of energy hit me like a wrecking ball. Great. Booby trapped and I had to go and set it off. Careless. Just plain, fucking, careless. To put it mildly I was pissed with myself. I wasn't sure what it had been that had hit me but I had encountered traps like that before. Ones where someone would leave some magickal charge for a person like myself. It made me wonder if whatever had taken the girl knew about me specifically. Or they had just taken precautions in case someone like me came along to investigate.

Adam looked in the room and saw me splayed out on the ground as I was picking myself back off the floor with blood running from my mouth. "What the hell happened in here?"

"Remember what you said, about something knocking you out of the closet the night your daughter disappeared?" I asked as I wiped at a bit of blood off my cheek.

"Yes, it was like something out of a horror movie."

"Well whatever took your girl left a surprise for me." I took another look at the closet and reached out to lightly touch it with my mind, wasn't going to be stupid enough to try and physically touch it again. The barrier that had thrown me out of the closet was still there and I think my touching it may have only strengthened it. That wasn't a good sign. That meant they were expecting someone like me, but that raised some other red flags.

"What do you mean?"

"It means that currently I'm not getting in that way. Don't worry I'm still going to get your daughter but it's going to take a while."

I took another look around the room and saw a picture on the girl's table. It was of two people, or to be correct it had been of two people, one person had been viciously ripped out of the picture. In the place of the second person there was now a face of the daughter. I picked it up and showed it to Adam. "Who's supposed to be in this picture with you?" I could guess easily enough but I wanted to have it confirmed.

"That's supposed to be of me and my wife. It was Charlene's favorite picture since she never knew her mom. Why would she rip the picture up like that?"

"Why would she be acting the way she has. Or more precisely why wouldn't it with the way it's been acting?"

"What do you mean?"

"Well I seriously doubt that the Charlene that you put in the hospital is at all Human. It may look, sound, and act Human, if a little screwed up, but I seriously doubt it's Human. There are all sorts of things it could be but I'm going to look around more to get a better idea of what's going on."

I looked around the room and opening the dresser drawers I got a nasty shock, sexually explicit nudes of kids and not just pictures of Charlene but several other girls as well. Whatever it was this thing had a sick sense of humor; they were probably there for the dad to discover and jerk off to. The question was why here in Charlene's room? Wouldn't it have made for sense for the thing to have put them in the dad's room?

I seriously doubted he was a predator but I wanted to be on the safe side. Just to be careful about the matter I slipped the pictures into my inner coat pocket. I would hand them over to the police to see if they knew anything about the kids in them. Not just because I was legally responsible to do so, but it was morally the only thing to do.

I thought about something he had said regarding his wife. With what was going on something sounded a little odd, and a bit too convenient. Adam was a fairly normal guy, at least as far as I could tell. Though with the pictures I needed to have a background check done on him. He didn't seem to have any training in magick. If he had, that scent of lust would have been overpowering and he would have fucked whatever it was that was masquerading as his daughter. That left open his late wife.

He had said that he didn't know much about his wife's past, as far as he knew she didn't have any siblings or parents, or any family at all that he knew of. But what if she didn't have them because she hadn't been Human either. I knew that a Daemon could give birth to a child, my niece was proof of that, but my niece was also half Infernal and half Divine. So while she was still a half-breed, she was still, in a sense, pure Daemon. I didn't know what would happen if a female Daemon gave birth to a half Human. I didn't know if the birth would kill her. I would have thought it would be far more likely for the child to die. What if…

There were other theories that I came up with but any theory that started to have any plausibility ended up with in a 'but what if?', and I needed more evidence to get a proper idea of what was going on. What I really needed was more information about the mother.

"Do you have anything that belonged to your wife? Like a piece of jewelry you kept of hers that that she wore a lot."

"I have a couple pieces like that."

"Good, let me see them." I followed him out of the room and waited for him in the hall. Damn that kid's room reeked. I could still smell it out here, then realized that whatever had hit me had left the stench to sink into my trench coat. Great now I may have to just burn the damn thing since I had no idea of how to get the smell out. I could probably cleanse it in my trophy room, but I wasn't sure if I wanted it in there. Everything in there was unstable enough already, and this wasn't so important that it would be really missed if it was simply destroyed.

Oh well, time to get fitted for a new one. It's a shame really, but that happens every few cases one way or another, so I've just grown used to it.

I waited in the hall as Adam walked into his bedroom, he came out a few minutes later holding a small jewelry box. "Her wedding ring and her favorite necklaces are in here. One of necklaces she never took off. She told me that she had been given it by her mother a long time ago. That was about all she had ever she ever told me about her mother."

"How about we take those into the dining room so I'll have better lighting to take a good look at them," I said.

Soon we were in a small dining room sitting down at the table and I picked up the necklace he had told me that his wife had never taken off. I immediately knew why she hadn't. The thing had a charge on it, something powerful too. I took an enchanted jeweler's loupe out of my satchel and put it on for closer examination just to make sure I had been right. There it was, plain as day. Written in tiny lettering was a binding spell of some sort. There was no longer any doubt about it. The guy's wife had been an Infernal, and she had been on the run. With this necklace, she would have been able to stay hidden from whatever had been looking for her. Things had just gone from bad to worse in a fraction of a second.

I sat back and just looked at the thing for a while. Here was my new working theory and it didn't end in a what if. The wife was an Infernal that had been on the run from something, probably some sort of Daemonic king. It was hard to say exactly what at the moment, and currently it was irrelevant to the case as it stood. Now that she was dead, I had no idea of what had happened to her but it seemed that whatever had been after her may have finally gotten its claws into her soul, and to further punish her it had grabbed her daughter. To make matters worse, more than likely it had sent that creature as a way to torment her husband and she'd have to watch everything through that thing's eyes. I couldn't imagine what it must have felt for her to see something resembling her daughter trying to fuck the poor guy. The wife must have been happy that her husband hadn't been seduced, but it still must have hurt like hell. I just hoped she knew that it wasn't her daughter that she was seeing. If she thought it really was her daughter doing all of this she would probably go through total torture. This was going to be a messy corpse case, which made me happy. I had a new supply of Daemon killers thanks to a shipment from my dad. I usually use banishing rounds but that's for kicking Daemons off this realm in very agonizing ways. This time I was going to be going into the Pit myself so I'd need to kill someone outright. You can't really banish someone who is already home.

The problem was trying to explain this to Adam. I didn't know if he was going to be able to handle it. I also needed a consultation on the necklace. I couldn't make out all of the spell, but it was enough to know what it was. I needed to talk to Felix, bastard son of Baphomet; the guy knew something about just about everything. He knew more about the Pit than I did. All I knew was enough to know that the language the spell was in was from the Pit. I also needed to talk to the Daemon masquerading as Charlene; this was going to be a whole lot of messy very quickly.

"Can I take the necklace with me when I leave, there is something written on the edge of it and I need someone to translate it."

"What do you mean? I know that necklace like the back of my hand, there is nothing written on it."

"Here put this on," I said giving him the jeweler's loupe. "Now take a closer look at the edge."

He took the loupe and did as I asked and I heard something catch in his throat. "What... what... is that?"

"I'm not sure. That's why I need to have an expert take a look at it."

I didn't know what had taken the girl, all I knew was that I was going to get her back before the unthinkable happened to her. If she was in there too long she may end up needing more help than I could provide, and I didn't just mean psychological. I was positive that she was going to need that once I got her out no matter what. I just didn't know what would have happened to her soul by now. No matter what, she was going to be a mess once I got her out there. Her soul may be in complete tatters, flayed from full Daemonic torture. I was good at making people beg me to kill them but I had nothing on a true Infernal. A full Infernal knew how to rip your soul out of your body and run it through the metaphysical equivalent of a shredder and then stuff it back into your body. Now that was a trick I'd love to learn.

CHAPTER

It was still early afternoon so I knew exactly where I had to go. I needed to talk to another half-Daemon, Felix, the bastard son of the Daemon of Hidden Knowledge. Other than both of us being half-Infernal there is little similarity between the two of us. We used our powers and resources very differently but we both got things done our own way. However we also work together fairly regularly so we have ended up as on and off friends.

As different as we are, we had both lucked out in the father department. You see most Daemons, whether Infernal or Divine, read Angel, aren't well known for sticking around with Mortals. A lot of people have a hard time grasping that a Divine would be a love 'em and leave 'em asshole because they're Angels. Rest assured that's nothing more than a good PR agency that gives them a nice guy reputation. Infernals are just as likely to stick around as Divines, which isn't very likely at all, but both of us got responsible fathers.

My dad stuck around because during the summoning he had agreed to marry my mother, and never regretted it. Even after all these centuries we still get together on the anniversary of mom's death, he still misses her. Baphomet though I think had different reasons. The only other half-Daemon I knew whose dad stuck around for a while was the

Super Spy known as Killroy. His father was a Divine who taught him a few tricks. My cousin, Sir David Booth of her Majesty's Secret Service, complete prat that he is, his dad hadn't stuck around. Though, according to my father, the Knight is related to me by blood.

If there was anyone in this realm of existence that would know what exactly that binding spell said it would be Felix. For a bastard son Felix had gotten lucky. Originally the thing had started out as a one night fling, truthfully I think Baphomet was blitzed on something, guy has a tendency to get lit up at times. Anyways nine months later a priestess shows up with a baby and calls upon him. The Daemon stepped right up and helped out.

There are several big differences between myself and Felix. For one thing Felix is an intellectual and prefers to do research and learn everything there is to know on a variety of subjects, though even he makes mistakes. I'm more of a hot lights and rubber hoses guy, make people scream for mercy to get the answers I need. There have been more than a few occasions where my way of doing things isn't practical for bringing useful results and I have needed my friend's help, and this was going to be one of those times. Of course there have also been times where Felix has called upon my assistance, like getting his apprentice back from being used as a trade by his mother to get back at her ex-husband. Poor kid was all but dead when I found him, but he is now under Felix's care and doing well.

I made my destination Dinky Town, a small neighborhood in Minneapolis bordering on the U of M. Felix has had his shop there since the college first formed and it has been a useful place for all sorts of people. Early on it had been on the other side of the street from its current location and had been a cramped store front filled with old books, some of them almost decaying. Okay I'm exaggerating on the almost decaying part, many of them were in various states of decay. The only reason that Felix had a store front was to have a legal way to extort money out of professors and students alike coming to him for help with studies in ancient cultures and various religious cults. He rarely sold books unless he had multiple copies of them, and even then you were assured to get the most stained copies, or the ones with the fewest notes in the margins. Some of his most useful books were covered in stains but were also so filled with some many notes cramped into the margins that you might as well have a couple extra books.

Over the last twenty years or so the place has gone through a major renovation including moving across the street. Felix still does a lot of consulting work, and still has a large collection of books that people can request if they know of their existence or can get Felix to open up about them, and good luck with that. Now Felix sold a range of modern occult tools and spell ingredients and the like, most of it's bull shit. Truthfully I think Felix just gets a kick out of people acting like idiots. Still he'd probably have the answers I'd need and that was all I needed of him, at least for now.

I pulled up in front of the store and got lucky and found a parking space right out front. I walked through the door and descended the steps into the current shop. There were a few people about the shop including a couple of employees who would be able to manage the store while I talked to Felix in private. "Well look what the Pit has dragged up," Felix said dryly as I walked down into the shop proper.

"Nice to see you too Felix."

"So, what can I do for you today, Black? I doubt I have anything you might need at the moment."

"Actually what I need is for you to do is a little translation work."

"Well that shouldn't be too hard, but what's in it for me?"

"The satisfaction that you helped rescue an eight-year-old from the clutches of something truly evil." Felix may be a jerk at times but even he had a well developed sense of right and wrong.

Felix shrugged. "That works for me. Step into my office," he said. He then turned to one of his staff members, "Janine please keep an eye on the shop, Mr. Black and I have some important business to discuss."

His office was cramped to say the least, not because of lack of square footage, it was simply crammed full of the more interesting stuff that only those in the know knew about. Everything from grave yard dirt to aborted fetuses could be found back here, along with blood and the skeletons of a whole host of creatures, including human, it was best not to ask where he came across some of this stuff. There was also a whole library of ancient texts on a variety of subjects of interest. "So what do you have for me?"

I took out the necklace and held it up in front of him. "This. I know it has some sort of binding charm on it, and I can't make out the language at all, so my guess is that it's pre-historic in origin, or at least of any currently known human languages. I was hoping you could tell me what it says since you know more about the Pit than I do."

"Well then let's take a look shall we?" I handed him the necklace and he made some interesting humming noises as he examined it from different angles. Eventually he pulled out an enchanted jeweler's loupe similar to mine, in fact I had gotten mine from him. "Well, well, well. This is most interesting I must say."

"So what can you tell me?"

"Well first off you're right, it is a binding spell, of sorts, however that's not really what makes this piece interesting. It's also not even the language that's interesting, which is, as you guessed an older alphabet out of the Pit. The region is thought to be uninhabited at the moment, but things like that are always changing, but that's neither here nor there. What makes this binding spell so interesting is that it is to a realm, not to a place or a person, and is worn voluntarily."

"Let me guess a Daemon using this would be able to hide on a different Realm from someone trying to find them?" I asked, though I was fairly sure I already knew the answer.

"Score one for the Black." His tone wasn't sarcastic either which was somewhat amazing. "That's exactly what this is meant for. The Daemon wearing this wouldn't be able to travel between realms, they wouldn't even be able to make it into the Mystic Wolf. On the plus side though it would be all but impossible for them to be tracked by someone from another Realm.

"Now the question is, where did you find it and what does it have to do with a missing eight-year old?" He asked handing the necklace back to me.

I looked at the necklace a bit and wondered if it would have helped the kid. "The kid's mother died during birth and according to the Daemon's husband she never took the necklace off. A couple days ago, something took the girl and left a bad copy in her place. The dad wants me to find out what happened to his daughter and get her back. I needed to get a better idea of what I was up against before I made another go at the kid's room to find more clues."

"Is that why your coat stinks so badly?"

"You noticed?" Stupid question.

Felix arched an eyebrow at me. "You're kidding me, right? I noticed it as soon as you walked into my shop. The thing reeks of the Pit, and a part I'm not familiar with, which isn't good. I know most of the Pit fairly well."

"Let me guess, you go on vacation down there?"

"I go to visit dad a couple times a year and he shows me around so yes. It's nice to be with him, no one is dumb enough to treat me like a nobody. Plus all the fun stuff is down there. His library is massive, and time doesn't work the same way down there as it does up here."

"Of course not." Time is of course relative, and while often linear, its length of passage can vary widely depending on where you are at the time.

"So, do you need a full translation? Cause that's going to take some time to finish or is the general concept all you really need?"

I shook my head. "I think I have all that I need. Now I have to question the copy.

"I do have a question for you though. Do you know if a female Daemon can die giving birth to a half Mortal?"

"Truthfully? I don't know," Felix said with a shrug, "it just doesn't come up. As you know female Daemons don't often have children, especially not a half Mortal so I really couldn't guess on the likelihood of something like that happening. I guess it is a possibility, but I honestly don't know."

I leaned back and looked at the necklace, and thought for a while. "Do you know how I could get into the part of the Pit this Necklace would have come from?"

Felix looked at me for a while, I think he was trying to decide whether or not I was joking. "You can't be serious."

"Why not? I need to find out where this came from, and if the language is from a part of the Pit that is no longer inhabited I want to make sure there is still nothing there. If something is there it is quite possible that's where I'll find the kid. Possibly the mother as well."

"You are certainly certifiable I'll give you that." Felix tone was bemused at best. "Tell you what. I'll look it up; it's going to take a while, and I may have to get dad up here for some answers, but I want a favor."

I sighed, I hated when people ask me for favors, it always leads to trouble. "What do you want?"

"I've heard about a book that's been uncovered in the Vatican, that I want. I want you to get it."

"You want me to go to the Vatican to steal something?" I asked incredulously. "Done and done. I may even start a fire on the way out to cover my tracks." Anything to stick it to a powerful organized religion, well Abrahamic anyways.

"That's the spirit. I knew I could count on you for something like that."

"So, you'll start figuring out how to get me down there?"

"Right away. I'll call you when I've got it all figured out."

"Thanks." I was about to leave the office when Felix stopped me.

"Oh and Jason?"

"Yes?"

"How much do you want for the coat?"

"This thing? Why?" To put it mildly I was puzzled. The thing reeked of lust. I could see it being used as an aphrodisiac that one would slip in to someone else's drink but other than that I couldn't really think of anything. Felix would never sell something like that and he had no use for it himself, the guy wasn't actually male, he wasn't female either. He had no sexual organs whatsoever and therefore no use for something like that. I was one of the few people who knew that about him, possibly the only person other than his dad who knew. It drove the Succubi at the Mystic Wolf nuts too. No matter how much they flirted with him he never tipped them well because he simply wasn't attracted to them or anything else.

"I want to study it of course. Anything that reeks that badly of the pit but hasn't been to the pit, and doesn't smell like any place I have been to, fascinates me. Makes me think that this may very well be from the place that necklace is from." I handed over the trench coat, making sure to take the envelope full of lewd pictures of little girls out of the pocket first.

"Keep it. I was just going to destroy the damn thing anyway."

"Well I'll let you get going. What's your next stop anyways?"

"The hospital the dad took the daughter's replacement to." It was going to be a simple enough job.

"Won't that be tricky?" Felix asked, which was probably one of the dumbest questions he had ever asked anyone.

"Not at all," I said with a wave of my hand. "I'm a consulting psychologist on the kid's case. With license to match."

"Let me guess, Court of Night University gave you your credentials?"

"Where else? Makes things go much faster when you can have fake paperwork for any job whenever you need it."

"High friends in low places. Must be nice to have those kinds of resources."

"Having the Countess Blood Wolf as an ally is always handy. Now I'll be on my way to get back to this case."

"As I said I'll call you once I have what you need."

"Thanks. I knew I could count on you."

As I headed out the shop I made a quick contribution to Pagan men and women who were fighting over seas. Never knew when the good karma I got from that would be needed.

CHAPTER

Now that I was rid of the reek of a sexualized Daemon of the Pit I was starting to think clearly. I didn't want to admit it to myself but while I had been wearing the coat those pictures had been very enticing to look at. Now free of that smell I was able to think about what I should realistically do with the pictures. In other words it was time to go to the cops. I really didn't think Adam was a pedophile but I didn't want to risk it.

I entered the St. Paul police precinct and waved at the various people at desks. I was well known so no one ever bothered to stop me. I took the elevator to the fourth floor where the division for sex crimes was. I stopped by a desk where an officer had his nose buried in a case file. "Hey Jackson. How ya' doing?"

Jackson looked up at me. He wasn't a court member so I couldn't pull rank on him. However we had worked together on various cases so we had a decent enough connection.

"What do you have for me Jason?"

"Found something for you at a client's house. With what's been going on with his daughter I'm willing to give him the benefit of the doubt on whether or not these are his." I dropped the envelope on Jackson's desk.

Jackson dumped the contents of the envelope on his desk and I watched his face turn several shades of red. The pictures were of seven different girls total, several pictures of each, the oldest maybe eleven. All of them in very sexualized positions. The ones at the bottom of the stack were the daughter. She'd have been a beautiful kid if she had clothes on. As it was this was just sickening. "What's been going on with the daughter? Is one of these girls her?"

I picked up one of the pictures of Charlene. "This is the daughter, her name is Charlene Johnson, her dad is Adam Johnson, and she apparently has been going nuts over the last few days."

"Define, going nuts?" Jackson asked as he dug several evidence bags out of his desk.

"She's been trying to seduce her dad, and elementary school teacher. Apparently she even literally jumped her dad while in the nude, and when he fell he blacked out and when he woke up again she had gotten his pants around down to his knees."

Jackson separated out the pictures into the different bags, each kid with their own bag. "That is bad. Of course, that could be a result of sexual abuse from someone other than the father. Anyone else with major involvement in the kid's life? Uncle? Aunt? Close family friend?"

"From what the dad told me there are no aunts or uncles in the kid's life. He didn't mention a friend, but I forgot to ask."

"I'm going to have to look into it. Thanks for bringing this in. Look, I'm going to get a judge to issue a search warrant for the place. We're going to have to go over his place with a fine tooth comb. I want to make sure if he's a predator we get him off the streets as soon as possible. With any luck if these are his pictures he hasn't actually touched a kid yet, but I want to make sure. So is there anything I can do for you?"

"Yeah, after the kid tried to get into her dad's pants he stuffed her into clothes and took her to Children's Hospital to put her in the psych ward. I need to get access to her."

Jackson looked at me for a bit. "That's a tall order. What did the dad hire you for exactly?"

"He says it's like someone had just up and replaced his kid. It's like she's been acting like someone he's never met."

"That sounds like something you'd be called in on. Okay I'll get you into the hospital, don't you have some sort of qualifications that will help? I seem to remember a degree somewhere."

"Yeah I have a PsyD so I can act as a consulting psychologist."

"Sounds good." Jackson picked up the phone and made a couple calls.

I simply sat there and thought about all of it. I didn't want to think that Adam was a pedophile, and if he was, I sure as hell hoped he hadn't touched a kid. Well at least not his daughter. If he had he wouldn't have objected when the girl had been pulling his pants off. Unless he didn't want to have sex with his own kid. It was a hard one to figure out. He had pictures of his own kid and it had been almost too easy to find the pictures. You would have thought the guy would have hid them better. Either that or Charlene's doppelganger had found them and put them there, but why? Was the doppelganger getting off on them as well and who were the kids, were they kids from Charlene's school?

Too many unanswered questions, finding the answers was going to be my job. I just hoped Adam was innocent, at least for my sake. If he was guilty of being a pedophile the cops would already have and I wouldn't have a chance to beat the ever loving tar out of him. For normal Humans, I can't stand pedophiles, and I love beating the crap out of them whenever I have the chance.

"The hospital is expecting you," Jackson said knocking me out of my own thoughts, and back to practical matters. "While you're out I'm going to run these kids through facial recognition to see if I can find any hits in any of the databases. Do you have anything else that may help me?"

I gave him the name of Charlene's school, just in case these girls were class mates. I thanked Jackson and then headed off towards the hospital.

CHAPTER 5

After talking to Jackson, I headed to Children's Hospital since they were now expecting me. Adam had dropped the kid that I was guessing was an Infernal here. I had my credentials listed in the system from other hospitals so when Jackson had called them it was a piece of cake getting a meeting.

When I parked I called up the office to check in with Jamie to see how Shadow was doing. "Hey boss," she answered once as soon as she picked up, oddly enough she sounded more than a bit distressed.

"Hey Jamie. How is Shadow doing, he was being a grouch this morning and I don't know why."

"Yeahhhhh, about that." Oh boy.

"What happened?"

"Shadow isn't here right now. I don't know what happened to him, only that a damn big raven busted through the window and snagged him and flew off with him." Oh shit! "There was nothing I could do to stop it, I mean I tried but it was like I was stuck in place. Then once I could move I found a note that reads. 'Shadow will be fine, as long as he lives up to his responsibility.' I'm kind of freaked out by this."

"Shit it must have been Muninn that grabbed him. Makes me wonder what that idiot has been up to. I knew I should have never let him start dating her."

"What do you think it means?" asked Jamie, who sounded as if she was still a bit shaken up by the situation.

"It's nothing, look I need to get back to this case. For now, I'm going to let that idiot worry about himself, I don't have time to. This case is getting scary and I don't have time to worry about Shadow. He's smart enough for a complete idiot and should be fine."

"If you say so boss." Jamie didn't sound so sure.

"So you know I'm at Children's Hospital right now, I have something to question, I just hope no one is going to be in trouble too deeply when I get there."

"I thought the girl was missing, what's she doing at the hospital?"

"The girl was replaced by some sort of doppelganger that is going nuts. It tried, and thankfully failed to seduce the father, and has done the same to other people."

"Oh joy. Is there anything I can do for now?"

"I don't think so, no. If something changes, I'll let you know."

"Okay. What about Shadow?"

"Don't worry about him for now. Right now the cops are getting ready to serve a warrant on my client's house."

"Are you going to warn him? That could be bad if they find something and they connect it back to you."

"I'm the one who requested that they serve a warrant. I found kiddie porn in my client's house, including pictures of his kid. I don't know what's going on but what I do know is that I sure as hell don't want to be caught up in that sort of mess. I'm not sure if the investigator is going to call my cell or phone the office. If he does call the office send him my way immediately."

"Got it boss. I'll talk to you later then." Jamie hung up.

When I exited the car I took off my shoulder holster and threw it in the trunk, then picked up my satchel and headed into the hospital. This was going to be a pain in the tail. I have a reputation among the medical community that wasn't exactly favorable. It always made things a bit difficult.

It had been a while since I had last been in this hospital since I don't usually work with children's cases, so once I was in I had to find information and get directions. They did a quick check of their records and found that I was indeed meant to be there. I was given a name tag and pointed in the direction. The ward was on the fifth floor of the building and took up most of that floor. I walked up to the desk and again signed in with a receptionist who had me sit and wait for one of the doctors on duty to escort me in. I was waiting for about ten minutes when a doctor appeared.

"Dr. Black?" the doctor inquired as he approached me.

"That would be me. The police have requested that I be sent to make my own evaluation of her case."

"That seems a bit odd given that she has only been here for less than a day. Why have you been brought in?"

"Well I had originally been called in by the patient's father to find an explanation for her behavior. I went to the home and started my investigation into Charlene's case and found pictures in the girl's room of underage girls wearing nothing, and in sexually explicit poses. I turned over the pictures to the police and they want me to come talk to the girl about them." This was all true enough.

"Why did they send you and not a social welfare officer?" It was an obvious question of course.

"I already have some knowledge about the girl so they felt that it would be easier for me to start the investigation."

The doctor shrugged as if to say it didn't matter to him one way or the other. "Exactly what kind of doctor are you then? I've never heard of you before except for interesting rumors. Some doctors refer to you as a quack that somehow gets amazing results using no known technique. Some even refer to you as a modern exorcist. So, which is it?"

"I'm more of an investigative psychologist. I try to understand the background of a patient by looking into their history and their natural surroundings before I meet with them. Hence why I was brought into this case in the first place." It was true enough, both what I had just said, and what the doctor had referred to me as being. I have indeed been called both.

"Well the police apparently want you to talk to her, and I assume get my opinion of her."

"That is what they have told me. From what I have gathered from talking to her dad and seeing her room, she has become a hyper sexualized individual who appears to have gone through hormones at an incredibly early stage of life. It has brought her to a nearly nymphomaniac emotional state."

"How far would you say this has brought her then?" The doctor sounded genuinely sounded interested.

"She has already tried to seduce her teacher in no uncertain terms. This morning she tried to get her father's pants off after she pulled all of her clothes off." The look of shock on the psychiatrist's face was palpable.

By this time, we were in the day room of the children's psych ward and I was trying to spot the doppelganger but was having no luck. "So where is the patient?" It was about then that I started smelling the creature.

The scent had changed, and had become more refined. I could tell from the way everyone was acting that it was starting to cause everyone to respond as if they were all on aggressive aphrodisiacs. The thing was adapting, it was hungry for sex, almost like a primitive Succubus. "What's that smell?" I asked. I already knew the real answer, I just wasn't sure the doctor would know.

"We've been trying to figure out that ourselves. It's strange, almost as if it is sexual pheromones being released in large concentration. It's been having some noticeable effects on many of the patients especially sex abuse survivors. Including sexual aggression and fear. Some of the staff have complained about sexual arousal since the smell became noticeable. I have to admit that it's been having a similar effect on me."

"Can't say I surprised about the arousal," I muttered, mostly to myself.

"What do you mean that you're not surprised?"

"I have come across this sort of thing before. Not often but I have dealt with it. It doesn't matter as to the reason though, at least not at the moment. Now on to the patient. Where is she?"

The doctor looked around for a second and suddenly became worried when he didn't see her. "She should be here, I don't know where she would be." He then looked around again and noticed something else that seemed to be troubling. "That's odd, two of our male patients are missing as well."

Ah shit. This was the last thing I needed. It was possible that a couple kids were getting it on with the doppelganger. "Is this something I should be concerned about?" I asked, well knowing that it was definitely something I should be very worried about.

"I hope not."

We tracked the smell to a large closet that had a mess of board games, movies, and the like spilled out in front of it. From inside I could hear moaning. Ah crap! The doctor opened the door and was horrified by what he saw, and unfortunately, I was far from surprised. There in front of us were two mid teenagers quickly pulling their pants up in front of a creature that looked like a ten year old girl that was on its knees and licking her lips.

"What is the meaning of this!" the doctor screamed. Several orderlies came running our way.

The two boys looked in shock at each other, then at the doppelganger, their mouths wide open. "It was her idea," one of the boys said.

"Yeah it was all her idea." The other kid confirmed.

"Of course it was my idea, doc. Just like it was with you earlier." That caused my head to snap 'round to look at the doctor. "And I see more people to have fun wi..." She cut herself off mid word when she saw me.

"Well, well, well, a fellow creature of the Pit." She smiled at me, licking her lips. "Do you want a part of my tender young flesh too?" That caused me to look at the creature, well at least we both recognized each other for what we were.

"What did she mean by it was her idea with you earlier today doctor?" I asked without taking my eyes of Charlene's copy. This was definitely a creature of the Pit, I didn't need to ask any sort of question to know that. It was a primitive Succubus as I thought. A true Succubus wouldn't pull a stunt this ridiculously stupid. This thing just wanted sex and it oozed that desire. I couldn't say I wasn't affected by it myself, but we both knew that I could hold out so it wasn't going to be worth her effort, though I'm sure she was still going to try.

"I... I... I..."

"Spit it out!" I was pissed, that guy had probably fucked this thing and I wasn't going to put up with that. I didn't care that this thing was an Infernal he should have better control of himself.

"The girl came on to me and it was like I couldn't control myself," he all but stammered.

I grabbed the thing by the arm to keep it from going after anyone else and called the cops from the receptionist's desk. I gave them all the information they needed after I had gotten a hold of a cop who was a member of the Court. Fifteen minutes later the detective and several other officers showed up and arrested the doctor as well as the two boys we had discovered in the closet with the doppelganger.

While that was all happening, I kept a tight grip on the creature, no way I was going to risk a chance of it escaping among the hustle and bustle. Soon enough I was able to use a private room to talk to it. This time I made sure I had the Court of Night police officer with me when I talked to it.

"Well let's see what can we talk about, Charlene?" I asked politely.

"How about we give up the charade. You know as well as I that I'm not Charlene, even her dad suspects it. It sucks having to look Human and so young, a bit harder to seduce someone when you look like a little kid. Still it is somewhat more satisfying I must admit, especially the doctor. He tries to act like a moral man, but really he's just as much of a sex fiend as anyone else, and it didn't take much to get him to sit up and beg. Still, pretending to be Human is incredibly degrading. So, what do you really want to know?"

"Where is the girl? Though I'm sure you're not going to tell me. At least not willingly."

"Ah the brat. Why should I tell you? I'm beginning to like it up here and if I was to tell you you'd just drag me back down there. I'm fairly certain you don't know where in the Pit I'm from yet otherwise you wouldn't be here. You'd already have the kid back with her dad and you'd be somewhere else."

"Then how about you tell me what you want with the girl? Surely you can tell me that." This was not going to be fun, I couldn't get the girl back to my office for proper questioning so torture was pretty much out of the question and there were so many questions that had cropped up that I needed answered. I also couldn't get much help from the Countess right now. She doesn't really have employees in Child Protective Services that I can rely on to get her out of here and under my control.

"Well, the girl is safe, I guess. I neither know, nor care what happens to her. I'm here to make the girl's mother and father suffer. Mostly her mother. You should know as well as I do that when an Infernal goes rogue you can't let that stand. My sister ran out on our lord and went into hiding on this awful realm. Why he was so angry with her I don't know, I'm much better in bed than she ever was. I guess it was probably just the principal of the matter."

"So, in order to make her suffer your lord made you show up looking like the girl in order to psychologically torture your sister? By pretending to be her kid and act the way you're currently acting you want her to think that part of her was transferred on to the kid."

"Aren't you the smart one?" The Infernal laughed a bit, and leered at me. "Why don't you try me on for size yourself right now. I'm more than certain it would be fun for both of us."

"I may be a bastard of the Pit but I do have standards. Fucking little kids is way beneath me, even if they really are Daemons like you. I don't know what you look like."

The Doppelganger stood up and started pulling her pants off. All of a sudden I could smell that daemonic scent of lust even stronger. "Are you sure you don't want to try me on for size. I can tell you right now, that at least this body's ass is still virgin and I know how many Humans like underage girls."

I grinned at her. "May I remind you that I'm not fully human. I know those tricks and they're not going to work on me. Now why don't you pull your pants back up, before I cuff you to that chair."

"I can tell you're going to crack." Ah fuck it.

I yanked her pants back up then grabbed out a pair of Daemon cuffs, and slapped her back into the chair with her wrists bent at awkward angles so that she couldn't escape. "Now we're going to have a nice conversation without you trying, and failing, to seduce me."

"And here I thought the handcuffs were going to be the start of some rough foreplay." The Daemon pouted and I could smell the scent of lust coming from her intensify. I so wanted to get truly nasty with her. Starting with smashing the butt of my trusty .45, Ace of Spades, across her face and knock that cocky grin off her face. Unfortunately, that wasn't going to happen for a while no matter how much the little bitch deserved it.

"So are we going to talk or what?"

"Oh fine, but I promise you are not going to get anything useful out of me. I'm just going to sit here and try to get your hard cock in me." The worst part of this was that the smell was beginning to get to me. I needed this thing in the trophy room, where I could beat the stench out of her and have it not affect me. That settled matters for me; I needed to make a call, I needed to get paperwork filled out yesterday.

I picked up my phone and dialed the Countess Blood Wolf's private number. There were few people who had this number. In fact I think I may very well be the only one with it, and I try not to use it unless I have to. "Hey Jason sweetie." She sounded chipper, good thing for me too, when she's pissed off at someone she often takes things out on me. "What can I do for you. I'm a bit short handed for muscle at the moment as a few revolutionary groups with money have contracted my people. If there is something else you need me to do though, by all means ask, I need a little distraction."

"Thankfully I don't need any muscle for the foreseeable future. I just need some paperwork filled out a couple years back. Is that possible?"

"Is that all? I thought you were going to ask for something hard. That's barely noticeable. Let me grab a piece of paper and a pencil and you can tell me what you need and I'll send it to the hackers as top priority." I could hear her shuffling around as she found something to write down. "Okay what do you need?"

"I need my home address put into the system as a private psychiatric clinic." I saw the Daemon grin at me and lick its lips excitedly. I couldn't wait to show it the trophy room. That would put a quick end to its attempts to seduce me.

"Hold on a second I need to check something out real quick on our current records regarding your license, that may already be the case."

"Really, that would speed things up with this case greatly." I looked at the Doppelganger and gave her an evil grin letting my eyes start to glow and did something I rarely ever did, let my teeth elongate and sharpen into ragged fangs. The teeth thing I rarely do because it can be quite uncomfortable when they return to normal and sometimes can take a while. During that time it looked like someone had made a good attempt to bash my teeth out, and had just broken them all instead. Still I wanted to get my point across to the creature. She was going to be put through a severe amount of pain and it wasn't going to be fun. Unfortunately it may very well have a masochistic streak since it had all but told me that it was a Infernal Lord's concubine.

"Oh, whips and chains? This is going to be fun," the creature said, apparently trying to give a suggestive wriggle.

"Not for you it isn't."

"You'd be surprised."

"Hey sweetie I'm back," Yvette said giving me good reason to ignore the Daemon, "I just checked, your house is already listed as a private psychiatric institute. We probably did that shortly after we did most of the slash and burn that lead to the court. So that paperwork's been filled out for a while."

"Great, I have an Infernal with me who's going to be a bitch and a half to crack, and I can't do anything right now because I'm stuck in a children's psych ward."

"I was beginning to wonder why you had all those officers sent over to the hospital, you'll have to tell me about it later. Do you want me to come over?"

I loved that about my friend, she loved seeing blood spilled as much as I did. "That would be great. The damn thing keeps trying to seduce me and it's getting rather annoying at this point."

"I can do that."

"Ooh more people to have fun with," it said, licking its lips. I so couldn't wait to beat the crap out of it.

"Thanks Yvette, meet me at the house in thirty minutes. I'm going to need your help here."

"I'll see you then sweetie," she said making a quick kissy noise into the phone.

"I love you too." I hung up after that.

"So we're going to have a three way then?" the doppelganger asked excitedly. "I can't wait to meet your friend. Is he as big as you? I hope he's a bit more fun, you're a boring stick in the mud." Just think about the scalpel old boy, just think about the scalpel and all the fun I'm going to have carving all sorts of interesting patterns on this thing.

"My friend's a woman and she has some interesting way to break people."

"Ooh, a challenge, I can't wait for the fun to start."

"Trust me you can." I smiled. "You won't be screaming in pleasure before I'm done with you."

"We'll see about that," she said licking her lips. "We'll just see about that."

CHAPTER

I gagged the damn thing on the way to my place, though not a physical one. Didn't want to attract attention after all. Instead I had used a spell to keep her mouth shut, and on the way out the spell forced the creature to say what I wanted it to say. It had been easy to get the thing to follow me out of the hospital without needing the handcuffs. After all it was willing to go. I was a going to be a challenge for it to seduce, which increased its desire to do exactly that. I think it felt that if it was at my home I'd be more likely to fuck it since there would be no witnesses. Boy, was it in for some nasty surprises.

I saw one of Yvette's limos parked in front of the house when we arrived. As we walked into the house I wasn't surprised to find the door unlocked. "You're late," Yvette said accusingly.

"Sorry more red tape than I expected."

Yvette's eye's drifted from me to the girl standing next to me standing a whole head shorter than Yvette. "Are you sure that little girl is an Infernal?"

"Aren't you a pretty one, I can't wait to get a taste of your juices," the Infernal said licking its lips and starting to give off her smell of lust.

"I stand corrected. This is definitely an Infernal, just going have to get past what it looks like."

"Just don't let the damn thing get undressed and we should be fine," I said. "This is just going to get annoying, because I think it's an extreme masochist, so breaking is going to take a lot of work."

"Oh I can think of all sort of ways for you to break me," the creature smiled, "but I don't think you would be willing to do any of them."

"I think I get what you want me to do and I'll immediately say no to most of them."

"What do you think it means?" Yvette asked.

"I think that she means everything I would have to do to get her to crack has something sexual attached to it."

"You wouldn't even think of doing that, would you?" Yvette sounded horrified, and rightly so.

"Of course not. Let's just…"

"Oh come on, you and I both know you want a taste of this young, nubile flesh." That was the last straw I thought, and I disfigured its face temporarily by smashing a fist into its jaw. Her face immediately started taking back its original look. "Mm, I like it rough."

I grabbed the creature by the hair and dragged it through the house up the stairs and into the trophy room. Yvette followed behind and once I slammed the Infernal into a chair she locked the door. "So which do we start with, whips or chains? Or do we…" the creature immediately stopped talking when it saw the horrors that were spread throughout the room. In one corner, sitting in an old electric chair, was the body of a Faerie king that had been turned into a grotesque ventriloquist dummy, the whole back of his head opened up and hollowed out. There were implements of torture from the inquisition that still had blood caked on them. Thousands of people had died at the hands of the inquisitors who had used these tools. Hanging on the wall still glowing gold were the continually bleeding wings of an Arch-Angel. Then the creature seemed to realize one of the scariest truths about the room. Most of the wood in the room, from the floor to most of the furniture, was made from Aokigahara, also known as the Suicide Forest of Japan. People went there to die. Even if you didn't go in there to die and just wanted to look around you had a good chance of being found dead, if you were ever found at all that is. These horrors and far more had shut the creature up quickly.

"So what do you think of this collection?" I asked happily. "I'm quite proud of this, and so you know there is no bed in here and your scent is completely muted, so neither of us can really smell it anymore."

"What kind of sick bastard are you?" This had just gotten fun. Now I had the upper hand.

"Oh that's cute coming from you, an Infernal that has been trying to fuck anyone and anything with a pulse, including your victim's father." I took a seat on the edge of my desk and looked the creature straight in the eyes. "Now you're going to tell me where Charlene is right now and you can go. Simple as that, you walk out of here without a single mark on your body, of course I'm not sure your master would want you back after that."

"And if I refuse?" The creature spat out.

"Then you find out what pain means." That time it was Yvette who growled it out as she started to shift accompanied by the sound of breaking bones and tearing flesh, into the most disturbing creature one could imagine. She looked like a cross between an old fashioned Nosferatu and the scariest modern cinema Werewolf one could think of. Almost hairless, her corpse white skin with its slight tinge of blue was stretched over a bony frame of a wolf like creature with Vampiric fangs, and cracked, talon like fingernails. Her voice was beautiful, sounding exactly like breaking rock. Her clothes unfortunately were now laying in a shredded pile at her feet.

"I've seen uglier..." was all the doppelganger got out before it was plucked out of the seat by Yevette and slammed into the desk. Blood sprayed out of its nose covering my waist and legs in gore and making a mess of the paperwork on the desk. Thankfully the paperwork was simply for show. I only used this place for storing disturbing mementos from my cases, and torturing people. Doing the one I had found greatly helped with the other.

"Now I don't think you want to insult my friend." It wasn't really an insult, Yvette knew she was horrifying in that form. I think it had to do with the idea that something being even more horrifying didn't sit well with her. She was Lovecraftian in appearance and took pleasure in it. Truth be told I had come to find it kind of cute. Of course I was also used to her throwing around tanks and gutting Nazis when she was like this, so maybe it was just good memories.

"Fuck you," the creature was at my feet so I kicked it in the head. Hard enough to hear bone break. Yvette grabbed it and slammed it back into the chair. Though she was fairly gentle about it. She knew I didn't want to get a new chair already. One had been destroyed when a Succubus friend of ours had slammed a prisoner through it. That chair had cost me over $50,000 to replace.

"I already told you that wasn't going to happen now. Your stink of the Pit is pretty much gone here so no more flirting with us. Okay." The creature snarled at me but kept its mouth firmly shut. "Well I guess if you don't want to talk I'll just have to start getting creative."

"Please do," it said leering at me, "let's see if you can get me to crack through torture, though I warn you I might just find the pain arousing."

This was going to be an issue. It sounded like this thing may be a true masochist in every sense of the word. With it being a Daemon it could take a ton of abuse and keep going. Threatening to kill it may not even work because it would call my bluff. I couldn't afford to kill it right now. With these limitations I found myself at a loss for what to do next. I looked to Yvette who seemed as much of a loss for how to get this thing to crack as I was.

"Yvette let's step out for a second, we need to talk," I said motioning my friend out of the room.

Yvette followed without saying a word and locked the door behind her without me mentioning it. "So, what's the plan?" she asked.

"That's the problem, I have no idea. That creature is a masochist so all of my normal methods are pretty much useless."

"Same problem here. I'm used to breaking Humans, not Daemons, especially not masochistic ones." She sighed in frustration; she could keep a person alive for days if she wanted to, she had even learned some new tricks for proper psychological torture. Unfortunately, none of the psychological tortures would work quick enough to get the results we needed, if they would work at all. Sensory deprivation would do a number on most Humans, but Daemons have more senses that I don't know how to block that they can use to entertain themselves with. They can also block out other senses more easily than a Human can. Putting her under a hot light, and beating her with a rubber hose would work if she was Human. Over loads on the two senses would break a normal person easily. For her it would be futile, she'd enjoy the pain and could easily block out the light. I couldn't use the scalpel on her, that was obvious. That was designed to exert maximum pain on a person, especially a Daemon, yet keep them alive with no real side effects except permanent scars to the psyche. This thing would probably have an orgasm if I did that so that dropped that out of my repertoire, along with pretty much every torture device at my disposal. I wondered.

"How long do you think it would take for it to crack just sitting there?" I asked.

"You mean let the room itself work its magick on her?"

"Not just that. We walk in and out of the room on occasion and we just ignore her. Let her stew, she can't try to get at us sexually anymore, her scent is too muted so she'll give that up. The longer we ignore her and let everything work its way on her mind she's got to give up at some point."

Yvette grinned like a mad woman, an interesting look on her nightmarish face. It would be a source of many nightmares for most people, yet here I am thinking of it as adorable in a perverse sort way. "That sounds like it just might work. Why don't you tell her you've got plenty of time to wait her out and just leave again."

I walked back into the room and smiled at the doppelganger of Charlene. "Well I guess we can't torture you, since we know it won't work on you."

"I made it more than clear that there are other ways to break me. You just have to set aside your morals for a few minutes and rape this pussy good and hard."

"Well see there is a big problem with that. My friend out there would rip me apart if I did that. Mostly because she's the jealous type."

The doppelganger smiled and licked its lips. "Well the more the merrier then."

"I know you would like that, but I have other means of finding out where you're from, but I can't simply let you leave. So, for now you're going to stay right here." I didn't smile, it was poker face time.

"You're kidding me? Here? Chained up? I can barely move and I've got nothing to do." I could tell she hadn't expected this development. She was too used to getting her way, or at least slapped around for a while. Being ignored was going to drive her nuts; in the Trophy room I was willing to bet she'd be a screaming wreck in a couple of days.

"Well, have a good night. Yvette and I will check in on you from time to time, just in case you decide to cooperate at some point." I left the room and locked it with an ancient ward, just in case she figured out a way out of the cuffs; it had never happened before but I was taking no chances. Looking at Yvette's now-Human face I could tell that she had heard it all.

"How long do you think she can hold out?" Yvette asked, heading for the guest room where I kept a couple spare changes of clothes for her.

"I'm guessing two, maybe three days before she cracks, depending on how strong willed she is," I said with a shrug. "However, that may not matter."

"Why's that? Don't you need her to take you to her home realm?"

I smiled slightly. "Felix is looking into that for me right now. You see when I was searching the victim's house the father showed me a necklace that her mother never took off."

"Let me guess, it was a protection symbol." She opened the closet and was poking around for something comfortable, not wanting to go too casual, and definitely not too formal.

"Not quite. The victim's mother was a Daemon who had been on the run for who knows how long. There is a binding spell on the necklace that would keep her from leaving the Mortal realm. In all practical effect, she couldn't be tracked down by whomever she had run from. It turns out that the alphabet the spell is in is from a part of the Pit that had been deserted at some point so it's possible that whatever had been there has returned. From what I have learned the mother, who died in child birth, is now having her soul tortured. To make things sick they decided to really go at it and send a doppelganger up to take the place of the daughter…"

"And have the mother think her daughter had turned into a psychotic nympho." Yvette shuddered. "That is absolutely sick. So, what's happening to the real kid?"

"I wish I knew. Unfortunately, I'm stuck right now. Felix is still trying to figure out how to get me down there, and this damn thing is being stubborn. Until something changes I'm forced to sit idly by and hope nothing too bad happens to the kid."

"Out of curiosity where's Shadow?" She asked after a while of looking around. "I know he isn't terribly fond of me, but this? I haven't seen him yet."

"The idiot got himself kidnapped apparently." As I have said Shadow was smart enough to get home safely. At least I hoped that feather brained idiot was.

"He's been kidnapped!?" Yvette yelped. "Why aren't you going bonkers right about now? He's your familiar after all."

"Simple. I know who took him and it's his own damn fault. He'll be fine, as long as he doesn't do something truly idiotic," I said calmly. "Would you like something to drink?"

"Who took him?" Yvette asked pushing off the wall and falling me down towards the small bar in the dining room.

"His girlfriend, Muninn, did. At least that's my impression. Either that or it was her brother, Huginnn, that grabbed him for her. Either way he's probably on Asgard getting chewed out for something. I wouldn't know what it's like though, and truthfully I'm glad I don't."

"So you're sure you're not worried?"

"Why would I be? Muninn isn't going to let Odin kill the feather brained half-wit. At least I hope not. Besides whatever he's done he probably deserves a good ass kicking. Besides after this he may explain to me why he's been such a sourpuss over the last few days."

"I hope you're right." It was kind of odd for Yvette to worry about Shadow like this since she and my familiar weren't exactly on the best of terms. Shadow thought she was using me, which she isn't, and Yvette thought that I was holding on to the past keeping him around, which I am not.

"Of course I am." Truthfully though? I guessed I was very worried, I just didn't want to show it. That idiot has been in the family for generations, as in pre-Roman invasion of Britain generations. I honestly don't know what I'd do without him, he's just always been there. A pain in the ass to be sure but he's just always been there when I've needed him. I hated to admit it I guess but I think I've just gotten to the point where I sort of take it for granted that he's always going to be there. Him not being in the house without me telling him to piss off made the place feel empty.

"Bullshit! Your scared, you just don't want to admit it. We both know that Shadow and I don't get along very well, but I think you're trying to pull some macho bullshit about not being worried. Not going to work with me Jason, so just admit it, you are scared."

"Fine! I admit it! I am scared! Does that make you happy?"

"No. What would make me happy though is a Power Driver." Yvette dropped into a chair and looked at me.

I took the hint. There were few people who knew me better than that little psycho, pretty much Shadow being the only one. "On the rocks? Or no ice?"

"No ice, and keep 'em coming." She leaned back and threw an arm over her eyes. "You're a real pain in my tail you know that, don't you?"

"I'm sure I am." I went to the kitchen to get a highball glass and the orange juice. Once I was back to the dining room I grabbed a couple bottles of Everclear and poured the highball most of the way with booze and finished with a splash of orange juice. "Here you go."

Yvette downed the drink in about a single swallow. That drink would drop just about any Human, but with her supernatural tolerance to pretty much any drug, getting her drunk on anything was pretty much impossible. Well anything easily purchased in the Mortal realm. "So, I'm the jealous type hmmm?"

"Trying to deny it?" I asked

"Not at all. I'm just wondering what you meant by that?"

"I don't know. I'm beginning to think we could work out as a couple though."

"Now this just got interesting. But as amazing as this is going to sound I don't want to talk about it right now, I just want this case to be over with as soon as possible."

"Worried about the kid? She's not your victim to worry about." I reminded her.

"I know you're the one being paid, but right now I don't care. She's a little kid stuck in an Infernal realm. I don't even want to think about what could be happening to her right now. Especially what it will do to her in the long run."

"I try to hold out hope that I'll be able to get her out before the damage is permanent." I sighed and looked back up the stair case to where that damn doppelganger was sitting hopefully going mad.

"You mean we'll be able to get her out. I'm coming with you."

"No point in even trying to talk you out of this I guess?"

"Nope." She looked at the empty glass in her hand. "Poor me another one. I want to try to get a buzz going at least."

"No problem." I took the glass and poured her another drink. Silently we both knew that it was going to be a time for a relaxed conversation about nothing important. Our relationship we seemed to mutually agree to leave off the table, though neither of us actually having said as much. Honestly I forget what we talked about it was so unimportant.

After a while I started getting hungry. "You want to go to Mystic Wolf for some dinner?"

"Aren't you worried about that thing up there getting out?" Yvette asked.

"Not really, no. I'm going to stop up there before we leave though just to see how it's doing. Though I'm not going to ask it if it's ready to talk."

"If you say so. I'll get ready while you do that."

I headed upstairs and heard thumping and impassioned cursing coming from the Trophy room. I unsealed the door and walked in. The creature was livid of course. Couldn't say I blamed it.

"What do you want?" it snarled.

I just went over to my desk and started shuffling papers around in one of the drawers, not even having bothered to look at it. All the papers were meaningless since, as I have said, I don't really do much in this room other than store trophies and interrogate people here.

"Let me go and we'll have a good time. You'll never forgive yourself if you don't have a taste of me. I can make Gods sing my praises at my touch, think what it would be like for you, half breed. You'd never look at another woman the same way again. They would all look plain and meaningless after a few minutes with me."

Blah, blah, blah. It kept running its pretty little mouth off, and I just ignored it as it kept going. The more I ignored it the more graphic it got about what it would do for me. Truthfully some of it sounded kind of fun, but Yvette would never go for some of what it talked about. She'd be too worried about cutting me too deeply.

Eventually I left and the Daemon started screaming vivid curses at me again. All sense of it wanting to prostitute itself so I'd fuck it for answers was gone. It was just pissed at me for the moment. Must be really annoying for it to not be getting its way I thought. Oh well, it would break soon enough.

"Ready to go?" Yvette asked once I got down the stairs.

"Let's."

CHAPTER 7

It was about eight when we got to the Wolf and the place was packed, more so than usual, but it was karaoke night which explained it. Looking for a quiet table for just the two of us was going to be impossible so we decided to find someone we knew. After a few minutes of searching we spotted my niece, Red Raven and one of her adopted moms, a Succubus named Sasha. "Mind if we join you?" I asked. Well tried to ask as I was cut off at the at the 'we' part.

"Uncle Jason!!!" Red hit me like a crazy, little, Daemonic cannon ball.

"Watch it shorty," I said as I picked her up and hugged her.

"Hi Sasha, hi Red," Yvette said from behind me.

"Aunty Bloodwolf!" Red absolutely adored Yvette and used her court name since she thought that 'Aunty Yvette' didn't sound right.

"So how are you two doing?" Sasha asked as she took Red out of my arms. "Come on Red, let them sit down."

Red wriggled out of Sasha's arms and ran up to Yvette jumped into her arms. "Hey kiddo." Yvette smiled at Red and then started tickling her until she almost fell out of her arms.

Sasha grabbed Red away from Yvette before my niece hit the floor. "Ok time to calm down Red. How about you draw them each a nice picture. Okay?"

"Okay!!!" Say what you want about the kid. Red Raven is one of the happiest kids you'll ever meet, and she was going to grow to be a beautiful woman, in who knew how many years. She had a lot going for her of course. She was a half breed Daemon, part Infernal, part Divine, and took after her actual mother, my cousin, may her soul rest in peace. Red's father I had the pleasure of killing, because he was an abusive asshole who had killed Red's mother and had tried to kill her. I had tortured the fuck out of the bastard before I killed him. It was his wings that now hung in my Trophy room. I hadn't needed to, but it had felt so damn good to do some major body work on him to release some of the pent-up frustration at the time. She also has a massive heart which I give credit to Sasha and her other mother Kara for. The girl was in a loving environment and I knew that it was doing her a world of good.

"So, what are you up to Jason?" Sasha asked. "You two here on date?"

"Oh wouldn't that be nice?" Yvette said jabbing me in the ribs.

I shook my head. "I wish. No we're here to take a break from letting a Daemon stew in my Trophy room for a while. The thing is being incredibly stubborn, and I can't torture it."

"Why not? You like torturing people." Sasha asked.

"The thing's a masochist and would enjoy any of my normal tricks…"

"Mom. What's does masochist mean?" Red piped up.

"A masochist is someone that enjoys pain." Sasha replied ruffling the little girl's hair.

"Why would someone enjoy being hurt. I don't like getting hurt. Like the time I fell down the stairs, and the time I hit my head on the counter, and the time…"

Sasha thankfully cut Red off mid-sentence, I really didn't need a list of all of her minor injuries. "Yes, I know most people don't like getting hurt. It's just that some people do for some reason."

"I don't know why anyone would be like that. It just doesn't make sense. I think Joey Marshall in class likes getting hurt though." I couldn't help but laugh.

"What makes you say that?" Sasha asked arching one eyebrow.

"Well he keeps making me mad to the point where I hit him. I do hold back, I really do, but one of these days I don't know if I'll be able to."

"Now Red Raven you shouldn't hit people." The Succubus scolded.

"But mom says it's okay to hit people if they're bad."

Sasha just shook her head. Her fiancé was a Valkyrie so hitting bad people was something she would definitely do. "Great now I'm going to have to lecture Kara about what she is teaching you."

At that point Yvette broke down in hysterics. "That's your fault, you know, your girl toy is a bad influence on her."

"Mom what's a girl toy?"

"It's an adult joke. Why don't keep drawing?"

"Ok."

"Please watch your language around her, she tends to repeat everything, and the last thing I need is for her teacher to call me again about her using foul language. It's kind of embarrassing, especially since I'm now spending some of my time subbing at her school."

I was grinning like an idiot at this point. "No problem. So anyway, where were we?"

"You said the Daemon you were torturing was a masochist so you were trying something new."

"Oh yes, that's right. I'm trying something completely new and I hope it works out. I'm going to let it sit in the Trophy room while all of the horrors of the room screw with its head."

"I can see how that would work. I was only in there for a few minutes and that place was disturbing enough for me, and I'm an Infernal. I don't know how you can stand being in there for any length of time."

"Two reasons: I built the place, and I don't stay in there very long. That place scares even me." That was truth of the matter, I didn't like being in that room at all. The place was pure evil, but it had its purpose so I kept it. I didn't trust anyone else to take care of that shit. Of course, I may end up moving it somewhere else eventually, but for the moment it stayed put. "I can only handle it for a couple hours at a time before I have to leave."

"And you're leaving a tied-up, Daemon stuck in there?" Sasha sounded understandably horrified. "What did they do to deserve that?"

"They kidnapped a little girl to torture her mother, who was a Daemon who had been on the run. The Infernal is a doppelganger that has been, acting like a Succubus, with everyone with a pulse."

"How old is the girl?" Sasha was sounded pissed and I couldn't blame her in least.

"Eight."

"By the All Father's beard that's horrible. Was it the mother who hired you?"

"The mother died during child birth and I guess her soul was tracked down."

"A stupid Sasha!" She yelled at herself, "Of course she's died."

"What do you mean of course she's died?" Yvette asked.

"What? Oh I just mean that for the most part Daemons can't give birth to half Mortals. That's why in all those legends about heroes that are the offspring of Gods, it's always the Human that gives birth. For the most part those heroes aren't the children of actual Gods, more likely an Arch-Angel but I digress. The mother wouldn't have survived childbirth. Which means that she basically knowingly committed suicide, which makes me wonder why she did it in the first place."

"Well she was married." It was a lame excuse.

"She really must have loved the guy if she was willing to give him a kid, knowing she was going to die in the process."

Now things had just stopped making sense completely. It was nearly impossible for any Daemon, Infernal or Divine to get a new body, if they did actually die on the Mortal realm they'd be stuck in whatever realm they were from as nothing more than a ghost at best. Though they're also nearly impossible to kill there so usually it's a moot point. So why had Charlene committed suicide just to give the guy a kid? And why would she even let herself get pregnant in the first place? Now nothing added up.

One of the Succubi waitresses, Stella, showed up and tapped me on the shoulder with her tail. "Hey sexy," that greeting got Yvette growling, "are you ready to order?"

"Why don't you start with Yvette."

Stella turned her attention to the Countess. "What would you like sweetie?"

"A Power Driver." Brisbane had made that a standard drink, not that many people actually ordered them.

"And you?" Stella asked turning back to me.

"Double scotch on the rocks." I said after a minute. Maybe the familiar taste would jump start my brain.

"Sasha, do you or Red Raven want refills?"

"That would be great."

"Okay let's double check. A lemonade for Red, and a Coke for Sasha, along with a Power Driver for the Countess, and a double scotch on the rocks for Black?" We all nodded except for Red who had her tongue rubbing her upper lip as she concentrated on her drawing. "I'll be right back."

I didn't bother to watch her walk off for two reasons. I was still trying to work things out, the other was that I didn't want Yvette blowing her top. I was mad as hell. With what Sasha had just told me I had even more questions than before.

"So where's Shadow?" Sasha asked.

"Funny story that. Isn't it, Jason?" Yvette said.

"What's funny?" Red asked.

"Apparently Muninn grabbed the idiot and flew off with him," I said, trying and probably failing to sound calm.

"She what?!" Sasha blurted out.

"Shadow has been acting like a sourpuss for a couple days, then while I'm out on a case a large raven broke into the office and grabbed Shadow and flew off."

"And you're not worried?"

"He's terrified, he just won't admit it." Yvette said, answering for me.

"I hope he's okay," Sasha sounded worried. "Do you want me or Kara to talk to Odin about it?"

"Don't worry I'm sure it's all going to work out."

"As I said, terrified." Yvette cut in.

Stella returned with our drinks and dropped them off in front of us. I picked up my scotch and took a slow sip and tried to figure out a few things. Why had the mother killed herself willingly just to give her husband a kid? Was the father a pedophile, or were those pictures put there by the doppelganger? What was the doppelganger's motive to set the dad up? Nothing about this case made sense anymore. The problem was that I had to wait until the damned creature broke, and I didn't know how long that was going to take. The worst part was that it wasn't going to be fast enough. The sooner it snapped the better but who knew how long that was going to take.

We talked with Sasha and Red for a while until Kara showed up and they went home together leaving me and Yvette alone. At about midnight we decided to call it a night, and head home.

CHAPTER

It was about one in the morning by the time we got home. As usual Yvette was stone cold sober, something she wasn't happy about. She often lamented the fact that she couldn't get even more than a mild buzz when she wasn't at the Wolf, which would quickly fade once she stopped drinking for thirty minutes. "Who gets to check on our guest?" she asked.

"How about you do it," I replied hanging up my jacket and hat.

"Not a problem." Ditching her shoes Yvette headed up the stairs to check in on the Succubus. I followed up the stairs fairly quickly and caught part of what the Infernal had to say. To put it mildly the thing could make a great living up here writing smut. She was nothing if not creative with the descriptions of what she would be happy to do with the Countess if she would just let her out. Every sort of foreplay from blood-letting rough to highly submissive was mentioned. She talked about every trick in the book, and many I had never heard of. I really should be taking notes for later. I was sure Yvette would want to try some of these out and I would need time to get properly warmed up. I wasn't that flexible, at least not enough to do even a quarter of what that Infernal was promising.

I couldn't see her face but I knew my friend was probably trying her hardest not to smirk at the thing. Yvette was straight but I was fairly sure that if the Infernal had been able to get her full scent going it could even seduce her. To make matters worse, as much as the scent was muted it was once again becoming noticeable. Maybe this had been a mistake. I couldn't air the room out because it wasn't really an airborne smell in any normal sense of the term. Yet it was building up and I knew it was going to be trouble.

As Yvette left I heard Charlene's double begging to be let out, that she'd do anything sexual if we'd just let her out. I shut the door behind the Countess and almost broke down in laughter. "How much longer until she fully breaks down do you think?" Yvette asked.

"Probably tomorrow, I'm hoping to get some information from Felix by then so I can give it a chance to cooperate without bluffing about killing it."

"Do you think it will be as simple as that?" Yvette asked.

"Probably not but I don't want to kill her if I don't have to." I couldn't explain why, but I couldn't really bring myself to be more than thoroughly mad at her. Yet, for some reason that I couldn't explain to myself, I didn't want to kill it, at least not yet. Apparently she was just as much of a pawn in this game as everyone else.

"Are you feeling okay Jason?" Yvette asked looking at me worriedly. "Normally you're a blood thirsty maniac about something like this.'

"I guess I kind of feel bad for that creature in there. I don't even want to think about what it's going through. I mean this sort of torture is bad even by my standards."

"I guess you have a point. I know you don't like spending much time in there yourself, leaving that Infernal in there is doing a number on it. We'll see if it's more cooperative in the morning."

"I guess." I looked back at the door to the Trophy room and really couldn't help but feel sorry for the thing. "Look do you mind if we don't sleep together tonight. I just can't..."

Yvette sighed and put an arm around me. "I know how you feel. I'll spend the night in the guest room. To tell you the truth I'm not in the mood anyway, this has got me sick." She hugged me again and headed off towards the guest room.

When I got to my own bed I looked over at Shadow's perch and got worried. The idiot was still gone, and I was worried that something might have happened, something serious. I hadn't heard from any of the Gods or Valkyries for that matter, and none of their familiars had showed up either. Yet either Muninn or possibly Huginnn had broken into my office and kidnapped my avian friend. The question was why?

As far as I know he hadn't mentioned anything to me about it, not that it meant much. I guessed it would explain why he had turned into such a grump lately. That still didn't offer a clue. He was always a grump but this had been different. He had been better since he had gotten involved with Muninn, not as cranky for such a continuously long streak. I wondered if this had to do with her. There really was no way for me to find out until he showed up again. I could only hope it would be sooner rather than later.

CHAPTER

9

I woke up to my phone ringing. "Hello?" I answered more than a little groggily.

"Did I wake you up, Jason?" It was Jackson which made me look at the clock and try to figure out why he had called me so damned early.

"Yeah but I needed to get up anyway. What do you have for me?" This had better be important.

"We got the warrant to search the dad's home, and to put it bluntly it's a damn good thing we have him in custody."

"Shit! What do you mean?"

"His computer is loaded with kiddy porn, and we have found records of conversations he's been having with several underage girls going back months. I don't know how far he's gone so far but we just got a predator off the streets because of that kid."

"Thanks, I'll talk to her about it, maybe things went farther with him than she originally told me."

"Well whatever happened you did a good job."

"Thanks Jackson." I hung up, I didn't want to think about what could have happened to who knew how many how many girls if he hadn't been caught. It always started small, how far it would it have gone? Now to talk to the Infernal.

I put on my robe and realized I could smell coffee, meaning that Yvette was up. Good I needed to talk this out now. As I walked to the kitchen I thought of how to broach the subject. "Morning sweetie," Yvette said as soon as I walked into the room, she was wearing a robe with kittens and a pair of pink bunny slippers. She had picked those out to keep at the house. Why? I didn't know, she was just weird at times and I had long ago given up trying to understand her.

"Good morning," I said. "We've got problems."

"Define problems?" Yevette asked me as she poured me a cup of coffee.

"Charlene's dad is a pedophile."

"So, where does that leave us with the kid? Assuming we can get her back. I know you well enough to know that you're not going to let her stay in the Pit."

"I guess she goes into the system as soon as we get her back, and to put it mildly I'm not happy about that. She has no other family that I know of, at least according to the dad that is, and as you said, I'm not leaving a little kid in the Pit."

"What about the Infernal we have stewing upstairs?" Yvette asked taking a sip of her own coffee her eyes drifting towards the stairs. "Do you think she knew that going into this?"

"It does make one wonder doesn't it." My eyes following hers. "There is only one way to find out though."

"You might want to change first."

"You should as well. You're not exactly intimidating dressed like that." Yvette smiled and walked past me leaving me to follow her upstairs.

Once we had both changed into more respectable clothing I opened the door to the Trophy room and saw the Infernal sweating profusely and breathing hard. "Okay what do you want to know?" she whimpered. "I'll tell you whatever you want to know just let please me out of the room."

"What do you think Jason?" Yvette asked.

"She answers our questions and I'll be happy to let her go provided she takes us with her to get the kid."

"Fine I'll do it just please let me out of this room." I saw tears forming around her eyes. Damn I had broken this one.

"This may not surprise you but Charlene's dad has been arrested as a pedophile."

"I see you found the pictures then. I was hoping you would, and that means my job is done."

"Wait, what?" Now I was confused.

"Charlene's mom wanted to keep her kid safe, when she found out that her husband was a pedophile she begged me to come here and switch with her child so I could help the cops nail the sick fuck to the wall."

"I thought you said that your master was torturing her soul?"

The Infernal gave me a ragged laugh then smiled like a maniac. "Master was pretty pissed off, but they had had fights before. She decided that it was time to return to him. She got pregnant to leave that scum husband something to remember her by, a person not just a possession. She had already been in contact with our master and he had a new body ready for her when she died up here."

This was just getting bizarre. "Charlene kept an eye on her husband and daughter. Eventually she realized that her husband was a pedophile and knew that it was only a matter of time before he raped a kid. She couldn't stand the idea that a man she had loved would do that, and she worried about her daughter. So with our master's permission I followed my dear sister's plan. As I'm sure you know we Infernals only have a bad reputation, one that isn't always justified. I don't want to see little kids get raped, I have better morals than that."

"And Charlene?"

"The kid's fine. Damned if her mother is going to let the brat get hurt." The Infernal looked at me and smiled. "Now can I please leave this horrible room. And yes I promise I will take you to where the kid is."

I uncuffed her. "There you go."

"Thank you. Do you mind if we get out of this room? It's going to give me nightmares for centuries to come." She still hadn't taken her true form.

"Not a problem. But would you mind taking your true form. It's kind of hard dealing with you when you still look like a little kid."

"I thought you would never ask, I'm sick of looking like this." In a flaming puff of brimstone she changed from a eight year old girl to a red, cloven footed Succubus standing nearly seven feet tall. Her wings were tattered, both looked to have broken in several places, and her horns were fully cracked with light seeping through them.

"You look like you've seen better days," I said.

"What? Where's a mirror?" I pointed her to the bathroom, and after a few minutes of looking she came back out looking angered and defeated. "Probably that damn room of yours. It really ripped into me. I feel like someone tried feeding me to a pack of ravenous hell hounds."

"Sorry about that, but you were being a pain in the ass." I really did feel sorry. The Infernal had been helping a kid, in a sick and twisted way sure, but she had helped. Problem was that she had been a real pain about it and this was the result.

"I know, but I had a mission to complete." Her wings were already starting to heal along with her horns.

"You were messing with the wrong person," Yvette said almost smugly so I gave her a quick kick. "Ow."

"So what do you want me to call you?" I asked the Infernal.

"Call me Coriss." she smiled and stretched a bit. "Now shall we go? I'm sure you want to see the kid."

"Please, I want to meet her and her mother." I looked over at Yvette. "Do you want to come along?"

"No I was planning to come if you needed some muscle to beat the crap out of someone, sounds like you're going to be fine. Besides I have to get back to the court and bust some heads." She hugged me and gave me a kiss on the cheek. "Have fun."

With Yvette gone Coriss smiled. "She loves you, you know."

"That obvious huh?"

"The way you looked at her when she had changed was cute. Besides, I'm several millennia old, I can tell these things." She smiled a bit, by now she was almost completely healed. "Shall we go?"

"Sure. How are we going to do this, via circle? Or some other way?"

She grabbed on to me in a tight hug. "Hold on." There was an explosive scent of brimstone and we were in the Pit. Where exactly I didn't know and the place seemed to be in the process of rebuilding. There were minor Daemons cleaning up rubble and carting it off. I guess that this had been exactly as Felix had said for the longest time, and abandoned for some time.

"A little run down isn't it?" I asked.

"Well we had a war here some time ago. This place had been pretty much destroyed, it's one of the reasons my sister left," Coriss looked around with a slow smile touching her lips, "but we're slowly rebuilding. It'll be beautiful again, an absolute wonder to behold." She seemed to be seeing something from the past that I would never see for myself. It was an image for her that seemed to be a source of inspiration for her. "There had been a library there, really more of a University. It had towers reaching high into the sky with majestic stained glass windows coloring the books inside. Even Baphomet himself would come here to study various knowledges."

"Shall you bring me to the kid now?"

Coriss tore her eyes away from a shattered building just long enough look at me, and I could tell she had been crying. "Come on, it's this way." Her eyes drifted back to the building for a few more seconds before she grew tired of the sight and led me on through some of the rubble to what looked like a small keep.

It was a slow walk as she seemed to have missed the place and was just happy to be home again. "Was the room that bad?" I asked.

"It was horrid. I saw the war that destroyed this place repeating over and over. I could hear the screams of hundreds of thousands of Daemons, including children as this city was destroyed and our people butchered." I didn't need to see her face to know that she was crying, I could hear it in her voice. "I could smell the burning flesh all over again. I have been tortured in more ways than you could possibly imagine, but that room was something I would never wish upon my worst enemy. It showed me horrors like I have never seen before in my thousands of years of life, and I will desperately pray I never will again."

"I'm sorry, I really am. I honestly didn't know it would do that to you." I reached out and put a hand on her shoulder. I was surprised when she turned to face me. She dropped to her knees pulling me down with her and started sobbing into my shirt. The sobs wracked her body as she tried to come to terms with what she had seen in the time in my Trophy room.

I just let her cry, because right now I felt like the world's big asshole. I hoped I'd never have to do that to another person. Coriss had just told me in no uncertain terms that she had been through an emotional hell remembering the worst part of her life over and over. I didn't want to think of the nightmares she would have for who knew how many centuries.

After a while she let me back up having regained her composure. "You okay now?" I asked.

"No. But a little better I guess." She turned around and started leading further down the road. She said nothing more to me, and I couldn't say I blamed her. I had tortured people before. I had done things that no sane person would ever think to do to someone. This though was different. I had torn at her very soul and the thought that I had done that to someone would haunt me. The fact that I had now found out that she had done what she had to help save a girl? I was thoroughly disgusted with myself.

When we reached the keep the doors opened letting us in. "Sister, you're home!"

A Daemon who still looked Human came running from a hall and grabbed Coriss and squeezed her. "Who is this?"

"This is a private detective named Jason Black, and he is the mortal realm's biggest asshole," she said with the faintest of smiles.

"Do I want to know?"

"Probably not, but if it wasn't for him I wouldn't be back here so soon."

"You mean the plan worked? My husband is going to jail?"

"Your fairly convoluted plan worked." I confirmed. "Mostly likely he'll be sexually abused himself while he's in prison. But that's where he's going."

The mom, who confusingly enough was also named Charlene, hugged me hard. Hard enough for my back to crack. "Thank you, thank you, thank you." She turned to look at her sister. "And thank you too sister, I don't want to think what would have happened."

"I was happy to do it." Coriss hugged her sister and then pulled back. "Now I need a long bath and enough alcohol to drown a horse to get the stench of his place off of me. As for you Jason, thanks for helping, even with what you did to me, I still have to thank you."

As Coriss stalked off I stopped her to apologize once again for what I had done. She stopped briefly and sighed before moving on. "What did you do to my sister?" Charlene, or whatever her name was asked.

"I did horrible things to her that I didn't intend to. I was worried that I'd never be able to rescue your daughter if I couldn't get her to talk, so I did something I have now promised myself to never to do to someone again."

"Please tell me you didn't…"

"Rape her? No. She offered to tell me what was going on if I did have sex with her. But she looked like your daughter and I wasn't going to do that to a little kid."

"Thank you. I'm sure you want to see Charlene just to make sure she's okay."

"That would be great. I need for you to take care of some paper work on the mortal realm to keep me from getting in trouble, but I just want to make certain that the kid is safe."

"That's not a problem. Follow me." We walked past a couple doors before she opened one, and there was the kid who I had been searching for. "Charlene?"

"Yes mom?" The girl sounded genuinely happy, which was a good sign.

"This is Mr. Black, he's here to help bring you back to the mortal realm if that's what you want to do." I could see the mother give her daughter a pleading look not to leave.

"You're kidding right?" little Charlene asked. "There is no way I'm leaving, as long as I can go back there every once in a while to see my friends, but other than that I want to stay here with you, mom." The mother sighed in relief and I couldn't blame her.

"Want to know something Charlene?" I said addressing the little girl. "Your mother is something special, and so is your aunt, just don't blame her for what she did to you."

"I won't, and thank you for coming here to find me."

"Mr. Black? Could you stay for a while?" Charlene the elder asked. "I'd really appreciate it. I have so many questions to ask you."

"Sure, I'd like that." I sat down for a long visit.

CHAPTER 10

When I returned to my home I simply wanted to collapse but I knew that wasn't going to be possible. Shadow was still out there and I had no idea where the idiot was. I had a good idea that he was in Asgard, but I had no way of getting there. I didn't know of any circle that would allow me to cross over there directly. Even going through the Mystic Wolf would be difficult since I wasn't currently on the guest list. That was the problem with this sort of thing, realm jumping was hard if you didn't know the right circles, and if you wanted to go through the Mystic Wolf certain places had guest lists. If you weren't on the list you were screwed.

On top of that I had calls to make for the sake of Charlene. It had been decided that the mother would play the kid's distant aunt who would take the girl in since she had nowhere else to go. It wasn't a big issue just a matter of having a false identity for the mother made. Yvette would be more than happy to do that. It meant a happy ending for the kid, and wasn't that the point of this. The girl got to be with her mother who, until these last few days, she had only known through pictures. True, she was in the Pit, but the part she was in seemed nice. Coriss and Charlene had really made an impression on me as to what it had been like before the war that had destroyed the place and now it was rebuilding. It would be a nice place for the girl to grow up, at least I hoped it would be. I had agreed to help out a bit by keeping the kid up to date with was going on in this realm as best I could. For the mean time though she'd spent the vast majority of her time living in the Pit with her mother. I thought about bringing Red Raven down there at some point. With her mothers' permission of course.

Still my main concern was my avian idiot. He wasn't home yet and it was getting worrisome. I wandered the house for a bit looking in all of his usual hiding spots in case he was already home and just too ashamed to look at me. Of course he wasn't anywhere to be found. Even trying to reach out mentally and take a look at where he was through his own eyes got me nowhere. To tell the truth I was beginning to feel sorry for myself. I was beginning to really come to terms with how much I had grown to rely on him just for emotional stability.

I had just finished getting ready to head to the Mystic Wolf and get thoroughly plastered and become thoroughly miserable when there was a loud knock on my door. I opened the door ready to tell whoever it was to take a flying leap when a hand reached out grabbed me round the throat and we both disappeared.

I knew I had passed out at some point because the next thing I remembered I was waking up on a stone floor to the sounds of jovial laughter. To put it mildly I wanted to find the nearest asshole and kill them. I reached in to my coat pocket for Ace of Spades only to find out that not only was her holster empty, it wasn't even there and I wasn't even wearing my usual clothes. "You honestly didn't think we'd let you keep your gun, did you?"

"I'm not in the mood to play around asshole," I roared as I leapt to my feet. All I had to do though was take a look at who I was yelling at to have a true, 'Ah shit' moment. "What do you want Odin?"

"Sorry about the rough treatment dear boy. Heimdall has been in a rather disagreeable mood recently, and I think sending him to fetch you just gave him a reason to hurt something, though I must say you do look much better than you did a few minutes ago."

"What did I look like? Ah shit never mind the question," I said looking down to find that my suit had been replaced with more Viking like garb, though I had to admit it was quite ornate.

"Your suit will be replaced. No need to worry about that. Now about why you're here."

"What has Shadow done to tick off Muninn?" It wasn't even a guess at this point. The only way I'd have been pulled up here is if that twit had done something monumentally stupid.

"Well they are about to get married," Odin laughed, but I knew there was more to be said, "in what you might call a 'shot gun' ceremony." Ah fuck.

"So Shadow got Muninn knocked up?" That idiot.

"The chicks have already hatched." Odin was giving me a dangerous grin. "So, as I'm sure you'll agree, I can't exactly let him go without him doing right by Muninn."

I sighed; the idiot had really gone and done it this time. "I see what you mean. I take it I'm here as his master to make sure he promises willingly to be a dad, and marries Muninn?"

"That pretty much sums it nicely." Odin confirmed.

"Well I guess there's not much I can do. I'm not about to break tradition. He messed up, he has to fix this mess. However that leaves me with a question."

"Ah yes. He is still your familiar, and that does make things a little confusing for both of us. It's simply never come up before that I know of."

"And you would know." I sat down and looked at the sky. "So, I guess we have to be the first people to set precedent in the matter. I mean I need him with me, he's been in the family for I don't know how long, and he's really the only connection I have left to my family. Plus he's my familiar which means he's pretty much part of me."

"And I of course need Muninn to help bring me information of what happens through Midgard." Odin gave a slight snort of laughter. "I really think that this is going to be a case of Shadow and Muninn really being the ones who need to figure this out for themselves. This will be an interesting situation."

"That it will, that it will."

"Well come on, Black. It's time to get to the wedding. Is there anyone else who should be here?" Odin asked.

"Could you please bring Jamie up? Preferably more gently than you brought me up here."

Odin clapped me on the back, nearly bowling me over. "I'll ask Frigga to pick her up. I'm sure she'd be more than happy to and she will definitely be gentler about it than Heimdall was with you."

"Can I go talk to the groom now?"

"Not a problem. Follow me."

I followed Odin into Folkvangr, Freya's hall, which was fitting since she was the Goddess of love. It was a beautiful place of course, beautiful men and women everywhere lying about the grounds in various states of undress with Valkyries in attendance. One of those things people often forget, Freya gets half of those who die in battle. This place just isn't one long feast and fight setting. As some people joke, with Freya being both a Goddess of Love as well as one of War, her motto should be 'If you can't lay 'em. Slay 'em', of course I wasn't stupid enough to say that to her face.

After a while of wandering endless corridors, which I think was Odin's way of getting me thoroughly lost so I didn't grab Shadow and make a break for it, which would be suicidal anyways, we came to what amounted to a chapel. He told me to wait and had a quick talk with Frigga who then quickly disappeared. "This way to the groom," Odin said.

He led me to a room that was directly off the chapel. He opened the door and ushered me in. Once inside I saw Shadow straining at a tether around his feet that was attached to a perch. Odin shut the door leaving the two of us alone. *Please tell me you're here to get me out of this mess.* Shadow begged.

"As if. This is your nest, you sleep in it." I dropped into a chair across from the condemned. "So you're a dad now. What do you have to say about that?"

Damn it boss!!! How I was supposed to know it could happen? We're two different species! This shouldn't be able to happen at all! Shadow was hopping up and down he was so mad.

"Well it did happen." I refused to feel sorry for the twit. "Anyways what's the problem? You love her don't you?"

Well yeah, but this is a commitment that I'm not sure I'm ready for. Great, I was beginning to feel bad for the idiot. *I haven't had a mate in well over three-thousand years. I don't know if I still have it in me.*

"What, the ability to stay loyal to someone? I'm sure it'll be just like riding a bike."

I can't ride a bike! Shadow shouted in my head.

I sighed, he was just being difficult at this point. "You know quite well what I meant. You'll be just fine."

I looked him squarely in the face making sure I had his complete attention. "Now I'm going to give you some advice as a friend. This is not an order from master to familiar simply as one friend to another. Marry her and be happy together, though the two of you are going to have to figure out a few things afterwards but for right now just do yourself a favor and marry her and be her husband and dad to your kids."

Shadow just cocked his head to one side and blinked at me a couple of times. *You're serious aren't you. You're not ordering me to do this. This really is all my decision?*

"This is all you buddy."

Shadow puffed up his chest a bit then sighed. *I'm ready. For better or worse I'm ready to marry Muninn.*

Truthfully, I was relieved he had decided to marry her on his own. If he hadn't I would have just ordered him to and had him resenting me for who knew how long. This was by far better.

I didn't know what the future held for him or myself any more but this was going to be an interesting ride. My familiar was marrying the familiar of a God and this was an issue that had simply never happened before. True I was immortal, at least for the most part, which meant Shadow himself was also an immortal so there was a good chance that they'd have an immortal life together. Still it was going to be a massive change and one I'd have to eventually get used to.

The big question of course was where would they live? Would they take turns on where they stayed the night? Would Shadow spend a fair chunk of time away from me until the chicks were fully grown? So many woulds it was hard to get my mind around.

I knew he was still my familiar, just as Muninn was still Odin's familiar, but familiars were never meant to have this much freedom. Besides, as Shadow had so bluntly pointed out this shouldn't have happened. Muninn was a raven and Shadow was a crow; children should have been impossible. Of course, Muninn wasn't a normal raven and maybe she loved my idiot enough to want to have children with him. I guess she was worried that he would leave her and this was her way of keeping it from happening. Of course both crows and ravens mate for life. From what Shadow told me he had had a mate before he had become a familiar. He still thought about her from time to time, and he had even once told me that as wonderful as Muninn was, and as much as he loved her, he still missed his first mate. That had been over three thousand years ago; the fact that he could remember exactly what she looked like that far back amazed me. He would tell me about the shine on each feather, the fact that her beak was slightly kinked in what most of the other crows thought was disgusting, but that he thought was kind of cute. Normally he told me this when he was drunk as a college student on his death march, but it never stopped him from telling me.

If he loved Muninn even half as much as he loved his original mate, the two of them would be happy for a long time. This was why I didn't want the Countess up here right now but had instead asked for Jamie. Yvette would have done her best to get Freya to marry the two of us. Truthfully I still wasn't sure if I wanted to get married. Yvette was probably the only one who could put up with me in a romantic sense, and we knew so much about each other that it was scary. Truth be told there would be a lot of benefits for the two of us to get married, but it would also mean changes that I wasn't sure if I was ready for. I knew neither of us would take the other's name, not that that really mattered.

It was a stupid thing anyway for anyone to be concerned with. It also probably meant moving, and that I wasn't ready for. I liked my house, all my stuff was there and some of it would be just plain dangerous to move. Plus there were all sorts of other issues, though mostly I think it was just because I didn't want to leave my house. I had it built back in the late eighteen hundreds and it was still important to me. I couldn't imagine Yvette wanting to move into the house either. She needed to be in total control of the court and that meant she had to be able to be ready to painfully break someone at any time so she lived at the old hotel the Court was stationed in, in a two-story apartment that had a great view of Saint Paul. So the idea of her going from the lap of luxury that the court provided, to my house was silly to say the least. Now though was not the time to think about that sort of thing; right now this was about Shadow getting hitched.

Please stop thinking about the Countess, Shadow finally said. *I'm the condemned party here, not you.*

I grinned. "Sorry, I always thought I'd get married before you."

You know as well as I do that this doesn't come up, so of course you'd get married before me, Shadow said hopping up and down. *Now let Odin know that I've agreed to marry Muninn of my own free will and that you didn't have to order me to do it.*

"You're sure you want to do this?" I asked teasing him.

Yes already!!!

I opened the door back to the chapel. It didn't take me long to spot Odin. He was standing with Frigga and my secretary. "Odin. This twit of a familiar of mine has agreed to marry Muninn of his own free will. I didn't order him to, he came to the decision on his own."

"That's good to hear. Then we will be ready to start this soon." Odin walked into the room with me and undid the strap that had held Shadow in place. "It's good to know that you're taking responsibility for what you did."

Shadow squawked indignantly at the God. "Shadow, stuff it," I hissed at him.

"I fully understood that, bird, and don't you forget that." I hoped Odin wasn't going to fry Shadow. "I speak all languages, including that of birds. So don't think you can get away with talking about me behind my back. Especially not with Muninn."

Shadow's feathers sprung up and swelled up to make himself look bigger. Odin merely laughed, probably much to Shadow's annoyance. "You think a little crow like you can take on a God? I must admit you have guts little bird. Not much in the way of a sense of self-preservation, but definitely guts."

"Shadow stop acting like an idiot," I said flicking him in the back of the head.

It was at this time that Jamie showed up wearing a beautiful Norse dress. "So here's the groom. Don't you look marvelous Shadow," she said. Shadow rubbed up against her hand which was his way of asking her to scratch the top of his head, something that she knew he loved.

"Come on Shadow. Let's get this over with." Odin told me where to go and following his directions we ended up at sort of altar with Freya in front of us. Then behind us stood I didn't want to guess how many Valkyries, along with a Succubus, Sasha, which meant Red Raven was around. The Valkyries parted ways and out came Red Raven, her horns polished, the feathers of her wings glossy, and her halo so dark that it warped the very light around it, was prancing down the aisles tossing rose petals. Following Red came Odin's two massive wolves, Geri and Freki, then flying slowly by Muninn's brother Huginnn. Finally at a slow and stately pace at last came Odin with Muninn on his shoulder.

Muninn had a necklace of precious jewels draped across her breast in the middle of which was a golden key. As much as crows love shiny objects, and Shadow is no exception to the rule, I knew the only thing that caught his eyes at this moment were Muninn's.

The ceremony itself was brief, a few words from Freya, a quick preening from each bird to the other, and that was about it. They were birds; this was more ceremony than they needed. By the Gods they were already married when Muninn had laid those eggs. Now it was just official in everyone else's eyes.

There were still practical things that needed to be settled, but for now that would be an afterthought. Though truthfully it should have been thought through a lot earlier. Still I was just going to be happy for the idiot. He was married and had every right to be happy. I just felt sorry for Muninn. I had put up with Shadow for centuries. Now she'd be dealing with him a fair amount of time, and that was as much of a reason to feel sorry for anyone as there ever was one.

A NEW JOB

A TALE FROM THE MYSTIC WOLF

Somewhere deep in an infernal realm, it really doesn't matter which one, they're all pretty much the same, an alarm clock started blaring.

"Shut the fuck up you wretched thing!" A Succubus flailed helplessly at her end table only to turn on the TV while threatening all out violence upon the alarm. Managing to grab the cursed object she threw it against a wall where it continued to scream out. Having not learned its lesson the Succubus decided to get really angry with the clock and obliterated it with a blast of fire.

She was all set to go back to sleep when she realized that the TV, which was far too expensive to kill, especially since she was all but broke, had on an early morning news show, not the usual afternoon report. She stared at it for a while trying to figure out why her clock had woken her up and this distressingly early time of day.

"Come on girl, think. Why would I set an alarm to go off this early?" The question was, of course, rhetorical since there was no one else in the room.

Her first clue came when her phone started playing GWAR's cover of *Carry On My Wayward Son*. She looked at the phone's caller ID and saw it was her friend, Angela. "Hello?" she asked wearily.

"Damn it Terry don't tell me that you're still asleep?"

"Why? Am I supposed to be awake? Do you have any idea how early it is?" Terry hated any time of day that started before noon. She picked up her watch off the table and saw that it was barely nine.

"You forgot didn't you?"

"Apparently I did. What is going on today?"

"You have a job interview today you idiot. So get yourself dolled up because I swear if you screw this up my boss is going to give me no end of trouble. I vouched for you, girl. I'm on my way to pick you up so get your sexy ass cleaned up and I want to see perk in your tail, tits, and wings, and a shine on your horns. Or so help me, I'll grind you up and feed you to my hell hound."

"Ah shit. I'll be in the shower in two shakes." Terry knew Angela was kidding about feeding her to her hell hound, and least she was fairly certain she was.

"Make it one. I'm on my way to your place now and I'll be there in twenty minutes. NOW MOVE!!!" Terry dropped the phone and ran off to the bathroom.

How could I have possibly forgotten that I had an interview at the Mystic Wolf today? Seriously! It's every Succubus's dream job to work there. Minor Infernal to Arch-Angel, now that would be a seriously awesome job. These thoughts and many more like them kept racing through her mind as she hit the shower working furiously to get super clean, so clean that she'd squeak.

After her shower she grabbed some horn polish and gave her horns a fast, yet thorough shine. Makeup and hair was easy enough with a little natural magick. She ran her hands from her chin up to and through her hair, and what would have taken a Human over an hour to do took her all of ten seconds. All she needed now was a touch of classy scent. She decided against anything she could produce naturally. Angela had told her that getting the job required class, natural scents were fine while on the job, but those were for sexually attracting victims, not for getting a job. She picked out her favorite perfume, the bottle of which was distressingly near empty, it was called Death's Dream and was insanely expensive, and she couldn't afford another bottle if she didn't land the job. However if using the last of it meant landing it she'd take the risk.

She was still wearing a towel and staring at her closet, when Angela buzzed on the bell to her apartment. "Are you ready to come down?" She asked as soon as Terry answered.

"I'm having a crisis. I don't know what to wear!"

"Oh for the love of... Let me in and I'll help you pick something out."

"Please help me, I need this job."

"Tell me something I don't know. Now let me in."

Once Angela was in the apartment she found Terry standing in front of her closet fully nude throwing stuff around in it. "Come on let's see what you have," Angela said pushing Terry aside. "By the way you smell classy. Not sexy, which you definitely don't need right now, but classy."

"Thanks. I think."

"It's a compliment." Angela was still rummaging through her friend's closet as she spoke. "No... not this... no... no... what were you thinking when you bought this... no... Ah this should do it. At least I hope it will." Angela came out of the closet holding a full length, black dress that was slit up to the hip on one side. The dress showed a fair amount of cleavage, but that described pretty much anything worn by a Succubus.

"That old thing? I haven't worn it in well over seventeen centuries."

"Look, it's similar to something that's made it into a modern style. Now throw it on and we'll head out to the transfer station."

As Terry got into Angela's car, a brand new, silver Sky Razor, a sleek and incredibly expensive sports car, dollar signs lit her eyes. She hadn't known until this moment just how much money there was in being a waitress at the Mystic Wolf. Up until this point she couldn't imagine these cars as anything but cramped, but she had enough room to flex her wings enough to keep from cramping up and the back of the seat was designed especially for Daemons with tails. "How much did this cost?"

"A lot, and don't drool on it. I paid for it in cash and don't want any marks on it for as long as possible." Angela slammed down on the accelerator and the car jumped into traffic with a bit of a fish tail. Causing Terry to slam back into the seat.

"Damn it Angela aren't you driving a little recklessly?"

"Your fault," Angela muttered. "If you hadn't slept in this morning we'd be at the transfer station already and you'd be ready to be summoned. Now let me concentrate."

They reached the transfer station with plenty of time. Long enough for Angela to give Terry some advice. "Okay we've got twenty minutes before you get summoned. So I'm going to give you some advice on what to do next. First be friendly, but remember not to flirt, you're not going there to seduce him, you're trying to get a job. His daughter will be there as well and she's going to be a major part of the hiring process. Sam, that's the daughter's name, is responsible for keeping us in line now and she's a hard ass. She also ranks God level there so whatever you do don't piss her off. Most of the time she's a sweet heart but she has the ability to get down right mean. So just be friendly but not overly so."

"I feel sick," Terry said looking slightly pale.

"Nervous?"

"Terrified."

Angela looked at her friend who was shaking slightly. "Don't worry, you'll do just fine. I wouldn't have recommended you for the job if I didn't think you could handle it."

"Okay," Terry said taking a couple deep breaths.

"Just relax, you'll do just fine." Angela kissed Terry full on the lips. "There will be more of that when you land the job. Now remember not to flirt with either Brisbane, he'll be the big guy, or Sam, and you'll be fine. And keep everything as perky as possible, I'll be there the whole time."

"Thanks."

Angela looked at her watch, it was five minutes until Terry got summoned, she had to get going. "Now let's get you in your circle and I'll see you in a few minutes.." She watched her friend step into the circle then using a rune sequence that was tattooed on her arm sent herself to the Mystic Wolf.

* * * *

Brisbane looked at the circle he was going to use for the summoning to make sure it was perfect. He then looked at his notes again, ah yes Terry Sumer. She was related to another waitress, but only enough to have the same last name. Angela had recommended her to him and she was a good judge of character so that already had points going for the Succubus in question. He had set up the circle the day before, it looked like any normal summoning circle, all sorts of ancient sigils laid out in chalk with candles around it and a couple sacrificial offerings. The only difference, and you had to be familiar with Daemonic bureaucracy to notice it, was that there was what equated to a departure gate number.

There had been a time when summoning a Daemon was risky work at the best of times. If you didn't know what you were doing, and for the most part no one did, it was easy to summon some random Daemon who was just sitting down on the toilet. That sort of thing led to all the problems with Daemons trying to figure out how to warp your commands and wishes to make them backfire. Now that the bureaucrats had taken over, which was some time in the late nineteenth century, things had gotten more stabilized. Daemons had to take turns waiting at a Transfer station for people who weren't calling someone specific. Knowing a Daemon's true name was dangerous as you could summon them at any time, including when they just went to bed, though they were a bit easier to control. Then there were departure gate circles like the one Brisbane had drawn. They allowed you to summon a specific Daemon as long as you had a prearranged summoning time, which was difficult but not impossible to set up. Daemons could also use them to send themselves somewhere specific on another realm that had a similar arrangement, mostly in other Daemonic realms of various types.

"Well, first time to do an interview, isn't it Sam?" Brisbane asked his daughter who was sitting on the side of his desk.

"Of course, most of the girls were here when you adopted me, and those that weren't you hired before you put me in charge of dealing with their Union."

"Well you're the one with the business degree. I'm just a drink slinger with a few community classes in business. I've been winging it the whole time."

"You've done a great job so far, but I do have some new ideas that I want to go over with you."

"After the interview we'll go over them."

Angela popped up behind the two Gods in a puff of fire and brimstone scented smoke. "Is your friend ready for her interview?" Brisbane asked without bothering to turn around.

"As ready as she is ever going to be I think."

"Okay then let's summon her up." Brisbane snapped his fingers and the candles that were placed around the circle jumped to life. He then let loose with a few sentences of a truly ancient language. (I'm not going to bother to even try to write it down phonetically, as the English alphabet is too limited to do so.) There was a great blaze of fire within the circle and a gush of wind that blew out the candles.

Terry came up from a crouch as smoke rolled off of her in waves. "Why hast though summoned me?" She asked, her eyes glowing red.

"Well you got style, kid," Brisbane laughed with a couple of claps. For her part Sam just laughed.

Terry gave a little bow. "I try to please." Her laugh was nervous.

"Don't worry about the dramatics and please calm down this will be pretty simple. So let's start with introductions. I'm Brisbane, the chief God of the Mystic Wolf. The young lady here is Sam, she's my daughter."

"Adopted daughter, it's why we don't look at all alike," Sam said.

"Anyways," Brisbane started, ignoring the interruption, "she is the one responsible for dealing with the Union on behalf of the bar. She works with your friend over there on negotiating contracts for you guys. And of course you're Terry, right?"

"Yeah, that would be me." To say she was nervous would be an understatement.

Brisbane smiled, hoping that it would help her calm down, everyone told him that his smile softened his imposing features. "It's okay, I'm not going to bite you."

"I'd lov..." As soon as Terry saw the look on Angela's face, she remembered her warning about not flirting.

Brisbane laughed, a grin splitting his face. "Let me guess. You were about to say something to the effect that you'd love it if I bit you, weren't you?"

Terry blushed furiously at being caught, and like most Succubi she hadn't known up until that point that blushing was possible for her. "Errr... sort of."

"Don't worry, it's pretty natural for the Succubi who work here or even just apply to say something like that. In fact Angela said pretty much the same thing when she interviewed. Actually, that was a bit of a test. You see, I want you girls to flirt, it comes naturally to you and it helps business but there are some limits. If we decide to hire you, you'll be given the exact limits you can go to. However we have other things to test you on."

"Like what?" That bitch Angela had gotten her worked up over nothing about the flirting bit.

"Well for one thing when you are working you're going to be waiting on up to fifteen tables at a time. That's usually on weekends or karaoke night. But often times this place is packed. The trickiest part for you will be remembering what people ordered at which table, when there is a lot going on." Brisbane stood up and motioned for Terry to follow him. Sam followed behind the Daemon and made a point of trying to step on the Succubus' tail. Like all of the other girls' tails it deftly avoided being stepped on, which was perfect. The other reason was that Sam just liked looking at the tails of all the Succubi who worked there and was envious of them.

"Now I've asked a bunch of the regulars and some of the staff to come in to help with your interview," Brisbane said as they entered the main part of the bar. At the moment it looked like a sports bar. With various levels that were a couple steps higher, or lower than the main room. The people that were there were in the easier part of the bar to deal with and were seated at eight of the tables. "Now here's where the fun begins. Angela will be helping you today and if we hire you, she or one of the other girls will be helping you get the hang of things for a couple nights."

Terry looked around the room with a petrified squeak. "Don't worry this part will only take about two hours, and no matter what you'll be paid for this even though it's a test. Right now I'm looking for accuracy and grace, you'll build up the speed as you get comfortable. Now the kitchen exists on a separate time line so this is what I want you to do. Get the drink orders of half your tables and write them down as you get them. Then go over to Fay and she'll show you how to set up the accounts for the different tables at the register. Next go to the other half of your tables and repeat the process. By the time you've gotten those orders back to the register the drinks for the first group will be ready. Take the drinks out to them and ask what they'd like to eat, collect the order…"

"Bring it back to the register and enter it in with the orders of the drinks. By that time the drinks for the second group of tables will be ready and I bring them out, and get their orders. By the time I get back the food for the first group will be ready for me to bring to their tables?"

"Well you do pick up things fast. You got it exactly. Now once everyone has their food you can begin to flirt a little." Brisbane took another look at Terry's dress; it wouldn't work for the test. "First though you need to change into a uniform. I don't want your dress getting ruined. Angela, get her a uniform."

"Certainly boss," Angela said as she came over and grabbed Terry around the waste and headed with her back to the dressing room.

"How am I doing?" Terry whispered, once she and Angela were out of ear shot of the two Gods.

Angela gave Terry a light slap on the arm. "You're doing great, just keep it up and you'll definitely land the job. Now let me show you the dressing room."

The dressing room was more like a locker room than anything else. Well like one used by a professional cheerleading team. Each Succubus had her own closet with multiple outfits. The bar had different themes and would take on a different form for those themes; much of the bar would stay relatively the same, but there could still be massive changes. It was one of the joys of working in a Divine Realm that its God liked to change things up all the time. For every theme the waitresses had a pair of different uniforms. The reason for two was in case there was a need to change because something happened to one, the Daemon would just go back and change and put the messy uniform in the laundry hamper. Ten minutes after it went in the hamper one of the Brownies who had come to live at the bar would clean the outfit thoroughly and put it back in the closet.

"Okay you're my size so you can wear my extra uniform, for the sports bar version of the Mystic Wolf. Now out of the dress and into this." The uniform was little more than a tiny, black halter top with the bar's logo embroidered on the left breast. The halter top was so small that it showed a fair bit of under cleavage. For a bottom she wore shorts that basically amounted to, coverage wise, high wasted panties, with a hole in the back for her tail. For shoes she was wearing black and silver cross trainers. Angela had her stand in front of the mirrors.

"Damn I look good," Terry said, wolf whistling at herself. "This is a normal uniform for us?"

"Yep we tried to get Brisbane to let us wear more revealing outfits, but this was as good as we could do. Trust me on this though, this, matched with a little flirting, makes us a lot of money. Besides he brought in a psychologist with a degree in fashion design and she went over how packaging that showed some, but not all of the goods, could drive people nuts."

"I know nothing about psychology but I love the packaging." Terry struck a few more poses in the mirrors. "Now I really want to work here."

"Vanity, thy names is Succubus," Angela laughed. "You keep modeling off for yourself in the mirror and I'm going to get changed into my uniform so I can help get you through this. And if I were you I'd change your makeup to fit the uniform."

"Oh good point." Angela ran her hands over her face and her blood red lipstick was replaced by silver and her eye shadow was a gradient from black to silver. "Now that's perfect."

A minute later Angela was dressed. "Okay, put this on," she said handing Terry a demi apron, "you'll keep your note pad, pen, and check presenters here."

Terry took it and tied it round her waist. "I guess I'm ready to go."

"Good, now let's prove to the bosses why I recommend you, but before we go I need to give you a little advice regarding flirting."

"Okay."

"Out there is a mix of clientele groups like you'd see on a regular day. After you bring everyone their food, spend a couple minutes at each table chit chatting. If it's a male female couple sit down next to the woman. For one thing the woman won't feel as threatened by you as if you were sitting with her man. The other reason is that it gives the guy a chance to compare you side by side, you'll almost always be the more attractive, so bigger tip. Next if the table is all guys bend down as far as possible when taking their order so that they see plenty of cleavage, bigger tips. Now sometimes a kid comes to the bar with a parent for whatever reason, I happen to know there is a young one here today, when you chit chat be sure you talk to the kid for a bit."

"What kind of person takes their kid here?" Terry was almost shocked.

"All sorts of people, especially if they want to come here and can't find anyone to watch the kid, in this case it's different. The child is the adopted daughter of another employee who now works as a part timer. In fact she's the one who left, leaving this job opening." As far as Angela was concerned Red Raven should be the only kid allowed in the bar since she was half Divine and half Infernal herself. "Now do think you've got it all?"

"Pretty sure I do."

"Well then let's go."

* * * *

"So, what do you think so far?" Brisbane asked Sam.

"Well she's definitely as good looking as all of the other girls who work here. She also knows how to keep her tail from being stepped on, and before you ask, I was doing my damnedest to step on it. I swear their tails have a separate awareness of what's going on."

"Talked to a couple of the girls about that very thing long ago. I was told that their tails are incredibly sensitive and that they sense even the slightest movement, and temperature changes, so you're not far off. I'm sure you've also noticed that they're prehensile so they can do all those light caresses that drive people nuts."

Sam nodded in agreement. "I can't remember who told me but they can also use their tails in some way to enhance the pheromone they release."

"That I didn't know," Brisbane remarked. "Not surprised of course but they never told me directly. When did you find that out?"

Sam shrugged as if it should have been obvious. "Right after you adopted me. The girls saw me as an honorary Succubus since I had been working as a prostitute when you met me."

"That explains why they wanted you to be the one in charge of negotiating with their Union," Brisbane said with a slight chuckle.

"Are you seriously telling me that you didn't know that?"

"Honestly no, but it does explain why they took such a shine to you so quickly."

Sam shook her head. Sometimes her dad was so dense. She looked towards the dressing room and saw Angela leading Terry out. The young Goddess whistled lowly. "Definitely sexy enough to work here," she told her father.

"Definitely, very athletic body type. Not too skinny and nowhere near plump, just perfectly toned. Just enough muscle definition to let us know that she takes good care of herself." Brisbane wrote down a few notes.

"Why do I feel like I'm reviewing a piece of art rather than looking at a real, breathing person? Is it fair to her?" Sam asked. "It almost feels a little trashy of me to objectify her in such a base way."

"Sam, honey, you must keep in mind that, for the most part, Succubi have a complete different set of moral standards than many other races," Brisbane said. "They take delight at being objectified in such a way. Very few of them want to change that about themselves."

"Sasha being one of the few?" Sasha had taken on a massive change at some point and had decided to go to college and study elementary education. She was now working as a substitute teacher.

"Sasha is one of the few, but even then, she finds herself caught at times between wanting to be taken seriously for her abilities as a teacher and her desire to come off as a bit of a sex object." Brisbane often found himself talking with his now part time employee about it.

"What does her fiancé say about it?" Sam was referring to a Valkyrie who was the Succubus's other half.

"Kara? I'm not sure. I know she loves having Sasha to herself and she trusts her completely. Those two are a perfect match, they also make great parents."

"That's true, Red Raven is lucky to have them. You'd almost think she was actually related to Sasha instead of adopted."

"Okay enough chatter, we are doing an interview and we need to study Terry."

Terry had just finished getting the first round of drink orders and was heading to the register. She looked at the thing in bewilderment. Programming her universal remote had been difficult enough for her, this though...

"Don't worry it's pretty straightforward," Fay told her. "First you type in your employee number here, then hit enter," she said pointing at a touch screen. "Since you're not an actual employee yet the number you will be using is 666, and yes it's a bad joke, blame Angela."

Terry typed in 666, and hit the enter button. It popped up a screen that was a list of table numbers. "Okay now what?"

"Now you touch the screen next to each table, that will bring up another window where you will type in each drink order."

Terry looked at her note pad and realized that she hadn't written down a table number for any of them. "Ummm..."

Fay smiled, knowing what had Terry worried. "Don't worry about that, we all forget to do that for the first few days. Just as long as you keep the tables consistent it won't be an issue. So go by the order you have in your hand."

Terry took a couple deep, calming breaths and started to type out the first drink order when on the second letter a group of drinks popped up to the side of the box she was typing in. "What's this?" She asked slightly bewildered.

"Okay that is a list of drinks that start with those letters, starting with the most commonly ordered drink. The more you type the smaller the list gets. Depending on the name you may get to the point where you can just scroll through the list to find what you're looking for. It takes a while to get quick at it, but once you do it speeds things up immensely," Fay said. "Now one you enter the first drink hit enter and it will pop up as seat one, if there is more than one person at the table you hit add person, then type in their order, repeat this until all drinks have been added. After that you hit the place order button here."

Terry did as Fay told her and was quickly done with the first order. "Now what?"

Fay looked at the order in Terry's hand and checked it against what was on the computer. Once she had confirmed the order she pointed at another button. "Okay next thing you do is hit the next table button. And you start all over again."

Terry repeated all the steps with only minor prompting from Fay. "Good, now once you get the orders from the next set of tables you come back, repeat the process and bring out drinks to the first set of tables."

Terry headed back out and was quickly picking up orders when she saw Red Raven who was insanely easy to spot. Seeing as she was the only kid in the place and the fact that she was an obvious half-breed Daemon it was impossible for her to be anyone else. On top of that there was a Succubus sitting next her and on the other side of the table was a Valkyrie. "Hello ladies what can I get for you?" She asked in the same perky voice she had been using today.

"I'll have a strawberry mead," the Valkyrie said. "Sasha will have a 1919."

Terry knelt down next to Red Raven. "And what would you like little lady?"

"I'll have a virgin strawberry margarita," the young girl piped up.

Terry wrote down the orders, but forgot the virgin part. "Okay I'll be back in a few minutes with your drinks."

"Um Terry," Angela, who had been following her friend the whole night started, "you forgot something with the order."

"What? A strawberry mead, a 1919 and a strawberry margarita. I got it right," Terry was certain she had gotten the order right.

"You missed the virgin part on the margarita."

"So?" It didn't sound like that big of a deal to her.

"The difference is that a regular margarita has alcohol in it, a virgin one doesn't." Angela explained. "Anyone under the human age of twenty-one can't legally have alcohol. Now we don't know exactly how old Red is, but in human terms she is way too young to drink alcohol."

"Oops. Um…" Terry blushed a deep scarlet.

"Don't worry, I caught it and it didn't get to the table, just be more careful next time. If makes you feel better you did a good job with Red by coming down to her level to ask for her order directly."

"Thanks."

They got back to the computer with the orders and Terry put them in with only minimal help. She was about to take the drinks out when she noticed that one of the trays had drinks with similar colors to it, she didn't know how to tell the difference. "Um… how do I tell the difference?"

Angela grinned. "You didn't think we'd make it easy on you, did you?"

Terry just stared at the tray for a bit. "Help me. Please."

"Take a close look at the tray."

"I'm looking," Terry said as she stared at the tray hoping he would figure out what she was looking for. "What am I looking for?"

"Do you see the bar's logo on it?"

"You mean right here on the edge?"

"That's it. Now all the drinks that were ordered are arranged clockwise in the order they were written in the computer with the first drink being just left of the logo."

"That makes sense," Terry said, relieved that it would be that easy.

"Okay back out there, now try to balance the tray on your left hand over your shoulder."

"You're kidding, right?" She wasn't sure she could do it.

Angela smiled at her friend; her response was pretty much as expected. "It's easier than it sounds. If you feel like you're losing control use your tail to help balance it, but only as a last resort. You want to get to the point where you can touch people with your tail, light slaps and gentle caresses that sort of thing, while holding a tray. If you drop a tray or two today don't worry about it. You'll even do it once you've been working here for awhile. I still drop a tray on occasion so it's really no big deal. Just try not to spill on anyone. Just think graceful."

Terry took a couple deep breaths to calm her nerves. "I can do this," she whispered to herself.

Easing the tray onto her hand she centered the weight as much as she could. She felt it begin to tip and quickly moved her tail up to brace it, while she tweaked the balance. "Okay girl, you got this," she whispered in another piece of self-encouragement.

"Now just bring the drinks out to the right tables and get them set down in proper order and you'll be doing well. Just remember to bring the tray down low enough so that you can see where the mark on the tray is." As Terry headed back to the tables Angela followed her, making low whispers of encouragement the whole time; she knew Terry needed the job so she was trying to do her best to help.

There were a couple of times when Angela had to remind Terry in what order people had ordered their drinks, but that wasn't a huge deal, even she occasionally screwed up. There were more tricks regarding recognizing drinks that she would teach her later, tonight was just a try out.

"Is everyone ready to order?" Terry asked, setting down her tray.

The table was men only; remembering what Angela had told her, Terry bent over a fair bit as she wrote down the orders, but it didn't feel it was the best way to seduce them. She quickly found that thinking of them more like potential victims than anything else made it easier for her. In a sense they were victims for her to feed on, not their souls of course, but instead their wallets. She played up every bit of her sexuality to the best of her abilities. She could do this, she could almost taste their lust for her, and it was a high she could get used to. She had never been a waitress before, but she had always been a temptress like all her sisters. As each of the men—though that was a bit of a stretch to call them anything but boys—ordered, she walked around behind them and let her tail drag across the backs of their necks. If they lost their concentration she'd bring the barb across their jawline and use her strength to pull them up to look at her.

"You have the most beautiful eyes."

"That's such a nice compliment," she purred in the boy's ear. "But what do want to eat?" She snapped her teeth shut right next to him causing him to swallow hard.

After the boy ordered, Terry sauntered away with a lot of sway in her hips and looked back over her shoulder and blew the boys kisses. "Now that was a good job, those boys are regulars and you just played them," Angela said giving Terry a quick slap on the ass.

Terry gave her friend a playfully wicked grin. "Hey I'm just trying to get hired, and if that means giving those boys something to have wild fantasies about, that's just going to be a bonus."

There was a man and a woman at the next table she took orders at. She could tell that the woman was straight but maybe a little curious; Succubi had perfect gaydar. She could smell nervous lust coming off her, mixed with a high amount of envy. She'd be the fun one to toy with. As she left the table with their order she let her tail slide across the woman's arm and could feel her tremble and her skin flush at the touch. The woman gave a slight hiss of pleasure as Terry's tail left her arm. Definitely a fun one there.

She followed all of Angela's advice; her friend had stopped talking at one point, though she couldn't remember where exactly. When she got to Red's table she went from sultry temptress to happy big sister.

"Now since you're Sasha," Terry said pointing at the Succubus, "that would make you Kara?"

"You got it."

Terry dropped down next to Red. "And I guess that would make you Red Raven then wouldn't it?"

Red gave her a massive grin, showing the most adorable dimples. "That's me."

"Well it's nice to meet such an adorable little lady. So what would you like to eat?"

"I'll have the beef tacos with extra cheese and no lettuce."

"You don't like lettuce?" She leaned in so she was whispering directly into the girl's ear. "I'm going to tell you a secret, promise not to tell." The little girl nodded. "I can't stand the stuff either."

Red gave off a cute giggle. "I won't tell," she said, trying, and failing completely, to sound like she was taking a solemn oath.

"And what would you two like?" Terry asked Red's moms. There was no reason to flirt with them; it would be reckless to flirt with Sasha since Kara was a Valkyrie and might pound on her. And flirting with Kara would be seen as poaching another Succubus's property. That meant playing big sister to Red. It was kind of weird but she thought she could easily get used to it.

"Good job with Red," Angela said a second later. "You played that table perfectly, Red's a sweet kid so keep treating her like you just did there. One thing you can do, and this doesn't mean you did anything wrong, is you can flirt with those two. Keep it relatively tame since they don't know you yet, but as you get to know them you'll figure out how far you can get away with."

"Won't Sasha think I'm poaching if I flirt with Kara?" Poaching victims was a major no no among Succubi. You didn't try to steal the soul of someone that another one of them had already been working at. The entire clientele of the Mystic Wolf was constantly up for grabs so you couldn't stake a claim on anyone, though according to what she had been told often times patrons would pick a favorite Succubus.

"By Brisbane no, in fact she gets a kick out of it, as long as you don't over do it you'll be fine."

"What about everyone else?" Terry was really hoping she got everything down just right.

"You're doing very well. Now what's the next step?"

"Food?" Terry asked, hoping she got it right.

"Yep appetizers go first. You've had five tables order appetizers so they're first up. Remember do them in order from first to last. After that, the tables that ordered entrees and then?"

"Entrees to the tables that ordered appetizers?" Terry was so hoping she didn't screw it up.

"Very good. On average over half of the tables order appetizers so always be prepared for that."

Once they got to the computer Terry double checked with Fay on the correct manner for putting in Red's request for no lettuce on her tacos.

"What do you think?" Fay didn't sound mad, more as if she wanted Terry to figure it out on her own.

"Would it be the same way as the way people order their steaks and burgers?"

"Not quite but close. First you go here." Fay tapped a button that read requests. "Here's where you let the kitchen know what kind of special things the guest wants. So here you write, no lettuce extra cheese, hit enter and you're done. Got it?"

Terry nodded slowly. "I think so."

"Good, now get those appetizers out on the tables."

Appetizers were easy, a few times she'd come back with drinks needing refills and requests for the bar. But she was starting to get the hang of it. Once the entrees were out she began to feel less nervous, and had begun to relax a bit.

"All the food is out, now here's the tricky part."

Terry's whole body tensed up at the thought that she hadn't gotten past the tricky part. "What's that?"

"You have to learn to mingle, flirt here and there for a couple minutes and move on all the while keeping an eye out for who needs a drink refilled and who seems to be finishing up their meal. You also need to be aware of plates becoming empty so you can get them out from in front of people." Terry gave Angela a deer in the headlights look. "Don't worry it's easier than it sounds. Keep in mind something, not everyone wants to be flirted with so pick your targets."

"Any suggestions?"

Angela laughed. "They're your victims now. You have fun."

Terry picked out a couple easy to spot targets. The couple from earlier with the straight but curious woman who she was going to turn fully lusting after women. Some tables that were all single gender were definite targets. She didn't know about the Dragon though. Elves could be prudish so she'd skip that table but keep an eye on their drinks carefully. Zeus and Hera she didn't want to push her luck with. Zeus had a well earned reputation and so did Hera so she was going to stick to drinks and plates with them. Red's table she might hang around a little bit. She wasn't going to try to flirt with either of the girl's mothers but she was going to take an interest in Red. Her first victims were the couple.

Terry sat down next to the woman, she appeared to be in her thirties and wasn't bad looking, at least as far as Humans went. The man was about the same age, maybe a little older, and smelled strongly of bull pheromones. She loosely wrapped her tail around the woman's leg letting the barb of her tail drag lightly from the woman's ankle to mid thigh and back down. She could feel the woman's heart beat jump a couple notches and her body temperature start to rise.

"Hello I'm Terry," the Succubus said with a smile. "I'm trying to get hired."

"We know about that, Brisbane asked to come in and see what we thought of you. I'm Kevin, and that's my wife you're sitting next to, Sally."

"H... h... hi," Sally stuttered as Terry let the barb of her tail drag slowly down. "It... it... it's nice to mee... gah... wow... I mean meet you."

"Are you okay dear?" There was a look of deep concern on Kevin's face.

Sally gnawed on her bottom lip to keep from squeaking, "I'm just fine," she just managed though the grip on her silverware showed the opposite.

After a couple minutes of chitchat and mercilessly tormenting Sally, Terry said, "Well why don't the two of you just enjoy your food, I'll be by later." Terry unwrapped her tail from Sally's leg as she stood up. She knew the woman wanted to share a bed with her, but Angela told her that was a one way trip back without chance to be rehired. Still she knew that Kevin was going to have a great time tonight.

After talking with them she saw that several tables needed refills on drinks. Once that was settled and she spotted another table that looked good for tips. As she talked with the young men, she guessed that they were in their twenties and a couple were kind of cute so the flirting was easy. While she talked with them her eyes constantly roved her tables. When she saw another table starting to run dry she told the kids she'd be back later, she grabbed their empty beers and went over to the other table to collect their glasses and take down another set of orders in case people wanted something different. After she brought drinks back to the tables, she found another table to talk to. After a few minutes she realized that she could average about three to six minutes with any table before she had to move on. It allowed her to make at least one stop at all of her targets. She had returned to Kevin and Sally at one point for a couple minutes and she had stopped to see Red Raven and her mothers twice.

At some points she had to ask people if they wanted dessert or their checks. Fay helped her with the computer a bit, but Terry realized it was fairly straightforward and had become self explanatory at this point. At the two hour mark Angela brought Terry over to Brisbane.

"Yes sir?" Terry had never been so scared in recent life. She looked over her shoulder and saw Fay and another Succubus take over; she almost felt like she had just had her victims poached, and her fear was replaced with a slight sense of anger.

"Well, shall we talk?" Brisbane asked.

"Okay." She followed Brisbane, Sam, and Angela into the office. She noticed that they had clipboards and notepads covered in ink.

"So Sam do you want to start?" Brisbane asked the young Goddess.

"Sure. So you know I was talking to people who had finished their meals and were leaving to get their impressions of you. I also collected the tips so you didn't get distracted by that." Sam wasn't smiling which scared Terry. When Sam dropped around three hundred dollars on the table in front of the Succubus her eyes went wide. Sam smiled at her. "And that's from only four tables. The other four are still being tallied so the customers like you. Overall people thought you were nice and friendly. The wife of one of the couples you served, Sally, asked if she could take you home with her, and that you had done things with your tail that had driven her nuts. I think Kevin had realized at some point that you were doing something to Sally but he hadn't been sure what. That's the kind of thing we like to hear."

"My turn," Brisbane said. "Fay told me about how well you picked up on the computer system which is impressive. Angela told me about your accident with Red's drink, and that was the only accident when taking notes. She said you needed a little help getting drinks in front of the right people. That is nothing big, you'll learn all sorts of tricks to getting faster at that. You definitely have the grace for the job, and I know you'll pick up speed. This also wasn't particularly fair to you. On most days you'll have one or two tables filling at a time and you won't be swamped from the get go. This was almost a worst case scenario to test you on."

Brisbane flipped through his notes some more. "Okay why don't you two step outside for a few minutes and while Sam and I have a quick discussion."

As Terry left the office she could feel the shakes really set in.

"Don't worry, you got the job. I'm damn near sure of it," Angela said.

"You really think so?"

"Dead on. You did great. You did better than me for my interview."

Terry wasn't sure if she could believe her friend. "You're not yanking my tail are you?"

"By Lilith no. You're a natural. What you did to Sally was pure artistry. I've never seen her get that worked up. You had her eating out of your hand."

"I hope you're right. I'm scared as heavens right now."

"Don't worry." Angela heard the office door start to open. "Okay tail, tits, and wings up. Time to get hired."

Terry took a deep breath and got ready for the worst. "Come on in," Brisbane said once the door was fully opened.

* * * *

The bar had taken on the look of a fifties diner with the girls on roller skates. "Don't worry, it gets easy after an hour of wearing them," Angela said.

Terry glared at her from where she had fallen for the third time in as many minutes. "It better or I'm going to be dropping trays all night."

"Now what do I expect to see?"

"Perk in my tail, tits, and wings," Terry sighed, it was practically Angela's motto.

"I saw someone here on the way in and apparently she can't wait for you to get your own holy symbol."

"Sally's here!?" Sally had become one of Terry's favorite victims… err patrons.

"And her husband isn't here either." Double joy. "Just remember flirting only. You can get her worked up as much as you want, but leave it at that."

"Of course." Terry knew what was the punishment for going overboard, and she did not want to lose her job, she had too many other victims, and she loved it all.

"All right girl, let's head out."